# DEAR DEAD DAYS

THE 1972 MYSTERY WRITERS OF AMERICA ANTHOLOGY

# DEAR DEAD DAYS

EDITED BY EDWARD D. HOCH

WALKER AND COMPANY
New York

Copyright © 1972 by Mystery Writers of America

First published in the United States of America in 1972 by the Walker Publishing Company, Inc.

Published simultaneously in Canada by Fitzhenry & Whiteside, Limited, Toronto.

ISBN: 0-8027-5267-5

Library of Congress Catalog Card Number: 72-80535

Printed in the United States of America.

TEXT DESIGN BY ELIZABETH BAECHER.

# Acknowledgments

"The Ptarmigan Knife" by Miriam Allen deFord. Copyright © 1968 by Miriam Allen deFord. First published in *Ellery Queen's Mystery Magazine* (September 1968). Reprinted by permission of the author.

"A Sad And Bloody Hour" by Joe Gores. Copyright © 1965 by Joe Gores. First published in *Ellery Queen's Mystery Magazine* (April 1965). Reprinted by permission of the author.

"A Fool For A Client" by Lillian de la Torre. Copyright © 1949 by Arizona Quarterly. First published in *Arizona Quarterly* (Autumn 1949). Reprinted by permission of the author.

# Contents

---- The Ptarmigan Knife
by Miriam Allen deFord     1
1593 A Sad and Bloody Hour
by Joe Gores     19
1699 A Fool for a Client
by Lillian de la Torre     40
1861 Chinoiserie
by Helen McCloy     57
1880 Decision
by Bill Pronzini     84
1892 The Other Hangman
by John Dickson Carr     92
1897 A Note on American
Literature by My Uncle,
Monroe Sanderson
by Henry Slesar     108
1901 The Ripper of Storyville
by Edward D. Hoch     115
1915 Proposal Perilous
by Morris Hershman     140
1919 All the Way Home
by Jaime Sandaval     147
1926 Belgrade 1926
by Eric Ambler     159
1929 The Austin Murder Case
by Jon L. Breen     182
1932 The Legacy
by Clayton Matthews     197
1938 The Gettysburg Bugle
by Ellery Queen     209
1942 The Adventure of the
Double-Bogey Man
by Robert L. Fish     231

# Introduction

THE STORIES in this book are all set in the past—a past that ranges from prehistoric France to wartime England, with stops along the way in sixteenth-century London, nineteenth-century China, the American West, New Orleans at the turn of the century, Paris during World War I, the Balkans between wars, and middle America during the 1930s. It is an impressive panorama, and the stories which comprise it are just as impressive.

For this volume I have chosen only stories which take place prior to 1945. That year seemed to me the most likely dividing line between past and present. It was the year World War II ended and the Atomic Age began. It was also, coincidentally, the year in which the Mystery Writers of America was founded.

Within this framework of the past, I have tried to include stories of every type—detection, crime, suspense, espionage, true crime, pastiche, parody, and at least one unclassifiable item. Mainly, I have chosen stories which I enjoyed reading, stories which puzzle and entertain, but which also evoke memories of the past. The dates assigned on the contents page are exact in some cases, approximate in others.

The majority of stories included here have never been reprinted before. A few are recognized modern classics, and here in the context of the anthology I think you'll find them taking on new life and vigor.

I'll have further comments on the individual stories as we go along. For now, my thanks to the authors who donated them, and to the entire MWA membership for their suggestions and submissions. Special thanks to my wife Patricia, who handled so much of the paperwork involved in editing a volume like this.

Edward D. Hoch

# DEAR DEAD DAYS

# The Ptarmigan Knife

## by Miriam Allen deFord

*By way of prologue we offer this story of the far distant past, perhaps as long ago as 25,000 B.C. Miriam Allen deFord, who has written both mystery and science fiction tales of prehistoric times, here offers us what must surely be the first detective in human history.*

OVER ALL THE LAND that one day would be known as the Valley of the Dordogne in a region called France lay the peace of deep summer. The day's quota of tribesmen came home from their hunting to the summer encampment near the great cave which was the focal point of their wanderings; they brought with them two stags. It was too late in the season for reindeer or bison which would return when the brief summer was over and the long winter had begun.

Bright-Morning's heart sang within him. It was his first hunt as an equal, not as one of the older boys who followed at a distance and were allowed to act only as beaters and to help bring in the game. At fifteen he was still too young to have a woman of his own to bear him children, but he had been initiated and now he was free to go into the bush at twilight with willing girls who were still unattached. Bright-Morning was a man.

And he had further reasons today for elation. His spear-point had finished off that second stag in the exact spot where, a few days earlier, he had for the first time been permitted by his father to paint a rather wavering but properly placed spear on the pictured animal—a painted beast which, after the ritual dance, had brought its living similacrum into the hunters' reach.

Bright-Morning was the only son of the tribe's Spirit-Sayer; his mother had died when he was a small child. Long ago his father had conceded that the boy had the Gift and would some day be his successor. For a long time now Bright-Morning had been allowed to hold the stone lamp and the stone bowls of paint in the deep recesses of the cave while his father with his marvelous skill depicted the animals which the tribe wanted the spirits to send them. Soon now, little by little, the young man would begin to draw and paint and model in clay on his own, just as he was already learning the sacred songs and how to interpret the marked pebbles. But he must keep his joy to himself, for until he was openly acclaimed this was secret between him and his father.

All the men, as soon as they entered the camp, with its summer huts of sticks and woven vines scattered on the grass-covered plateau before the mouth of the cave, felt a subtle change in the ordinary routine. The women had come back from their gathering of seeds and roots and fruit, the cooking fires were lighted and ready for the stew, but there were little clumps of whisperers, and the children who usually played and shouted around the fires were being peremptorily silenced. Bright-Morning abruptly left the other hunters who mingled with the women to hear what had happened, and went straight to his father's hut, which was larger and more isolated than those of ordinary families.

The Spirit-Sayer sat on the ground studying the contents of his magic pouch. He was an old man; he had seen nearly fifty winters. His son stood respectfully at the entrance and waited until his father had replaced the bones and herbs and knots of hair in the pouch and beckoned the boy to sit beside him.

"What is it?" Bright-Morning asked.

"They have found Swift-Walker."

Three nights before, on the Eve of the Midsummer Festival, Swift-Walker—a young man a few years older than Bright-Morning, a fine hunter, no great thinker but taller and more handsome than most of the men of the tribe— had lain down to sleep with the other men who did not yet share a hut with a woman and their young ones. In the morning Swift-Walker was gone, and he had not been seen since. At first no one noticed; he had gone perhaps to bathe in the river, or he had followed some fox or other small animal that one hunter could handle by himself. But when night came again and still he had not returned, his mother and her kinsmen—his father was long since dead —had begun to search. There had been no trace of him. Perhaps he had drowned.

"Where? Alive?" Bright-Morning asked.

"No, dead. Two women went deep in the forest to find a honey tree and discovered the body. It is still there. At first light I shall send a party out to carry him back for burial."

"What animal killed him?"

"No animal. The birds and beasts had been at him, but his throat was cut deeply, with the clean slice of a knife."

Bright-Morning reflected. Beasts of the wide fields, perhaps, could inflict such an injury—a horse's sharp hoof, the claws of a lion—but none of the animals of the forest that covered the foothills.

"Cloud-Woman was one of the two who found him. She is very discreet. She picked up this beside him, hid it in the folds of her garment, and brought it directly to me. She will not speak of it to anyone."

The Spirit-Sayer reached again into his pouch and took out an object that he laid carefully on the ground between them. It was a bone knife, sharpened and polished, but stained now with dark rusty spots. Its handle was a beautifully carved ptarmigan.

Bright-Morning caught his breath.

"But—but that," he stammered. "I know it. It is Red-Sky's that he carved and carries; it is his chief treasure. Why haven't you called him to you and accused him?"

"Red-Sky is no fool," said his father dryly. "Aside from other good reasons, if he had killed Swift-Walker with that knife, do you think he would have been foolish enough to leave it there? Perhaps somebody stole it from him and left it so that Red-Sky would be blamed, as you just blamed him."

Bright-Morning was silent, chaotic thoughts whirling in his mind.

"I shall call a council of the tribe after we have eaten," his father went on, "and I shall ask for volunteers to go at first light tomorrow to bring back Swift-Walker's body. I want you to be the second to volunteer."

"Why not the first?"

His father smiled.

"Because the first will be Rain-in-the-Face, as usual— he never misses a chance to be conspicuous. He is a harmless show-off; we need not suspect him."

The Spirit-Sayer was right; as soon as he had told the tribe what they already knew, and asked for volunteers, Rain-in-the-Face jumped to his feet. When he had been accepted, Bright-Morning then held up his hand. To his astonishment his father shook his head.

"You are too young," he said. "The task is beyond you."

That stung, and Bright-Morning retorted hotly.

"I am a man!" he asserted. "I have been initiated. What a man can do, I can do."

"Very well, then," said his father, frowning. "Since you insist, you may go."

Then Bright-Morning understood. By refusing him at first and then reluctantly agreeing, the Spirit-Sayer had removed suspicion that he might be sending his son as a spy.

"I shall want two more," said the Spirit-Sayer, "and Cloud-Woman will go to show the way."

From the shadows in the back a heavy-set, burly man arose. It was Horse-Slayer.

"Swift-Walker was my sister's son," he said. "Take me."

"You may go. Now one more."

"Why?" asked a voice. Bright-Morning peered through the darkness, but could not identify the speaker. "Does it take four men to bring one from the forest? Swift-Walker was not a bison or a mammoth."

"We do not yet know just how Swift-Walker died," said the Spirit-Sayer. "The body was badly mutilated, as if hacked by teeth or claws or a sharp knife. There may be danger, more than three can cope with and protect Cloud-Woman as well. Who will be the fourth?"

"I will go," suddenly announced Snow-Born, Red-Sky's half brother—they had the same father, but different mothers. Bright-Morning sensed a shock of surprise among the listeners. Everybody knew that there had been bad blood between the half brothers; Snow-Born was proud of his beautifully flaked spear-points, and Red-Sky, that gifted carver, had openly derided them. And Snow-Born was a dour and surly man, not given to offering himself for extra duties. The Spirit-Sayer accepted him with a nod.

Bright-Morning caught his father's eye as the meeting dispersed, and understood the message. As soon as sleep settled on the others, he rose quietly and went soundlessly to the Spirit-Sayer's hut.

"I shall not keep you long," said the old man. "You must have your sleep and be ready to leave at dawn. I shall give you only these instructions: keep your ears and your eyes open and your mouth shut. Notice everything, however trifling, that seems the least bit unusual, and remember it to tell me when you return. Say nothing and above all accuse no one, even if you should be certain you have discovered the killer. Keep in mind that I need the answers to four questions: Who lured Swift-Walker into the deep forest at night? Who had reason to wish him dead? Why did Snow-Born volunteer? And why has Red-Sky made no complaint of the loss of his precious knife?"

The four men came back before noon, bearing Swift-Walker's corpse on a litter of woven vines. As soon as they had left at dawn, the Spirit-Sayer had ordered a grave dug in the floor of the cave, well behind the living quarters which they had used now for several winters. The hole was lined with red ochre from his own store of paints, and Swift-Walker's mother, White-Deer, brought out his shell necklaces and armbands to be buried with him.

After the cleansing of the dead body and of those who had touched it, the funeral was held. The men sang the death chant and the women wailed, and the Spirit-Sayer performed the traditional ritual, and Swift-Walker was placed in his grave and the earth thrown over him and stamped down by the bare feet of the young men of his own puberty group. Then Bright-Morning left the watching mourners and followed his father to the privacy of his hut. The Spirit-Sayer motioned his son to sit beside him.

"What did you observe?" he asked.

"Not very much, but a few things. When Cloud-Woman led us to the place, Snow-Born hung back and began pacing around the trees and bushes, his eyes downcast."

"Looking for the knife?"

"I suppose so, but when he saw us watching he joined us at once."

"Was there anything else? Did anyone say anything not to be expected?"

"Not really, I think. Unless I had known beforehand, I should have believed Swift-Walker had been slashed to death by tusks or claws. Rain-in-the-Face examined him carefully and exclaimed, 'Yes, our poor brother is indeed dead!' "

"Hardly unexpected, from that buffoon," commented the Spirit-Sayer.

"When he heard that, Snow-Born laughed. Horse-Slayer looked angry; he told them both to be quiet."

"Of course. Swift-Walker was his sister's son."

"It was he who lifted the body and laid it on the litter after Rain-in-the-Face and I had woven it. He and I carried it, and Cloud-Woman walked beside us, just as we showed ourselves when we came into camp. Rain-in-the-Face walked ahead of us and cut down twigs and branches that blocked our way, and Snow-Born walked behind. I glanced back once when we had just started and saw him stop and paw the earth with one foot, like a horse."

"Still hoping to find Red-Sky's knife."

"You think he knew who stole the knife and used it to kill Swift-Walker?"

"Not so fast, my son; there are still questions to be answered. Tell me, when I spoke to the meeting last evening, do you remember a woman who began to sob and then hushed abruptly?"

"Yes. I supposed it was Swift-Walker's mother."

"White-Deer is a custom-observing woman. She would never have let herself give way to grief before anyone outside her closest kin. I am old; I am not fleet of foot or strong of arm as I was once, but my sight is still keen. It was Red-Sky's woman. And my hearing is still sharp; the man who tried to prevent me from sending still another volunteer was Red-Sky himself. He may have feared that Snow-Born would offer to go, as he did."

Bright-Morning gazed at his father, completely mystified. He could figure out that for some reason of his own Red-Sky had not wanted his half brother to volunteer; but what had his woman to do with it? She was fat and beautiful, a girl just nubile, and half Red-Sky's age. The mother of his grown children had died the year before. It was rumored that Red-Sky had paid an incredible number of fine flint tools and spear-heads to She-Bear's father, He-Who-Dares, for her—had contracted for her even before his woman had died, while the girl was still an uninitiated child; but neither he nor She-Bear's father would talk about it. Swift-Walker, like all young unsettled men, had of course dallied with many girls, but so far as Bright-Morning knew he had never had anything especially to do with She-Bear.

He thought it over, and then a light broke on him. The Spirit-Sayer sat watching him quizzically. The youth burst out, "I think I see it now. Swift-Walker was going out with Red-Sky's woman whom he had paid so much for so that she would bear him many babies. Red-Sky caught them, or learned about it. So he—but how could *he* get Swift-Walker to go into the forest at night? Oh, I know— he would order his woman to lure her lover there; he could tell her that she must do it or he would kill her too. And then—"

"Red-Sky was here all that night. And as we agreed, in any event he would not have left his knife behind."

"Then he lent the knife to Snow-Born to do it for him —no, he and Snow-Born are on bad terms, so he would never—"

"They quarrel, but they are still half brothers, and that would have been a matter for near kinfolk to handle. But Snow-Born was here all night, too. You forget it was Festival Eve. Both men were among the dance leaders who spent the night with me in an inner recess of the cave while I painted their bodies. To keep the sacred paint ceremony secret, we rolled a heavy stone against the opening to the chamber. Nobody could leave until morning. Nobody did leave."

Bright-Morning shook his head. It had all got beyond him again.

*"Somebody* must have been missing from camp," he murmured. "Somebody besides Swift-Walker, I mean— the one who killed him. Or could it possibly have been someone from an enemy tribe?"

"What tribe? We have not seen strange hunters for many months, and we are at peace with all so long as we keep off one another's territory. Besides, what would Swift-Walker—or any man—have been doing in the deep forest at night? No, the killer must be of our own."

"But who?"

"I do not yet know, but when I do it will be because the spirits have whispered it in my ear. You are very ingenious, my son, but they do not yet whisper to you."

Bright-Morning gave up. He waited for his father to say more.

But the Spirit-Sayer waved him to his feet.

"Go now," he said. "I must be alone to consult the spirits."

Bright-Morning could not keep his mind off the mystery while he waited for his father to announce the revelation which the spirits had made to him. With every other possible suspect eliminated, only She-Bear herself was left. But that solution had difficulties too. If she had yielded to Swift-Walker and taken the risk of stealing into the forest with him while Red-Sky was absent, then why kill him when she got there? Once more he decided it was beyond human ability to solve.

The night passed, and the new day, and not only Bright-Morning but all the people waited in vain. Until the Spirit-Sayer had spoken, the strange unexplained death of Swift-Walker lay like fog between man and man, something wrapped in uncomfortable silence but always in men's minds. Only Swift-Walker's nearest kin mourned him aloud, as was the custom, and would do so until the moon stood again in the same phase as on the night he had died.

Then the Spirit-Sayer emerged from his hut, where he had sat fasting and in seclusion that had kept him visible but reverentially unapproachable even by his son; and in the hour when the hunters were home again and the day's meal had been eaten, he summoned them once more around the all-night fire.

He stood before them now in full regalia—not the animal mask he wore for the Hunting Ceremony, but with his body painted in red and white, his head crowned with the feathers of the Sacred Bird of the Sun, his hands clasping the bone insignia of his spiritual power, his pouch of holy secret objects dangling from his belt. He looked over the bowed heads as if counting them, or seeking to make sure that certain ones were among them. For this council even Swift-Walker's mother and kinfolk had come from their mourning to listen to the Spirit-Sayer's great disclosure.

"Hear me, my people," he began in his deep voice. At the tone a shiver moved the communicants as wind shakes the grass in a field.

"By grace of the spirits of our dead, and the High Gods of lightning and air and mountain and sky"—it was the formula, but it always pierced the hearts of the listeners— "it has been granted to me to discover and reveal the fate of our brother Swift-Walker. Hear me. Swift-Walker died by a human hand that held a knife. . . . Red-Sky, why did you make no outcry when you found that your knife carved with the ptarmigan was missing?"

Red-Sky rose trembling to his feet, and suddenly all present realized that he was no longer a strong man of ripe age, but old and past his manly strength.

"I was afraid and ashamed, Spirit-Sayer," he said humbly. "I was ashamed because I thought that in my absence one close to me had taken my knife, and I was afraid because it might have been done to impute to me an act I did not commit."

"You were with us all that night in the cave, so how could you have been accused? And who among those near to you would have wished to do you such an injury?"

"My half brother—" Red-Sky muttered. Snow-Born stood up angrily.

"Am I a thief?" he shouted. "No, I can feel no love for my half brother, who makes jest of my handiwork and is jealous of my skill lest it compete with his. But I did not steal his knife and I did not use it. You all know that I was with him and the other dance leaders throughout the night when Swift-Walker vanished."

"We know that, Snow-Born," said the Spirit-Sayer calmly. "And if Red-Sky wishes you suspected, it may be to hide another." So, thought Bright-Morning, it *was* She-Bear. But why? "But tell us, then, why did you volunteer to help bring back Swift-Walker's body? No, you need not answer that—I know. It was because you hoped to find the knife there, which means you knew it was lost. Whether you would have restored it to Red-Sky, in the loyalty that two sons of the same father should show each other, or would have displayed it in accusation, to cause your half brother shame and grief, I do not know—though I should like to believe it was the former you had in mind. It does not matter, since you did not succeed. Cloud-Woman found the knife when she discovered the body and brought it to me, and only my son has known that I had it; and he I know has not spoken.

"But now, Snow-Born, I want to know how you guessed the knife was missing, since Red-Sky has given no word of it—and how you guessed it was the weapon with which Swift-Walker's life was ended?"

There was a long silence. The Spirit-Sayer gazed piercingly at Snow-Born. But before the man could bring himself to speak, a figure rose from among the huddled crowd of women and children. It was She-Bear.

"I will answer for Snow-Born," she said clearly. "I know it is not seemly for a woman to speak in council, but I will take it upon me. When you, Spirit-Sayer, said that Swift-Walker had been hacked as if by a sharp knife, and when Snow-Born offered himself as a volunteer, fear overcame me and against my will a sob burst from me. For, earlier that day, Snow-Born had approached me and told me that he too was carving a knife. 'Since my brother is jealous of my skill,' he said, 'I cannot humble myself to ask him if I may see his knife with the ptarmigan, but in all admiration I would like to behold in what manner he accomplished the joining. Will you ask him on my behalf?'

"His words were friendly but his face was not. I was frightened, but I said only, 'It would be useless. Red-Sky does not lend and least of all to you.' Then he said, 'He has not worn his knife of late. Will you, when he is not here, take it from its hiding place and let me only examine it and return it at once to you?' My fright kept me from speech, and then he said softly, 'Or perhaps Red-Sky has lost his knife? And perhaps you alone know how he lost it, and for what use and where it is now?' And I was so over-come with fear that I started from where I stood and ran to the company of other women where he would not fol-low me."

"Do not believe her!" cried Snow-Born.

She-Bear stood weeping. "It is the truth," she said. "It was because I knew he suspected me that I sobbed aloud."

"What of that, Snow-Born? Does she speak truly?"

"I suppose so," the man said sullenly. "Yes, before Swift-Walker's body was found I had noticed that Red-Sky no longer wore his knife, and after I heard of the killing I did indeed suspect that She-Bear was somehow responsible. I was not sure enough to accuse her directly, but my thought was that I might frighten her into confes-sion. She eluded me, as she told you, and so all that was left was to go myself and try to find proof that my suspi-cion had been right."

"You took upon yourself authority that did not belong to you, Snow-Born," the Spirit-Sayer rebuked him. "If you had such suspicions, and any grounds for them, you should have come to me with them. The spirits do not approve of private vengeance. Now, She-Bear, did you kill Swift-Walker with the knife you stole?"

Red-Sky leaped up.

"What am I hearing?" he cried wildly. "Am I hearing that the woman for whom I paid He-Who-Dares so dearly was so bad a bargain? Are you telling me that Swift-Walker was invading my rights, and that the woman—whether in remorse or in fear of his threat to inform me if she refused him further, does not matter—then took from me my fine weapon and slew him with it? . . . It was my half brother I thought the thief."

"You fool!" exclaimed Snow-Born bitterly. "What had I to do with Swift-Walker? And have you become so old and besotted that you are the only one among us not to know that Swift-Walker had tried in vain to buy She-Bear from her father for himself?"

"I never considered him," grunted He-Who-Dares. "He had nothing to offer worth such a one as my daughter, beautiful and fat and surely fertile as she is."

There was stifled laughter; everybody knew He-Who-Dares for a greedy man.

The Spirit-Sayer raised his voice to a commanding shout.

"Be quiet, all of you! You are blaspheming against the spirits and against me as their spokesman, quarreling among yourselves even as I bring you their judgment. She-Bear, cease weeping and answer me in the fear of the High Gods. Are you guilty?"

Almost inaudibly, but firmly now, the girl spoke.

"I did not slay Swift-Walker. I did not steal Red-Sky's knife."

Bright-Morning, from his vantage point near his father, felt a thrill of surprise. He had been waiting with a mixture of excitement and revulsion for judgment to be made against She-Bear: would the Spirit-Sayer turn her over to Red-Sky, or would he himself perform the ritual punishment of death?

Yet now his father listened to her disclaimer without dispute. He said only, "Swift-Walker was a rash and stubborn youth. Many of us had observed how his desire was set upon you and how angered he was when He-Who-Dares sold you to Red-Sky instead of to him."

A shrill voice interrupted him.

"She bewitched my boy!" screeched White-Deer, the mother of Swift-Walker. "She laid an evil spell on him!"

"Silence!"

Horse-Slayer pulled his sister down and she sat muttering to herself.

The Spirit-Sayer went on, "Did you welcome Swift-Walker's desire? Would you have been pleased if your father had given you to him instead of to Red-Sky?"

"Would that matter?" asked She-Bear simply. "It is for a daughter to obey. And when I passed into Red-Sky's keeping it was my duty to bear his children if the High Gods so willed. I have followed always the God-given laws of our tribe."

"One law you did not follow, woman. I am your Spirit-

Sayer, appointed to be your guide and counselor. You should have come to me for help against Snow-Born or any other. But you are a weak girl, confused and frightened. Now, before us all, in the safety of my protection, I enjoin you to tell us what happened between you and Swift-Walker on Festival Eve."

Not a sound could be heard from the gathered people. Even White-Deer's low lament was hushed. She-Bear summoned all her strength. She stood alone in a little space made by those who had involuntarily shrunk from her.

"Late at night, when I lay alone in the hut, Swift-Walker awakened me. He seized hold of me roughly and laid his hand over my mouth so that I could not cry out. 'I have long wanted you and now I shall have you,' he said. Even if I had not been given to Red-Sky to be his woman, any feeling I might ever have had for Swift-Walker would have died within me after that.

"I struggled as best I could. I got one arm loose and stretched my hand under the skins of the bed, for that is where Red-Sky conceals his belongings of value, and I felt the handle of the knife. I am not sure whether I would have had the courage to thrust it into Swift-Walker's body. But I had no opportunity; he twisted my hand and snatched the weapon from me.

"But even so the High Gods took pity on me and protected me from the sin of disobedience to our laws. For then, holding the knife, Swift-Walker raised himself from me and stood a moment staring down at me in the half-darkness. I was beyond outcry or attempted flight, too weak from terror to stir.

"He seemed like one possessed who suddenly has been freed of the demon. He made a strange sound, half-groan, half-sigh, and darted from the hut. I stumbled from the bed and I could see him running down the path that leads to the forest, the knife still in his hand. I never saw him again until his dead body was brought back for burial.

"The next day was the Summer Festival, and I saw Red-Sky among the dancers. I had time to call my thoughts together. I dared not tell Red-Sky what had happened; I dreaded the moment he would find his knife was gone. But he kept silent about his loss, to me as well as to others; I know now it was his half brother he blamed. And before I could make up my mind to speak, word came of the finding of Swift-Walker, dead. The rest you know."

A shiver ran through the throng of listeners. In the memory of the tribe no other of them had ever destroyed his own life.

But the Spirit-Sayer shook his head.

"Your story was well told, She-Bear," he said gently. "You learned your lesson well. But your story is not true. I believe that Swift-Walker crept to you in the night and seized you. And I believe that you reached beneath the bed and brought out the ptarmigan knife.

"But it was not Swift-Walker who wrested the knife from your grasp and ran to the forest with it. It is not in nature for a man inflamed with lust suddenly to feel remorse for no reason; only fear could drive off one in Swift-Walker's state of passion. And you did not see him take the path to the forest. The opening of Red-Sky's hut faces the other way."

She-Bear stood silently weeping again, her face in her hands.

The Spirit-Sayer's voice grew stern. "Now I will say what really happened.

"Only the dance leaders were with me in the cave on Festival Eve. Who among the other men had reason to worry and watch when Red-Sky was absent? Who did not sleep, but kept his eyes on Swift-Walker, and saw him rise and leave? That man followed him at a distance where he would not be seen, and when he came upon him he did indeed find She-Bear resisting attack.

"It was that man who caught up the knife. When Swift-Walker, unarmed, was startled and leaped up at his arrival, and saw in the half-darkness who the invader was, he was terrified. He ran from the hut and sought to lose the other in the forest, for he knew well that even if he won a struggle he would bring down upon himself exposure and disgrace.

"The pursuer caught up with him deep in the dark forest, and they fought. Swift-Walker was younger and stronger and he beat down the other man, so that he was bent over his opponent with his throat exposed. Then the other must have seized his opportunity. He slashed with the ptarmigan knife, still in his hand, and Swift-Walker fell, dying or dead.

"The knife dropped as the victor got to his feet and in the darkness he could not find it; perhaps he did not know how easily it could be traced to its owner. This is mid-summer, and dawn comes early; the killer had to get back to camp and to his hut before the sleepers began to wake at daylight."

The Spirit-Sayer paused. It was so still that the people seemed to have ceased even to breathe.

"She-Bear is indeed a good and obedient woman; she was so to her father and is so now to her man. What she was commanded to say if she should be accused, she did say. But only one man had cause and opportunity for what was done, and it was he who taught her what to answer.

"He-Who-Dares, come forward and stand before me!"

She-Bear's father jumped up and turned as if to flee. Two of his nearest neighbors caught him by the arms and dragged him to the cleared space between the Spirit-Sayer and the crowd. There he brushed them aside and raised his head.

"I was protecting my daughter," he said truculently.

"You were protecting your wealth, which has always meant more to you than all your children," the Spirit-Sayer retorted. "We all know your greed. You knew that if Swift-Walker succeeded in ravaging the girl and Red-Sky learned of it, he might cast her off and demand from you the return of what he had paid for her. She would have no value to you then, for she would be any man's for the taking.

"Your evil has found you out. Through the very weapon you used, the spirits have guided me to discover your guilt. You took the life of one of our own tribe, and for that life you must pay with your own.

"Hold him and bind him," he commanded the men who had brought He-Who-Dares forward and who still stood behind him. "When the sun rises tomorrow, He-Who-Dares must be slain according to our rites and customs.

"Red-Sky, you are to keep and care for She-Bear as before, without holding against her any blame or accusation; of her own will she has committed no offense against you. Snow-Born, you and your half brother will both do penance for your ill feeling to one another, to wipe out the possession by evil that has made dissension between brothers who should be loyal friends. . . . The ptarmigan knife I myself shall bury as tribute to the Gods.

"Go now, all of you, to your huts and resting places and cleanse yourselves and pray in preparation for tomorrow's sacrifice."

Turning, the Spirit-Sayer in all his regalia walked away while the people waited, not daring to move until he had left them. The old man touched Bright-Morning as he passed, and when the crowd had dispersed the youth followed his father's signal.

For a long time the Spirit-Sayer sat in his hut in silence. Then he sighed deeply and said, "This is not yet the end. Tomorrow I must preside over the ritual slaying of He-Who-Dares—who was one of my own puberty group. The people will not soon forget. They will obey me, but that will not erase this trouble as if it had never existed.

"I must watch that Red-Sky does not harbor ill will against either She-Bear or Snow-Born; that Snow-Born represses his resentment of his half brother if he cannot overcome it; that Horse-Slayer and White-Deer do not plot against She-Bear because they blame her unjustly for Swift-Walker's death. It is a heavy responsibility to be the Spirit-Sayer of our tribe."

"But you will succeed, my father," said Bright-Morning confidently. "I know well that it was through you alone that the spirits revealed the true events of this great mystery. What none of us could understand by human reason was made plain to you who are under the guardianship of the holy powers."

The Spirit-Sayer smiled slightly.

"My son," he said slowly, "I have great hopes that when my time is over it will be you who will take up my office. You are learning from me to paint and model the animal likenesses that will reward our hunters, to receive my knowledge of our songs and dances and our secret rites. You are very young still, but I can see already that you have skill and thoughtfulness beyond mine when I was your age and under instruction from the Spirit-Sayer of my own youth.

"So today I shall tell you the first of the high secret sayings, which you will keep in your own heart and ponder over and never tell and never forget.

"Remember this, my son: for their peace of mind the weak and ignorant need to believe that when the Spirit-Sayer consults the sacred objects, the spirits reveal to him directly the truth he seeks. But it is not so. All the spirits can do is enable him to use the understanding that sets man above all lesser beings.

"The spirits work solely through the intelligence of man. *I myself* reasoned out the truth of the murder of Swift-Walker."

# 1593

# A Sad and Bloody Hour

## *by Joe Gores*

*England in the late sixteenth century—with further comment by the author when you have finished reading this remarkable tale.*

PERHAPS IT WAS UNSCANNED self-love, concern for the first heir of my wit's invention, that brought me back to London from the safety of Dover where The Admiral's Men were presenting Marlowe's *Tragical History of Doctor Faustus*. It was a grisly visit, for eleven hundred a week were dying of the plague. This scourge of God had carried away few of my acquaintance save poor Kit, but his loss was heavy: our friendship had been much deeper than mere feigning.

I finished my business with Dick Field and in the afternoon returned to my rented room on Bishopsgate near Crosby Hall. When I ascended the dank, ill-lit staircase to my chamber I found a lady waiting me within. As she turned from a window I saw she was not Puritan Agnes come to see her player husband, but a pretty bit of virginity with a small voice as befits a woman.

"Thank God I found you before your return to the provinces!"

Her words, and the depths of her steady blue eyes, made me realize that she was only about five years younger than my twenty-nine. With her bodice laces daringly loosened to display her bright red stomacher beneath, and wearing no hat or gloves, she might have been a common drab: but never had I seen a bawdy woman with so much character in her face. As if reading my thought she drew herself up.

"I am Anne Page, daughter to Master Thomas Page and until recently maid to Mistress Audry, wife of Squire Thomas Walsingham of Scadbury Park, Chislehurst."

All things seemed that day conspired to remind me of poor Marlowe, for Walsingham had been his patron since Cambridge.

"Then you knew Kit?"

"Knew him?" She turned away as if seeking his swarthy face in the unshuttered window. "With his beard cut short like a Spaniard's, full of strange oaths and quick to quarrel for his honour! Knew him?" She turned back to me suddenly. "Were you truly his friend? By all the gods at once, I need a man to imitate the tiger!"

"I am young and raw, Mistress Page, but believe me: sorrow bites more lightly those who mock it."

"Say rage, rather! Oh, were I a man my sword should end it!" Her eyes flashed as if seeing more devils than hell could hold. "Didn't you know that last May when Tom Kyd was arrested, he deposed that Kit had done the heretical writings found in his room?"

"The players were scattered by the closing of the theatres."

"On the strength of Kyd's testimony a warrant was issued; Kit was staying at Scadbury Park to avoid the plague, so Squire Thomas put up bail. But then a second indictment was brought, this time before the Privy Council by the informer Richard Baines. On May twenty-ninth I was listening outside the library door when the Squire accused Kit of compromising those in high places whose friendship he had taken."

I shook my head sorrowfully. "And the next day he died!"

"Died!" Her laugh was scornful. "When he left the library, Kit told me that two of Squire Thomas's creatures, Ingram Frizer and Nicholas Skeres, would meet him at a Deptford tavern to help him flee the country. I begged him be careful but ever he sought the bubble reputation, even in the cannon's mouth; and so he now lies in St. Nicholas churchyard. And so I wish I were with him, in heaven or in hell!"

"But why do you say cannon's mouth? His death was—"

"Murder! Murder most foul and unnatural, arranged beneath the guise of friendship and bought with gold from Walsingham's coffers! Kit was stabbed to death that afternoon in Eleanor Bull's tavern!"

I shivered, and heard a spy in every creaking floorboard; it is ever dangerous for baser natures to come between the mighty and their designs, and Squire Thomas's late cousin Sir Francis, had, as Secretary of State, crushed the Babington Conspiracy against the Queen.

"But what proof could you have? You were not there to see it."

"Do I need proof that Rob Poley, back from the Hague only that morning, was despatched to the tavern two hours before Kit's end? Proof that Squire Thomas, learning that I had been listening outside the library door, discharged me without reference so I have become . . ." She broke off, pallid cheeks aflame, then plunged on: "Oh, player, had you the motive and cue for passion that I have! I beg you, go to Deptford, ferret out what happened! If it was murder, then I'll do bitterness such as the day will fear to look upon!"

She admitted she was a discharged serving wench with a grievance against Walsingham; yet her form, conjoined with the cause she preached, might have made a stone capable. I heard my own voice saying staunchly: "Tomorrow I'll go to Deptford to learn the truth of it."

"Oh, God bless you!" Swift as a stoat she darted to the door; her eyes glowed darkly back at me from the folds of her mantle. "Tomorrow night and each night thereafter until we meet . . . Paul's Walk."

She was gone. I ran after her but St. Mary's Axe was empty. Down Bishopsgate the spires of St. Helen's Church were sheathed in gold.

Kit Marlowe murdered by his patron Thomas Walsingham! It could not be. And yet . . . I determined to seek Dick Quiney and his advice.

The doors wore red plague crosses and the shops were shuttered as I turned into Candlewick toward the imposing bulk of St. Paul's. In Carter Lane the householders were lighting their horn lanterns; beyond Tom Creed's house was The Bell where I hoped to find Dick Quiney. Though he's now a High Bailiff in Warwickshire, his mercer's business often calls him to London. I hoped that I would find him now in the City.

The Bell's front woodwork was grotesquely carved and painted with red and blue gargoyles, and a sign worth forty pounds creaked over the walk on a wrought-iron bracket: it bore a bell and no other mark besides, but good wine needs no bush to herald it. Through the leaded casement windows came the tapster's cry, "Score at the bar!" When I asked the drawer, a paunchy man with nothing on his crown between him and heaven, if Dick Quiney were staying there, he gestured up the broad oak stairway.

"In the Dolphin Chamber, master."

The room faced the inner court on the second floor. When I thrust open the door, Dick, with an oath, sprang for the scabbarded rapier hung over the back of his chair: forcible entry to another's chamber has been often used for hired murder. But then he laughed.

"Johannus Factotem! I feared my hour had come. How do you, lad?"

"As an indifferent child of earth."

"What makes the handsome well-shaped player brave

the plague—oho! September twenty-second tomorrow!" He laughed again, a wee quick wiry man in green hose and brown unpadded doublet. "The upstart crow, beautified with their feathers, will give them all a purge."

" 'Let base conceited wits admire vile things, fair Phoebus lead me to the Muses' springs,' " I quoted. "You ought to recognize Ovid—we read him in the grammar long ago. As for the translation, I had it from Kit last spring."

"Still harping on Marlowe, lad? We all owe God a death."

"What reports have you had of the cause of his?"

"Surely it was the plague. Gabriel Harvey's 'Gorgon' says—"

"That's now disputed." Over meat I recounted it all. "I fear Walsingham, but if I should be fattening the region's kites with his—"

"Would you number sands and drink oceans dry? In justice—"

"—none of us should see salvation. Not justice, friendship: forgotten, it stings sharper than the winter wind."

"Pah! Marlowe was hasty as fire and deaf as the sea in his rages. You'd do him no disservice to leave his bones lie." Then he shrugged. "But as you say, use men as they deserve and who would escape the whipping? So you'll off to Deptford, seeking truth."

"I will. If you could go to Harrison's White Greyhound—"

"I'll oversee your interests." He clapped me on the back. "Give tomorrow to gaunt ghosts the grave's inherited, tonight there's excellent *theologicum* and humming ale made with fat standing Thames water."

I could find no boats at Paul's Pier; and at Queenhithe, the watermen's gathering place of late years, were boats but no pilots. As I started for the Red Knight, a boy hailed me from the dock.

"John Taylor, boatman's apprentice, at your service." Barely thirteen, he had an honest open face, curly brown hair, and sharp eyes. "Do you travel to escape the plague?"

I sat down on the embroidered cushions in the stern of his boat. "No, I'm a journeyman to grief. Westward ho— to Deptford, lad."

The ebbing tide carried us toward the stone arches of London Bridge, sliding us beneath her covered arcade and crowded houses like an eel from the hand. As we passed the Tower the boy spoke suddenly.

"Weren't you a player in *The True Tragedy of Richard, Duke of York,* at The Theatre last year?"

"You know much of the stage for one so young," I grunted. Yet I was pleased that he had recognized me, for all men seek fame.

The bells of St. Saviour's on the Surrey Side were pealing eight far behind us when Deptford docks came into view around a bend in the river, crowded with the polyglot shipping of all nations. A sailor with one eye directed me to St. Nicholas Church, the mean stone chapel not far from the docks where Anne Page had said Kit was buried.

The rector was a stubby white-haired man, soberly dressed as befits the clergy, with his spectacles on his nose and his hose hanging on shrunken shanks.

"Give you God's blessings, sir." His piping voice would have been drowned in the Sunday coughings of his congregation. "Even as the holy Stephen gave soft words to those heathens who were stoning him."

"Let's talk of graves and worms and epitaphs. I want to see your register of burials for the present year."

"Here are many graved in the hollow ground, as was holy Lawrence after that naughty man Valerian broiled him on a slow grid." He squeaked and gibbered like the Roman dead upon the death of Caesar, but finally laid out the great leather-covered volume I desired. "Seek only that which concerns you: sin not with the eyes. Consider Lucy of Syracuse; when complimented by a noble on her beautiful eyes, she did tear them out and hand them to him so that she might avoid immodest pride."

"I search for only one name—that of Christopher Marlowe."

"Marlowe? Why, a very devil, that man, a player and—"

"Churlish priest! Kit will be singing when you lie howling! And why have you written only: *First June, 1593, Christopher Marlowe slain by Francis Archer.* No word of his monument or epitaph."

The old cleric, ruffled by my words, chirped like a magpie. "His bones lie tombless, with no remembrance over them."

"But he had high friends! Why, after a violent death, was he given such an unworthy burial?"

"Squire Walsingham himself so ordered." Animosity faded from his whizzled walnut face in the hope of vicarious scandal. "Surely his death was a simple tavern brawl? It was so accepted by William Danby, Coroner to the Royal Household, who held the inquest since Her Gracious Highness was lying at Kew."

"The Queen's Coroner would not be corrupt," I said brusquely. But could he be misled? "Now take me to Kit's grave."

In an unmarked oblong of sunken earth in the churchyard, under a plane tree, was Kit, safely stowed with flowers growing from his eyes. I felt the salt tears trickling down my own face.

"Even as St. Nicholas once restored to life through God's grace three boys who had been pickled in a salting-rub for bacon, so may we gather honey from the weed and make a moral of this devil Marlowe. The dead are as but pictures—and only children fear painted devils—but Marlowe was so evil that God struck him down in the midst of sin."

"Pah!" I burst out angrily, dashing away my unmanly tears. "Your preaching leaves an evil taste like easel! Speak only from the pulpit, father—play the fool only in your own house."

"My Father's House! In His House are many mansions, but none—"

I left his querulous anger behind to search for Eleanor Bull's tavern. Walsingham might have ordered just such a hurried obscure funeral if Kit had died of the plague; but then why had the burial record shown him slain by Francis Archer? And why had Anne Page given me Ingram Frizer as Kit's killer? Had her tale been more matter and less art than it had seemed? Perhaps Eleanor Bull would have the answers.

Playbills were tattered on the notice-post beside the door and Dame Eleanor would have made a good comic character upon the stage herself: a round-faced, jolly woman with a bawdy tongue and a nose that had been thrust into more than one tankard of stout, by its color. She wore a fine scarlet robe with a white hood.

"Give you good morrow, sir."

"Good morrow, dame. Would you join me in a cup of wine?"

"By your leave, right gladly, sir." She preceded me up the narrow stairs, panting her remarks over her shoulder in beery lack of breath. "I get few . . . phew . . . other than seafarers here. Rough lot they be, much . . . phew . . . given to profanity." She opened a door, dug me slyly in the ribs as I passed. "La! If I but lodge a lonely gentlewoman or two who live honestly by their needlework, straightway it's claimed I keep a bawdy house!"

I laughed and ordered a pint of white wine each. It was a pleasant chamber overlooking an enclosed garden; the ceiling was oak and a couch was pushed back against the cheap arras showing Richard Crookback and Catesby on Bosworth Field. A fireplace pierced one wall.

"Tell me, mistress: did a man named Christopher Marlowe meet an untimely end in your house some months ago?"

"You knew Marlowe, in truth?" She regarded me shrewdly. "For all his abusing of God's patience and the King's English with quaint curses, he was a man women'd run through fire for. Lord, Lord, master, he was ever a wanton! I'll never laugh as I did in that man's company."

I kept my voice casual. "A brawl over a wench, wasn't it? And the fellow who killed him—Francis Archer?"

"La!" She jingled the keys on her silver-embroidered sash. "You must have seen the decayed cleric of St. Nicholas Church—he can scarce root the garden with his shaking fingers, let alone write right a stranger's name. Ingram Frizer was the man who shuffled Kit off."

"I would be pleased to hear an account of it."

"Heaven forgive him and all of us, I say; he died in this very room, on that very couch. God's blood, I don't know what he was doing in such company, as Nick Skeres is a cutpurse and Frizer a swindler for all his pious talk; but all three were living at Scadbury Park and once spied together for the Privy Council. Rob Poley, another of the same, arrived on a spent horse in the afternoon, and two hours later the fight started. By the time I had run up here, Kit was already flat upon the couch, stabbed through the skull above the right eye."

"Wasn't Frizer charged when the guard arrived?"

"Right speedily: but the others backed his story that Kit, who was lying drunk upon the couch, had attacked him through an argument over the score. Frizer was watching Skeres and Poley at backgammon, when Kit suddenly leaped up cursing, seized Frizer's own knife from its shoulder sheath, and started stabbing him in the face. Frizer got free, they scuffled, Kit fell on the knife." She shrugged. "The inquest was the first of June; by the twenty-eighth Frizer'd been pardoned by the Queen and was back at Scadbury Park in the Squire's pay."

I sat down on the couch, muscles crawling. Kit had been as strong and agile as myself from the tumbling and fencing at which all players excel; and even in a drunken rage would the creator of haughty Tamburlaine and proud Faustus stab from behind? *The room seemed to darken; four dim figures strained in the dusk, Kit's arms jerked back, feet thrust cunningly between his, a cry—silence—* murder.

I looked up at Eleanor Bull. "Do you believe their story?"

"I'll not put my finger in the fire." But then her gaze faltered; her thumb ring glinted as she clutched the arras.

She turned suddenly, face distorted. "La! I'll speak of it though hell itself forbid me! It was I who saw him fumble at his doublet, and smile upon his fingers, and cry out 'God! God! God!' It was I who felt his legs and found them cold as any stone. And it was I who now declare that here was cruel murder done!"

Her words brought me to my feet. "Then I'm for Scadbury Park to pluck this bloody villain's beard and blow it in his face!"

She cast her bulk before me, arms outstretched. "Oh, master, that sword which clanks so bravely against your flank will be poor steel against the viper you seek to rouse. These other swashers—la! Three such antics together don't make a man. Skeres is white-livered and red-faced; Frizer has a killing tongue and a quiet sword; and Poley's few good words match as few good deeds. But Squire Thomas! Cross him to learn that one may smile and smile and be a villain."

"I'm committed to one with true cause for weeping. Go I must."

"Then take one of my horses—and my prayers with you."

After a few miles of gently rolling downs whose nestled farmers' cots reminded me of my own Warwickshire, I came to Chislehurst. Beyond a mile of forest was Manor Park Road curving gently up through open orchards to the moated main house of Scadbury Manor, a sprawling tile-roofed timber building over two hundred years old.

I was led through the vast unceiled central hall to the library, which was furnished in chestnut panels. His books showed the Squire's deep interest in the arts: Holinshed's *Chronicles;* Halle's *Union;* Plutarch's *Lives;* Sir Philip Sydney's *Arcadia,* chief flower of English letters. These were bound in leather and set on the shelves with their gilt-edged leaves facing out to show the gold clasps and jewelled studs. On the other shelves were rolled and piled manuscripts—*Diana Enamorada, Menaechmi*—which I was examining when a low melancholy voice addressed me from the doorway.

"Who asks for Walsingham with Marlowe's name also on his lips?"

He looked the knight that he so ardently sought to be, elegant as a bridegroom and trimly dressed in silken doublet, velvet hose, and scarlet cloak. His voice was like his thrice-gilt rapier in its velvet scabbard: silk with steel beneath. Lengthened by a pointed beard and framed in coiling hair, his face had the cruel features of a Titus or a Caesar: Roman nose, pale appraising eyes, well-shaped disdainful lips. A face to attract and repel in an instant.

"A poor player who begs true detail of Marlowe's quick end."

He advanced leisurely into the room, giving his snuff box to his nose. "Your clothes make your rude birth and ruder profession obvious. I knew Marlowe slightly and sponsored his serious work—not the plays, of course. But why ask me about his death when the plague—"

"I had it from An——from a mutual friend that he was slain, not by plague, but in a Deptford tavern brawl by your man Ingram Frizer."

"Did you now? And this gossip—the trollop Anne Page?"

"No," I retorted quickly, "Tom Kyd in Newgate Gaol."

He sneered and rang a small silver bell. "A quick eye and open ear such as yours often make gaol smell of home; and your tongue runs so roundly that it may soon run your head from your irreverent shoulders. But perhaps even the meanly born can honour friendship."

The man who entered was easily recognized as Nicholas Skeres: he was indeed beet-nosed and capon-bellied, and when he learned of my errand he advanced bellowing as if I would melt like suet in the sun.

"Why, you nosey mummer, Kit was a bawcock and a heart of gold! Why, were he among us now, I'd kiss his dirty toe, I would; for well I loved the lovely bully." He laughed coarsely. "Of course now he's at supper with the worms; but here's Frizer to set you right."

Ingram Frizer had a churchwarden's face but the eye of a man who sleeps little at night. His mouth was an O and his eyes were to heaven, and he aped the cleric's true piety as ill as the odious prattler replacing the well-graced actor upon the stage.

"Poor Marlowe," he intoned unctuously, "He left this life as one who had been studied in his death. Here am I, watching backgammon; there is Kit, upon the couch. He leaps up, seized my knife—" He moved, and the deadly blade whose hilt was visible over his left shoulder darted out like a serpent's tongue to slash the dancing dust-motes. "He strikes me twice in the face, I pull loose, we grapple, he slips . . . sheathed in his brain. I pluck away the steel, kiss the gash yawning so bloodily on his brow. He smiles a last brave time, takes my hand in feeble grip —but his soul is fled to the Eternal Father."

"Satisfied now, Mars of malcontents?"

"Just one more question, Squire." As my profession is counterfeit emotion, my tone matched Frizer's for buttery sorrow. "Then I will take my leave."

"Nothing will I more readily give you."

"Why did Poley, fresh from the Hague as from the seacoasts of Bohemia, come hurriedly that day to Dame Eleanor's tavern?"

"Question my actions, player, and you'll yield the crows a pudding!" Poley advanced from the shadows; huge, silent-moving, dark and sensual of face, his eyes falcon-fierce and his nose bent aside as if seeking the smell of death. His arms were thick and his chest a brine-barrel beneath his stained leather doublet.

Squire Thomas's sad disdainful smile fluttered beneath his new-reaped mustache like a dove about the cote. "He was just come from Holland. Where better than a tavern to wash away the dust of travel?"

"What of Baine's indictment of Kit that was sure to embarrass you and the others of Raleigh's Circle if it came to court? You had learned of it only the night before; this had nothing to do with Poley's despatch to the tavern on that day?"

His face went ashen, his lips bloodless; his pale eyes flashed and his voice shook with suppressed rage. "Divine my downfall, you little better thing than earth, and you may find yourself beneath it!" With an effort he controlled his emotion. "Apes and actors, they say, should have their brains removed and given to the dog for a New Year's gift."

He held up a detaining hand. "Soft, you—a word or two before you go. I have done the state some service and they know it. Beware! You said Tom Kyd gave you the news of Marlowe's death, then prattled details only Anne Page could have told you. No murder have I done—yet she spreads her scandals. Seek her out in secret and you will feel that the very cobbles beneath your feet do prate to me your whereabouts."

Such a man bestrides my narrow world like a Colossus; yet was he more fully man than I?

"You despise me for my birth, Walsingham; yet nature cannot choose its origin. Blood will have blood if blood has been let, and murder will out for all your saying."

But I didn't feel safe until good English oak was between us.

Ten had struck before I arrived, in defiance of Squire Thomas, at St. Paul's Cathedral Church. During the hours of worship the shrill cries of the hawkers and the shouts of the roistering Paul's Men compete among the arches with the chants of the choir; but then only my boots echoed upon the stones of Paul's Walk, the great central nave.

I loosened my sword, for one may as easily have his throat cut in the church as elsewhere. When a slight figure in homespun darted from behind a pillar, I recognized Anne Page's eyes glowing beneath the coarse grey mantle just before my steel cleared the sheath.

"You come most carefully upon your hour, player. Tell me, quickly, what did you learn?" Present fears forgotten, we patrolled the nave in measured steps. When I had finished she cried: "Oh, smiling damned villain! From this time shall my thoughts be only bloody!"

I cautioned: "Squire Thomas said that he had done no murder."

"Then you're a fool, or coward! On May eighteenth Walsingham sent Poley to find Kit a place to hide in Holland from the warrant brought by Kyd's deposition. But Baines's charge of blasphemy was too serious—Walsingham feared he would be compromised by helping Kit defy it. More, he determined on murder to prevent the public disclosures of Kit's trial." Her voice writhed in its own venom like a stricken serpent. "Oh, player, I would lay the dust with showers of that man's blood. But hold—enough! My quarrel is yours no further."

"I'll not leave you, Anne," I declared passionately.

"You must. Had I met you before Kit—" Her fingers brushed my lips in sexless caress, and regret laid its vague wings across her face. "Too late! Hell has breathed contagion on me; I am fit only to drink hot blood."

I shook my head and declared flatly: "I will walk with you, Anne; take you through the dark night to your home."

Outside the Cathedral it was cold and the air bit shrewdly. Rank river fog, driven by the eager nipping wind, obscured all about us. Noxious plague odors assailed us, and from the muffling smoke came the clop-clop of hoofs as a death cart rattled about its grisly business, the cartmen leaping down with iron tongs to drag the sprawled and sightless corpses from the slops and urine of the gutters.

Through the swirling fog of Dowgate Hill I could see the cobbler's house where last year Rob Greene was lost in death's dateless night. Here Anne broke in upon my reverie.

"Now surely twelve has struck—the moon is down, and it goes down at twelve. It's the witching time of night; in my soul shriek owls where mounting larks should sing. And now I must leave you."

"Now? Here? Surely not here, Anne?"

For we had arrived at Cold Harbour, where criminals

impudently mock our English courts and the filthy tenements breed every vice.

"Yes, here," she whispered. "Here night cloaks me from my own sight while my body buys me sustenance to nurse revenge; and here I live only in hope of one day taking Walsingham about some act with no salvation in it, so his heels may kick to heaven while his soul is plunged to deepest hell."

She led me down a narrow alley where rats scuttled unseen and my boots slithered in foul mud; suddenly a man was silhouetted before us, naked steel glittering in his right hand.

"Back—this way!" I warned.

Too late! Behind were two more figures. Light glinted off bared swords, a spur chinked stone. I felt so unmanned with terror of my sins that I could not even draw my sword—for thus conscience makes cowards of us all. But then one of the men called out.

"Stand aside—we seek only the woman."

But I recognised the voice; and with recognition came anger.

"Booted and spurred, Rob Poley?" When I cried his name Anne gasped. "You three have ridden hard from Scadbury Park this night."

"You know us, player? Then by these hands you *both* shall die!"

"If hell and Satan hold their promises." My sword hissed out like a basking serpent from beneath its stone, barely in time to turn his darting steel. "Aha, boy!" I cried, "Say you so?"

But as he gave way before me Anne Page flashed by, dagger high.

"Murderer! Your deeds stink above the earth with carrion men!"

His outthrust rapier passed through her body, showed me half its length behind. She fell heavily sideways. Before his weapon was free I might have struck, but I was slow, for never before had I raised my blade in anger. Then it was too late. He put a ruthless foot against her neck, and jerked free.

"Stand on distance!" he bellowed at Skeres and Frizer. "Make him open his guard. He must not live!"

But by then my youthful blood was roused, and like all players I am expert in the fence. I turned Skeres's blade, shouting: "Now, while your purple hands reek and smoke," I lunged, skewered his dancing shadow in the throat so sparks flew from the stone behind his head, and jerked free. "I know these passes . . . these staccadoes. . . ."

My dagger turned Frizer's sword, I covered, thrust, parried, thrust again, my arm longer by three feet of tempered steel. ". . . they're common on the stage . . . here . . . here . . the heart!"

Frizer reeled drunkenly away, arms crossed over his punctured chest; but what of Poley? Fire lanced my arm and my rapier clattered from my nerveless grasp. Fingers like Hanse sausages closed about my windpipe. I felt myself thrust back so his long sword could reach me.

"Say you so now?" His voice was a snarl of triumph. "Are you there, truepenny?"

My head whirled giddily for lack of blood. In an instant his steel would—but then my dagger touched his belly. "How now!" I cried. "Dead for a ducat, dead!"

With my last despairing strength I ripped the two-edged cutter up through his guts, sprawled over his twitching corpse.

Silence. Moisture dripping from overhanging eaves, hot blood staining my fingers. A rat rustling in the gutter. The turning world turning on, aeons passing. Yet I lay silent in the drifting smoke. Then from beyond eternity a weak voice called me back to life.

"Player—my gashes cry for help—" Somehow I crawled to her, cradled her weakly lolling head against my shoulder. Her voice was small, so very small. "The churchyard yawns below me. I'll trade the world for a little grave, a little, little grave, an obscure grave. . . ."

My salt tears gave benediction to her death-ravaged face; her body now was lead within the angle of my arm.

"Anne!" I cried. "Anne! Oh, God! God forgive us all!"

"Let not this night be the whetstone of your sword." Her heart fluttered briefly within the frail cage of her body; her whispers touched my ear in failing cadence. "Let your heart be blunted. This death is—a joy unmixed with—sorrow."

No more. I lowered her gently to the waiting earth, struggled erect. My breath still rasped and rattled in my throat; dark walls weaved, receded, shifted; lantern bright above Cold Harbour Stairs, stone slimy beneath my vagrant gory fingers, cold Thames below, whispering its litany *she is dead she is dead she is*

Falling. Nothing else besides.

Movement aroused me. I lay on the cushions of a waterman's boat, river fog upon my face. Peering forward I saw a familiar figure.

"Lad, how did I come here?"

John Taylor turned anxious eyes on me. "I found you at the foot of Cold Harbour Stairs." He indicated my sword at my feet. "Your blood upon the cobbles led to this—and one that was a woman. But rest her soul, she's dead. Two others were there also, one with his wizand slit, the other drawn like a bull in the flesh shambles."

I thrust my arm into the clear Thames water, found the wound only a painful furrow in the flesh. Frizer had escaped. Anne was dead. I needed time—time to think.

"The Falcon, lad. I'll see what physic the tavern acords."

I gave the boy my silver and went through the entrance, narrow and thick-walled from pre-Tudor days, to the taproom. Here I was met by a blast of light and noise. I kept my arm against my side to mask the blood. A jolly group was gathered by the bar.

> *A cup of wine that's brisk and fine*
> *And drink unto the leman mine:*
> *And a merry heart lives long-a.*

"Before God, an excellent song!"

"An English song," laughed the singer. "Indeed, we

English are most potent in our potting. I'll drink your Dane dead drunk; I'll overthrow your German; and I'll give your Hollander a vomit before the next bottle's filled!"

But this was Will Sly, the red-faced, jolly comedian I'd left in Dover! At sight of me he threw his arms wide.

"Out upon it, old carrion! You can't have heard: The Admiral's Men have been disbanded! By William the Conqueror who came before Richard III, Will Sly finds himself in the good Falcon with bad companions swilling worse ale." He suited actions to words, then leaned closer and lowered his voice as he wiped the foam from his moustache. "But you look pale, lad; and your tankard's dry. Ho! Drawer!"

"Anon, sir."

I had barely drawn him aside with my story when a blustery voice broke in. "Players in the corner? Then some man's reputation's due for a fall. In faith, it's better to have a bad epitaph than the players' ill report while alive. But let me tell you what I'm about."

"Why, two yards at least, Tom Lucy," laughed Will Sly.

Lucy was from Charlecote, a few miles from my home —a trying man with severe eyes and beard of formal cut, and the brains of a pecking sparrow.

"Perhaps two yards around the waist, Will Sly, but now I'm about thrift, not waste."

He was always full of wise saws and modern instances, so I cut in curtly: "We'll join you at the bar presently, Master Lucy."

After he had turned about I went on; soon Will Sly's face was as long as his cloak. When I told of the meeting with Anne in St. Paul's he burst out bitterly: "Fool! What if you were seen with this Anne Page? If—"

"Anne Page?" said Lucy to me. "I wondered at the name of the doxy you walked beside on Dowgate Hill hard upon midnight, player."

Will Sly matched his name. "Then you've been seeing double, Tom Lucy; he's matched me pot for pot these four hours past."

"I'm not decieved in her," said Lucy. "In the Bankside Stews her eyes have met mine boldly, like any honest woman's."

"Then the sun shone on a dunghill!" I burst out.

"Now vultures gripe your guts, player!" Lucy clapped hand to sword dramatically. "This'll make you skip like any rat!" When I stiffened he laughed loudly. "What? A tiger wrapped in a player's hide—or merely a kitten crying mew?"

Will Sly drew me away with a hasty hand. "Make nothing of it, lad—bluster must serve him for wit. He lives but for his porridge and fat bull-beef. But never before have I seen you foam up so, like sour beer, at any man. Is this my honest lad, my free and open nature—" He broke off abruptly, eyes wide at the blood upon his fingers.

"They set upon us in Cold Harbour. I left them stiff."

"How many? All? Dead? Why, you hell-kite, you!"

"There were three—Frizer lived, I think. Man, they made love to that employment! They're not near my conscience."

He shook his head. "Until tonight I'd have thought you incapable of taking offence at any man—nothing deeper in you than a smooth and ready wit. But yonder fat fool may yet breed you unnatural troubles."

"Just keep him from me," I said. "My blood is up."

But Lucy stopped me at the door, still not plumbing my mood.

"Hold, puppy! When a man mouths me as you have done, why, I'll fight with him until my eyelids no longer wag!"

Then he winked broadly at the company, waiting for me to turn away as is my wont. But suddenly I found myself with my rapier in hand, and saw, through the red mists, Lucy's mouth working like a netted luce's.

"Softly, master player!" He backed off rapidly. "I only jested. Er—I hold it fit that we should shake hands and part. You as your desires point you and me—why, I'll go pray."

I saw that he would pass it off as a joke, so I thrust away my sword and ignored his hand to stride from the place with Will Sly behind.

"Why so hot tonight, lad? The rightly great stir only with great argument. When honour's at stake find a quarrel in a straw—"

"Before my eyes they killed her!" I burst out. "Killed Anne!"

"No!" His homely face crinkled in honest sympathy; he turned away. "And you had begun to feel something more for her than pity?"

"I know not, but she and Kit cannot lie unavenged. What is a man if all he does is feed and sleep?"

"A beast, nothing more. And yet, lad, two carrion men crying for burial also shout to me of vengeance taken."

"But Walsingham—"

"Leave him to heaven. Look: he said no murder had he done. Are you God, to judge him false? They might have struck for private reasons, or for hire other than his. Can you be sure they didn't?"

We were at the verge of the river. I could smell the mud and osiers. Across the broad reach of gliding water a few firefly lanterns winked on the London side, for the mist had lifted; from downstream came the creak and grumble of the old bridge in the flood tide.

*Could* I be sure of Walsingham's guilt? If killing is once started, where did it end?

The calm gliding river had begun to calm my own troubled spirit. My nature was not bloody, my trade was not revenge. Kit had died as he had lived, in violence; but his death, perhaps, had shown me the way to even greater things than he had done: plumb man's nature to its depths, transfigure with creative light the pain and sorrow and suffering of the human spirit—yes! White hairs to a quiet grave mean not always failure, nor does a life thrown away upon a gesture mean success. Perhaps in all of this my mettle had been hardened.

Perhaps . . .

Will Sly spoke as if divining my thoughts: "Forget

these sad and bloody hours, lad; the night is long indeed which never finds a day. In these bones of mine I know the world yet shall hear of you. Don't toss your life away upon revenge, as the tapster tosses off his pot of ale, for one day the mass of men will come to honour and revere your name—the name of William Shakespeare."

*A Sad and Bloody Hour*

AUTHOR'S NOTE:

When this story was first published, even as perceptive a reader as the late Anthony Boucher expressed dismay that I should consider identifying William Shakespeare as the narrator to be any sort of a challenge. This misunderstanding was due, I am sure, to a deficiency in my art rather than in Tony's comprehension.

For I *intended* that Shakespeare lovers would make the identification instantly. The title is a direct quote. There are forty-four physical clues unmistakable to the cognoscenti. Examples: The Admiral's Men (The Chamberlain's Men were not formed until 1594); Dick Field (Willy's boyhood friend who published *Venus and Adonis*); the "rented room on Bishopsgate near Crosby Hall"—an allusion to a house on which Shakespeare was assessed five pounds in 1598.

If one knew only Shakespeare's work, not his life, he could hardly miss my shameless plagiarisms—396 lines quotes or paraphrased from eighteen plays and two sonnets.

No, the challenge was the same I offered Tony verbally at the time he raised the point: how many clues can you recognize? how many stolen lines identify (with their sources)? When I dug out the manuscript for inclusion in the present volume, I picked up the gauntlet myself I had thrown down for Tony years before.

And failed miserably.

Joe Gores

# 1699

# A Fool for a Client

## by Lillian de la Torre

*Lillian de la Torre, creator of the well-known detective series about Dr. Sam: Johnson, is one of our foremost practitioners of historical mystery in both fact and fiction. Here we present her fascinating and little-known essay on the trial of Spencer Cowper, at Hertford in the year 1699.*

ON MONDAY, MARCH 13, 1699, Lord Chief Justice Hatsell rode into Hertford for the assizes. He was attended by a string of lawyers, scriveners, advocates, and hangers-on of the court, booted and spurred and cloaked, riding in the rain.

As the bedraggled procession neared the heart of town a girl in Quaker garb came from her door and stopped one of the riders. She was Sarah Stout, a beautiful, gay, rich, and very un-Quakerish Quakeress. The young man whose bridle she took was a brilliant young lawyer, Spencer Cowper[1] by name.

What business brought him to the Hertford assizes that rainy March day is not recorded. It is certain he was not

[1]Grandfather of Cowper, the poet.

there to defend any murderers, because in 1699 persons accused of murder were not allowed to be represented by counsel. They had to speak for themselves by mother wit, an arrangement which made it comfortably easy to convict in murder cases.

Four months later, the young lawyer again appeared at the Hertford assizes. This time he had an accused murderer to defend—himself. Sarah Stout lay in six feet of earth, and in the dock, accused of her murder, stood Spencer Cowper. A lawyer who takes his own case has, they say, a fool for a client; but Spencer Cowper had no choice.

The trial of Spencer Cowper made history. This time the rough and sudden justice of the days of good King William had caught a Tartar—a man who could defend himself against the law with the law's own weapons. Young Cowper, his excellent wits sharpened by his danger, even invented a new legal weapon for the defence. The trial of Spencer Cowper was the scene of the first battle of expert witnesses. The battle was notable for the fame of its champions, and for the classic pattern which it set. At the trial of Spencer Cowper, and even after, it is a commonplace that the doctors do differ.

"Spencer Cowper, hold up thy hand."

At the bar of the Hertford Assizes the young attorney held up his hand for blood. He listened to the charge against him as the clerk of the arraigns read it off. The crime of which he stood accused was triple-studded with verbiage; the law never uses one word where three will do. In effect the document set forth that Spencer Cowper, not having the fear of God before his eyes, but being moved and seduced by the instigation of the devil, had violently, feloniously, voluntarily, and of his malice aforethought, strangled Sarah Stout, in the peace of God and our sovereign Lord the King then and there being, and had thrown her lifeless body into the millstream; the whole proceeding being against the peace of our sovereign Lord the King, his crown and dignity.

"How sayest thou, Spencer Cowper, art thou guilty

of the felony and murder whereof thou standest indicted, or not guilty?"

"Not guilty."

"Culprit, how wilt thou be tried?"

"By God and my country."

"God send you a good deliverance," the clerk of the arraigns closed the old formula. Spencer Cowper had heard it rattled off a hundred times; but this time it must have been more than a formula to the young lawyer. A man cannot unmoved stand up in court and take his trial for murder.

With Spencer Cowper were indicted three other young men of the law who had ridden the circuit to Hertford. The grounds of their indictment was a perfect specimen of a mare's nest. It might serve as a warning to young lawyers against sitting up late drinking wine and talking nonsense; as grounds for prosecution it was patent rubbish. The three young men had entered their lodgings soaking wet from riding in the rain. Over their wine they had jested about Sarah Stout, and referred to some money they had received. When, next morning, Sarah lay dead, they not unreasonably preferred to avoid touching the clammy body. At the murderer's touch, thought Hertford in 1699, the murdered corpse bleeds. When the young lawyers avoided this test, Hertford thought the worst of them. Their landlady upon this got to hearing the voice of the dead girl: "Divulge, conceal nothing." So she divulged, and concealed nothing, actual or imaginary, and the three young men of the law stood in the dock beside Spencer Cowper, where they considerably beclouded the issue; and there we may leave them.

But we cannot so quickly acquit Spencer Cowper.

The first witness sworn for the prosecution was the dead woman's maid, Sarah Walker. Walker proved that Spencer Cowper was the last man to see Sarah Stout alive.

"May it please you, my lord, on Friday before the last assizes, Mr. Cowper's wife sent a letter to Mistress Stout, that she might expect Mr. Cowper at the assize time; and as he came in with the judges, she asked him if he would alight? He said 'no; by reason I came in later than usual, I will go into the town and show myself,' but he would send his horse presently."

The horse duly arrived, according to Walker, but his rider tarried until the impatient Quaker girl had to send after him. Then he came and dined with her, and went away about his legal business, promising to return. He did return at nine o'clock at night. He wrote a letter, and had milk for supper, and he and Sarah sat chatting.

"She called me in," said Walker, "and they were talking together, and then she bid me make a fire in his chamber; and when I had done so, I came and told him of it, and he looked at me, and made me no answer; then she bid me warm the bed, which accordingly I went up to do as the clock struck eleven, and in about a quarter of an hour, I heard the door shut, and I thought he was gone to carry the letter, and staid about a quarter of an hour longer, and came down, and he was gone, and she; and Mrs. Stout, the mother, asked me the reason why he went out when I was warming his bed. And she asked for my mistress, and I told her I left her with Mr. Cowper, and I never saw her after that, nor did Mr. Cowper return to the house."

When Walker had had her say, the accused man took her in hand. He was not lost and at sea, like an ordinary culprit, but well armed for the battle, the first lawyer to defend a murder case. He was prepared for Sarah Walker.

First he attacked her accuracy, pointing out that she had originally said he went out at 10:45. He only succeeded in establishing that the Stout clock was one-half hour fast by the town clock. He then drew attention to a curious point: Sarah Stout's maid and Sarah Stout's mother had taken her night-rambling with strange calm. Cowper suggested that they were used to it. Then he began establishing the line the defence would take:

"Pray, Mistress Walker, did you never take notice that your mistress was under melancholy?"

"I do not say but she was melancholy;" (but the maid

saw what the lawyer was after, and side-stepped him) "she was ill for some time, and I imputed it to her illness, and I know of no other cause."

Cowper let her go, and the prosecution called the miller.

"I went out in the morning to shoot a flush of water by six o'clock," said the miller, "and I saw something afloating in the water. No part of her body was above water, only some part of her clothes."

This didn't suit the prosecutor; he depended on the floating of the body to prove the girl was murdered, not drowned. But the miller stuck to it, and Prosecutor Jones went on to his next point, to establish that she had been strangled.

"Did you see any marks or bruises about her?"

"No," said the contrary miller.

Spencer Cowper must have smiled.

Then followed the countrymen who had seen Sarah in the stream, or laid upon the bank. Not one would say that there was a livid mark about her neck, although the prosecutor urged it; but they testified to a discoloration under one ear. They described her in the stream, caught between the stakes that held back trash and rubbish—and dead girls—from drifting into the millpond. They described her lying dead in the meadow in her petticoats, strait-laced in her stays and perfectly lank, not swelled at all. (It was the prosecutor's turn to smile.) Froth came from her mouth and nose, but no water flowed from her.

Cowper cross-examined each, and Baron Hatsell, on the bench, commenced to fidget. Time was running on. He began to snap at the accused man.

"Now, my lord," said the prosecutor, "we will give an account of how she was when she was stript, and they came to view the body. Call John Dimsdale, Junior."

And Spencer Cowper arose and flung his bombshell.

"My lord, if your lordship pleases, I have some physicians of note and eminency that are come down from London; I desire they may be called into court to hear what the surgeons say?"

"Ay," assented the lord chief justice, "by all means."

They filed into court, sombrely splendid in their great periwigs and stiff-skirted coats, their tall canes set with pomanders to smell against the infection. They were a formidable array, numbering ten of the age's most famous medical men; to name but three, Dr. Hans Sloane, founder of the British Museum; Dr. Samuel Garth, urbane friend of the poet Pope and author of "The Dispensary;" and Mr. William Cowper[1] (who as a surgeon rated no higher title), great anatomist, discoverer of Cowper's glands, and teacher at one remove of a later, greater anatomist, John Hunter.

These big guns the defence now trained upon the prosecution's rather smaller-bore medical men, who fired the first salvo.

Surgeon Dimsdale was among the first to see the body. He proved the blackness under her ear. Spencer Cowper put it to him that he had reported it to the coroner's jury as no more than a common stagnation usual in dead bodies; but Dimsdale could not remember saying a word of it. He did, however, admit that there was no circle around the neck.

"My lord," said Surgeon Coatsworth, "in April last I was sent for by Dr. Philips, to come to Hertford to see the body of Mistress Stout opened, who had been six weeks buried; and he told me, that there was a suspicion she was murdered. Her face and neck, to her shoulders, appeared black, and so much corrupted, that we were unwilling to proceed any further."

But Mrs. Stout was very much enraged, because a great scandal had been raised, that her daughter was with child; and she said she would have her opened to clear her reputation.

So the gruesome autopsy went on. The doctors found that Sarah Stout was not with child. They also found, to their surprise, that the vitals were perfectly dry, and well-preserved in comparison with the decay of the upper parts; and they concluded that so dry a corpse could not

[1] No relation.

have been drowned. Spencer Cowper tried to mix them up a bit about whether water can enter the thorax; but nothing came of it.

Mr. Jones opened his expert testimony: "Now, my lord, we call these gentlemen that are doctors of skill, to know their opinions of them that are found floating without water in them, how they came by their death."

All Spencer Cowper's medical big guns took notes assiduously.

Those that are found floating, in the opinion of the prosecution's medical men, came to their death by foul play on dry land. Cowper kept them busy on cross-examination, whether their observations were on bodies six weeks buried, whether on persons who drowned by accident or on purpose; and the red herring of water in the thorax was much in evidence.

The doctors were followed on the stand by seafaring men, who deponed that men killed aboard ship were committed to the deep weighted with shot, lest they float. Edward Clement said he saw Beachy fight, and the wreck of the *Coronation,* and saw the men in the water like a shoal of fish, and he was categorical that the living sank and the dead floated. Richard Gin was sullen. He would only repeat what "they say" on the matter, and when the prosecutor tried to qualify him as an expert by asking, "Are you a seaman?" he replied grumpily, "I went against my will in two fights." The prosecutor dropped him.

The lord chief justice had his say: "Dr. Browne has a learned discourse in his Vulgar Errors, upon this subject, concerning the floating of dead bodies; I do not understand it myself," said Baron Hatsell vacuously, "but he hath a whole chapter about it."

A lord chief justice ought to have understood it. Sir Thomas Browne says plainly that drowned bodies sink, and are raised again by corruption.

Now the mare's nest of the three young lawyers was aired, and the prosecution rested.

It is remarkable that not one word of testimony was offered by the prosecution to suggest why Spencer Cowper should have strangled Sarah Stout, or paid the young lawyers to do it. Sarah's mother had a reason to offer, and she offered it later on with great bitterness. Now she sat in court glowering at the defendant; but her mouth was closed. She was a Quaker. A Quaker could not take an oath; and nobody could testify in court without taking an oath.

Now the accused lawyer rose to open his defence, and urged it so eloquently that Baron Hatsell sourly brought him up short.

"Do not flourish too much, Mr. Cowper."

Cowper dropped the flourish and produced his witnesses. First came the parish officers who had drawn the dead girl from the water. They proved over again how she was jammed between the stakes, and how froth purged from her.

"It rose up in bladders, and run down on the sides of her face, and so rose again; and seeing her look like a gentlewoman, we desired one Ulse to search her pockets, to see if there were any letters that we might know who she was; so the woman did, and I believe there was twenty or more of us who knew her very well when she was alive, and not one of us knew her then; and the woman searched her pockets; and during all this while of discourse, the froth still worked out of her mouth."

Now Spencer Cowper unmasked his battery of experts, and they set the precedent for generations of experts to come by flatly contradicting their brother experts of the prosecution. They set another precedent. They had been testing the question at issue experimentally. A prodigious mortality among the dog population was put in evidence. Luckless canines living and dead had gone into the water by the score to settle the matter. Did a body that floats enter the water already dead? Must a drowned body be full of water? To both questions, after their experiments, the defence experts replied, not necessarily.

Dr. Garth added a contemptuous dismissal of the seafaring men, as a superstitious people, who fancy that whistling at sea will occasion a tempest.

So much for the experts. Now Spencer Cowper addressed himself to a question which is not always faced in murder trials, and which, indeed, he was not obliged to face: assuming the innocence of the accused, how is the death of the victim to be accounted for?

Sarah Stout drowned herself, said Spencer Cowper, in a fit of love-melancholy. Everybody in court knew about love-melancholy. Sir Richard Burton had written a great tome upon it, and the symptoms were well known. Sarah had them, by what the witnesses said. Walker had admitted she was melancholy. She had left off company, the defence witnesses added, and applied herself to reading; she went about with her head-cloth disordered, saying carelessly that it would serve her time; she had been heard to threaten that she would drown herself out of the way. Her conversations with her friends were foreboding and dark:

"I asked her," recalled Mr. Bowd, "what is the matter with you? Said I, there is something more than ordinary; you seem to be melancholy. Saith she, you are come from London, and you have heard something or other: said I, I believe you are in love. In love! said she. Yes, said I, Cupid, that little boy" (said Mr. Bowd with classical elegance) "hath struck you home: she took me by the hand; truly, said she, I must confess it; but I did think I should never be guilty of such folly: and I answered again, I admire that should make you uneasy; if the person be not of that fortune that you are, you may, if you love him, make him happy, and yourself easy. That cannot be, saith she; the world shall not say I change my religion for a husband."

This dark saying seems to refer to a marriageable suitor; but not so a gloomy interview she had with one Mrs. Low. That lady had expressed the same opinion, that a young woman of Sarah's fortune might have anybody. Oh, no, said Sarah; it was a person she could not marry.

Upon these girlish confidences, and upon the testimony of his experts, Spencer Cowper might advantageously have rested his case. But he pressed forward, and put a name to the person whom she loved and could not marry: Spencer Cowper.

He began by his witnesses to paint a picture of Sarah Stout as she was in life, a very extraordinary picture for the days of good King William. The Quaker girl was twenty-six years old, rich, and independent. Her father, a malster of Hertford, had been a political supporter of the Cowpers, who habitually represented the borough in Parliament; the then M.P. for Hertford was Spencer's elder brother William, later to be first lord chancellor. The families were close, and exchanged visits. Spencer and his young wife were especially fond of Sarah. When the rich malster died, he by-passed his elder son to leave Sarah all his assets. Sarah coolly set out to realize and reinvest her heritage. She could not so much as discuss business when her mother was in the room. She went up to London unchaperoned, lodged at a goldsmith's, and did as she pleased. She did as she pleased at home in Hertford, too. She had her own maid, and her own friends, whom she entertained at her pleasure with a bottle of wine in the summer-house. She spent her evenings where she pleased, and stayed as late as she liked; a schedule confirmed by Mrs. Stout's inaction when her daughter went out with a man at eleven o'clock and didn't come back. So brazen was her behavior that Theophilus, an eloquent Quaker waterman, was brought down to reprove her, which he did publicly in a tirade of such "canting stuff" as infuriated the subject of his discourse.

It was this strong-minded young woman who set her heart on Spencer Cowper. He betrayed her frailty in open court. No one else could have told the story, and Mrs. Stout and her stepson John, no matter how angrily they glowered, could not disprove it. Such items as could be proved by another were proved by the persons concerned.

It was through him, Cowper said, that Sarah Stout met Mr. Marshall, a relation of Mrs. Cowper's.

"When she was first acquainted with him she received him with a great deal of civility and kindness, which induced him to make his addresses to her, as he did, by way of courtship. It happened one evening that she and Mrs. Crook, Mr. Marshall and myself, were walking together, and Mr. Marshall and Mrs. Crook going some little way before us, she took this opportunity to speak to me in such terms, I must confess, as surprised me."

The Quaker girl's advances to the handsome lawyer were couched in such terms as would hardly surprise us two hundred and fifty years later. They prove that the words of a maid to a man have hardly changed their guise over the centuries.

"Mr. Cowper," said the forward young woman, "I did not think you had been so dull."

Dull Mr. Cowper rose to the bait: "Dull? Wherein?"

"Why," says she, "do you imagine I intend to marry Mr. Marshall?"

Mr. Cowper thought she did; and if she did not, she was much to blame in what she had done to encourage his suit.

"No," said the brazen girl, "I thought it might serve to divert the censure of the world, and favour our acquaintance."

Mr. Thomas Marshall of Lyon's Inn, the subject of this conversation, now admitted on the stand that he "was never a very violent lover" and gave an account of his lukewarm courtship.

"When I came to town, my lord, I was generally told of my courting Mistress Stout, which I confess was not then in my head; but it being represented to me as a thing easy to be got over, and believing the report of the world as to her fortune, I did afterwards make my application to her; but upon very little trial of that sort, I received a very fair denial, and there ended my suit; Mr. Cowper having been so friendly to me, as to give me notice of some things, that convinced me I ought to be thankful I had no more to do with her."

The lukewarm lover put in evidence a billet-doux from the lady, gay, riddling, not in earnest, signed "Your Loving Duck." Mr. Beale, an old suitor of Sarah's who, though a Quaker, did not boggle at an oath, bustled officiously forward and identified the handwriting.

William Cowper, M.P., also spoke for his brother. He had known of the Quaker girl's importunities. He recalled one occasion in particular, when his Joseph of a brother, threatened with an unchaperoned call from the lady, had fled to Deptford, and Sarah when she heard of his defection changed color and went into "a woman's fit of swooning."

Now the luckless Sarah's love-letters were read into the record. Busy Friend Beale proved the hand again. Baron Hatsell thought they ought to ask her relatives, oath or no oath, but he got no help from them.

"How should I know!" said the angry Quaker matron. "I know she was no such person."

Nevertheless the letters were read. The sender and the receiver had been surreptitious about the correspondence.

"My lord," said the accused lawyer to the judge, "I must a little inform you of the nature of this letter. It is on the outside directed to Mrs. Jane Ellen, to be left for her at Mr. Hargrave's coffee-house. For her to direct for me at a coffee-house, might make the servants wonder and the postman might suspect, and for that reason she directed it in that manner."

Apparently the scruples of the man who ran away to Deptford rather than receive a lady in his chambers did not extend to a clandestine correspondence with the same lady.

The reckless Quaker girl addressed Mrs. Jane Ellen as "Sir." The riddling style was the same, but with this correspondent the writer was in dead earnest. Under date of March 5, hardly eight days before she died, she wrote:

"Sir,
I am glad you have not quite forgot that there is such a person as I in being; but I am willing to shut my eyes, and not see any thing that looks like unkindness in you, and rather content myself with what excuses you are pleased to make, than be inquisitive into what I must not know. I should very readily comply with your proposition of changing the season, if it were in my power to do it, but

you know that lies altogether in your own breast: I am sure the winter has been too unpleasant for me to desire the continuance of it; and I wish you were to endure the sharpness of it but for one hour, as I have done for many long nights and days; and then I believe it would move that rocky heart of yours, that can be so thoughtless of me as you are: But if it were designed for that end, to make the summer the more delightful, I wish it may have the effect so far, as to continue it to be so too, that the weather may never overcast again; the which if I could be assured of, it would recompense me for all that I have ever suffered, and make me as easy a creature as I was the first moment I received breath. When you come to Hertford pray let your steed guide you, and do not do as you did last time; and be sure to order your affairs to be here as soon as you can, which cannot be sooner than you will be heartily welcomed to

Your very sincere Friend."

There is no record of what Spencer Cowper thought as the clerk of the court droned out the words of the dead Quaker girl, nor of what the crowded courtroom thought; but they cannot have doubted that there had been summer between the married lawyer and the passionate girl before she vanished into winter and night forever.

But the year with Sarah Stout was freezing fast. She must have had a letter from Spencer Cowper, full of reservations about the inconvenience that might result from their "cohabiting," for in her last letter on earth she had dropped her pretty fancy of the seasons and picked up that lawyer's word instead:

March 9.

"Sir,

I writ to you by Sunday's post, which I hope you have received; however, as a confirmation, I will assure you I know of no inconvenience that can attend your cohabiting with me, unless the grand jury should thereupon find a bill against us; but I won't fly for it, for come life, come death, I am resolved never to desert you; therefore ac-

cording to your appointment I will expect you, and till then I shall only tell you, that I am
Yours, &c."

It was this letter which the dubious young lawyer, blowing hot and cold as now gallantry, now prudence, got the upper hand, took to his brother for advice. The brothers were undecided whether to save Spencer's chastity or the price of a lodging, and in an unlucky hour chose the cash. William engaged to write and cancel the Cowper's standing reservation at Barefoote's. This on second thought he did not do; he seems to have felt that Spencer would be safer at the inn. Spencer reached the same conclusion, and refused to alight at Stout's, but pushed on to Barefoote's. There, still prudent, he made sure the lodgings had not been "unbespoke." Assured that his brother would have to pay the bill, he sent for his bag and settled down to take his ease at his inn.

He could be firm as long as there was no expense involved. But when a free dinner was in prospect he weakened, and dined at Stout's. Even more weakly he returned to sup there. On that occasion, he said, he paid Sarah the interest on some money he had invested for her. She pocketed the six pounds odd, but left the receipt on the table unsigned.

In the unsigned receipt, old Mrs. Stout was to allege later, lay the key to the whole affair. Her daughter, she said, left the receipt unsigned because she was unsatisfied with Spencer Cowper's stewardship of her investments. He had made away the whole of her fortune, the story went, and when the girl betrayed suspicion she had to be silenced.

Though this accusation was never made in court, Cowper had heard it, and replied that he had never invested for her but once, and owed her no more than the six pounds odd; and that though his mind was on business, hers was on other matters than signing receipts:

"I would rather leave it to be observed," said the accused lawyer, "than make the observations myself, what might be the dispute between us at the time the maid speaks of. I think it was not necessary she should be present at the debate; and therefore I might not interrupt her mistress in the orders she gave; but as soon as the maid was gone, I made use of these objections . . . but, my lord, my reasons not prevailing I was forced to decide the controversy by going to my lodging."

"I believe you have done now, Mr. Cowper?" prompted weary Baron Hatsell.

But he had not. He had one more shot in his locker. Walker had sworn that he left Stout's about 10:45. The Barefootes had proved he entered his lodging at a little after eleven by the town clock. Now he filled the interval. A brace of servants from the Glove and Dolphin swore that he entered the inn as the clock struck eleven, and asked for his bill for horse-keeping, and paid it on the spot, going away in about a quarter of an hour.

Now the jury was in a hurry:

"We have taken minutes of what has passed. If your Lordship please we will withdraw."

This was to cut his Lordship out of his big moment, his charge to the jury. He frowned upon them:

"They must make an end first."

The prosecution wanted to bring some character witnesses for poor Sarah, whose character had been so mangled by the defence. But Baron Hatsell had heard enough, and he brushed them aside:

"I believe nobody disputes that; she might be a virtuous woman, and her brains might be turned by her passion, or some distemper."

He launched into his charge, which cannot have helped the jury much:

"You have heard also what the doctors and surgeons said on the one side and the other concerning the swimming and sinking of dead bodies in water; but I can find no certainty in it. The doctors and surgeons have talked a great deal to this purpose, and of the water's going into the lungs or the thorax; but unless you have more skill in anatomy than I, you would not be much edified by it. I acknowledge I never studied anatomy; but I perceive," said the lord chief justice of the first battle of experts, "that the doctors do differ in their notions about these things."

Thus unedified, the jury withdrew to consider their verdict.

Medical jurisprudence has matured into a science since its first appearance at the trial of Spencer Cowper. Can we find more certainty in the matter than judge or jury in 1699?

There is no certainty to be reached through the battle of the experts. The defence experts, we now know, were right: every body sinks, until raised again by corruption, and a very little water in a man's body can drown him. But the entire dispute is beside the point, since it is clear from prosecution and defence testimony alike that the body of Sarah Stout was found neither sinking nor floating, but entangled in the stakes of the weir.

Was she drowned, or was she murdered and thrown into the stream? Does science provide an answer? Writing of the case in 1931 in his "The Scientific Detective and the Expert Witness," C. Ainsworth Mitchell said regretfully that there is, as a rule, no single simple test for determining that point. Nevertheless, I think the evidence at the trial can be made to yield the answer. In the *Encyclopedia Britannica* article on the medical jurisprudence of drowning, Dr. Henry D. Littlejohn cites a number of the appearances which are found in the bodies of those who drown. If we find the most important of those appearances in the body of Sarah Stout, we must conclude that she was drowned.

The victim of drowning is unrecognizable; twenty acquaintances failed to recognize Sarah as she lay in the meadow. The head and neck of the victim of drowning decompose with marked rapidity; it was that phenomenon in the exhumed body that first surprised the doctors who performed the autopsy, though they interpreted it backwards to Spencer Cowper's disadvantage. Most characteristic is the froth that marks the mouth and throat of the victim of drowning; nine witnesses on both sides saw the froth work from her mouth.

Sarah Stout was drowned. Did Spencer Cowper drown her? His alibi, unlike poor Sarah, is water-tight; he did not.

Was he morally guilty of her death? It is plain that he was. His conniving at the "Mrs. Jane Ellen" subterfuge plainly convicts him of intrigue with her. His prudence became alarmed, and he tried to break off with her, though with wavering resolution. When he walked out of her house at 10:45 that night, she must have followed to plead or upbraid. To escape the embarrassment of being followed to his lodging by a railing woman, he did what otherwise makes little sense at that hour of the night—he turned in at the Glove and paid a bill. Sarah, left in the street, made her way in headlong grief and anger to the millstream.

In half an hour the jury was in.

"Spencer Cowper, hold up thy hand."

At the bar of the Hertford assizes the young attorney held up his hand for his mistress's blood, and knew in his heart that he was guilty—guilty of unkindness to the girl who loved him too well, of betraying her to the man who might have given her honorable marriage, of driving her with rocky heart to her death in the millstream. He was already punished at the best event by the care, the shame, the expense, and the political loss involved in the trial. Now he would learn whether his folly would cost him a shameful death on the gallows.

"Look upon the jury. Jury, look upon the prisoner. How say you? Is he guilty of the felony and murder whereof he stands indicted, or not guilty?"

*"Not guilty!"*

# 1861

# Chinoiserie

## by Helen McCloy

*Helen McCloy's first detective short story, this richly detailed evocation of China in the middle of the last century has become a modern classic. It has been widely translated and was recently produced in a Chinese version on Singapore television. Come with us now to old Peking—a city much in the news since President Nixon's visit there.*

THIS IS THE STORY of Olga Kyrilovna and how she disappeared in the heart of Old Pekin.

Not Peiping, with its American drugstore on Hatamen Street. Pekin, capital of the Manchu Empire. Didn't you know that I used to be language clerk at the Legation there? Long ago. Long before the Boxer Uprising. Oh, yes, I was young. So young I was in love with Olga Kyrilovna. . . . Will you pour the brandy for me? My hand's grown shaky the last few years. . . .

When the nine great gates of the Tartar City swung to at sunset, we were locked for the night inside a walled, medieval citadel, reached by camel over the Gobi or by boat up the Pei-ho, defended by bow and arrow and a painted representation of cannon. An Arabian Nights' city where the nine gate towers on the forty-foot walls were just ninety-nine feet high so they would not impede the flight of air spirits. Where palace eunuchs kept harems of their own to "save face." Where musicians were blinded because the use of the eye destroys the subtlety of the ear. Where physicians prescribed powdered jade and tigers' claws for anemia brought on by malnutrition. Where mining operations were dangerous because they opened the veins of the Earth Dragon. Where felons were slowly sliced to death and beggars were found frozen to death in the streets every morning in the winter.

It was into this world of fantasy and fear that Olga Kyrilovna vanished as completely as if she had dissolved into one of the air spirits or ridden away on one of the invisible dragons that our Chinese servants saw in the atmosphere all around us.

It happened the night of a New Year's Eve ball at the Japanese Legation.

When I reached the Russian Legation for dinner, a Cossack of the Escort took me into a room that was once a Tartar general's audience hall. Two dozen candle flames hardly pierced the bleak dusk. The fire in the brick stove barely dulled the cutting edge of a North China winter. I chafed my hands, thinking myself alone. Someone stirred and sighed in the shadows. It was she.

Olga Kyrilovna. . . . How can I make you see her as I saw her that evening? She was pale in her white dress against walls of tarnished gilt and rusted vermilion. Two smooth, shining wings of light brown hair. An oval face, pure in line, delicate in color. And, of course, unspoiled by modern cosmetics. Her eyes were blue. Dreaming eyes. She seemed to live and move in a waking dream, remote from the enforced intimacies of our narrow society. More than one man had tried vainly to wake her from that dream. The piquancy of her situation provoked men like Lucien de l'Orges, the French Chargé.

She was just seventeen, fresh from the convent of Smolny. Volgorughi had been Russian Minister in China for many years. After his last trip to Petersburg, he had brought Olga back to Pekin as his bride, and . . . well, he was three times her age.

That evening she spoke first. "Monsieur Charley . . ."

Even at official meetings the American Minister called me "Charley." Most Europeans assumed it was my last name.

"I'm glad you are here," she went on in French, our only common language. "I was beginning to feel lonely. And afraid."

"Afraid?" I repeated stupidly. "Of what?"

A door opened. Candle flames shied and the startled shadows leaped up the walls. Volgorughi spoke from the doorway, coolly. "Olga, we are having sherry in the study. . . . Oh!" His voice warmed. "Monsieur Charley, I didn't see you. Good evening."

I followed Olga's filmy skirts into the study, conscious of Volgorughi's sharp glance as he stood aside to let me pass. He always seemed rather formidable. In spite of his grizzled hair, he had the leanness of a young man and the carriage of a soldier. But he had the weary eyes of an old man. And the dry, shriveled hands, always cold to the touch, even in summer. A young man's imagination shrank from any mental image of those hands caressing Olga. . . .

In the smaller room it was warmer and brighter. Glasses of sherry and vodka had been pushed aside to make space on the table for a painting on silk. Brown, frail, desiccated as a dead leaf, the silk looked hundreds of years old. Yet the ponies painted on its fragile surface in faded pigments were the same lively Mongol ponies we still used for race meetings outside the city walls.

"The Chinese have no understanding of art," drawled Lucien de l'Orges. "Chinese porcelain is beginning to enjoy a certain vogue in Europe, but Chinese painters are impossible. In landscape they show objects on a flat surface, without perspective, as if the artist were looking down on the earth from a balloon. In portraits they draw the human face without shadows or thickness as untutored children do. The Chinese artist hasn't enough skill to imitate nature accurately."

Lucien was baiting Volgorughi. "Pekin temper" was as much a feature of our lives as "Pekin throat." We got on each other's nerves like a storm-stayed house party. An unbalanced party where men outnumbered women six to one.

Volgorughi kept his temper. "The Chinese artist doesn't care to 'imitate' nature. He prefers to suggest or symbolize what he sees."

"But Chinese art is heathen!" This was Sybil Carstairs, wife of the English Inspector-General of Maritime Customs. "How can heathen art equal art inspired by Christian morals?"

Her husband's objection was more practical: "You're wastin' money, Volgorughi. Two hundred Shanghai taels for a daub that will never fetch sixpence in any European market!"

Incredible? No. This was before Hirth and Fenollosa made Chinese painting fashionable in the West. Years later I saw a fragment from Volgorughi's collection sold in the famous *Salle Six* of the Hotel Drouot. While the *commissaire-priseur* was bawling, *"On demande quatre cent mille francs,"* I was seeing Olga again, pale in a white dress against a wall of gilt and vermilion in the light of shivering candle flames. . . .

Volgorughi turned to her just then. "Olga, my dear, you haven't any sherry." He smiled as he held out a glass. The brown wine turned to gold in the candlelight as she lifted it to her lips with an almost childish obedience.

I had not noticed little Kiada, the Japanese Minister, bending over the painting. Now he turned sleepy slant-eyes on Volgorughi and spoke blandly. "This is the work of Han Kan, greatest of horse painters. It must be the finest painting of the T'ang Dynasty now in existence."

"You think so, Count?" Volgorughi was amused. He seemed to be yielding to an irresistible temptation as he went on. "What would you say if I told you I knew of a T'ang painting infinitely finer—a landscape scroll by

Wang Wei himself?"

Kiada's eyes lost their sleepy look. He had all his nation's respect for Chinese art, tinctured with jealousy of the older culture. "One hears rumors now and then that these fabulous masterpieces still exist, hidden away in the treasure chests of great Chinese families. But I have never seen an original Wang Wei."

"Who or what, is Wang Wei?" Sybil sounded petulant.

Kiada lifted his glass of sherry to the light. "Madame, Wang Wei could place scenery extending to ten thousand *li* upon the small surface of a fan. He could paint cats that would keep any house free from mice. When his hour came to Pass Above, he did not die. He merely stepped through a painted doorway in one of his own landscapes and was never seen again. All these things indicate that his brush was guided by a god."

Volgorughi leaned across the table, looking at Kiada. "What would you say if I told you that I had just added a Wang Wei to my collection?"

Kiada showed even, white teeth. "Nothing but respect for your Excellency's judgment could prevent my insisting that it was a copy by some lesser artist of the Yüän Dynasty—possibly Chao Méng Fu. An original Wang Wei could not be bought for money."

"Indeed?" Volgorughi unlocked a cabinet with a key he carried on his watch chain. He took something out and tossed it on the table like a man throwing down a challenge. It was a cylinder in an embroidered satin cover. Kiada peeled the cover and we saw a scroll on a roller of old milk-jade.

It was a broad ribbon of silk, once white, now ripened with great age to a mellow brown. A foot wide, sixteen feet long, painted lengthwise to show the course of a river. As it unrolled a stream of pure lapis, jade and turquoise hues flowed before my enchanted eyes, almost like a moving picture. Born in a bubbling spring, fed by waterfalls, the river wound its way among groves of tender, green bamboo, parks with dappled deer peeping through slender pine trees, cottages with curly roofs nestling among round hills, verdant meadows, fantastic cliffs, strange wind-distorted trees, rushes, wild geese and at last, a foam-flecked sea.

Kiada's face was a study. He whispered brokenly, "I can hear the wind sing in the rushes. I can hear the wail of the wild geese. Of Wang Wei truly is it written—his pictures were unspoken poems."

"And the color!" cried Volgorughi, ecstasy in his eyes.

Lucien's sly voice murmured in my ear. "A younger man, married to Olga Kyrilovna, would have no time for painting, Chinese or otherwise."

Volgorughi had Kiada by the arm. "This is no copy by Chao Méng Fu! Look at that inscription on the margin. Can you read it?"

Kiada glanced—then stared. There was more than suspicion in the look he turned on Volgorughi. There was fear. "I must beg your excellency to excuse me. I do not read Chinese."

We were interrupted by a commotion in the compound. A giant Cossack, in full-skirted coat and sheepskin cap, was coming through the gate carrying astride his shoulders a young man, elegantly slim, in an officer's uniform. The Cossack knelt on the ground. The rider slipped lightly from his unconventional mount. He sauntered past the window and a moment later he was entering the study with a nonchalance just this side of insolence. To my amazement I saw that he carried a whip which he handed with his gloves to the Chinese boy who opened the door.

"Princess, your servant. Excellency, my apologies. I believe I'm late."

Volgorughi returned the greeting with the condescension of a Western Russian for an Eastern Russian—a former officer of *Chevaliers Gardes* for an obscure Colonel of Oussurian Cossacks. Sometimes I wondered why such a bold adventurer as Alexei Andreitch Liakoff had been appointed Russian Military Attaché in Pekin. He was born in Tobolsk, where there is Tartar blood. His oblique eyes, high cheekbones and sallow, hairless skin lent color to his impudent claim of descent from Genghis

Khan.

"Are Russian officers in the habit of using their men as saddle horses?" I muttered to Carstairs.

Alexei's quick ear caught the words. "It may become a habit with me." He seemed to relish my discomfiture. "I don't like Mongol ponies. A Cossack is just as sure-footed. And much more docile."

Olga Kyrilovna roused herself to play hostess. "Sherry, Colonel Liakoff? Or vodka?"

"Vodka, if her Excellency pleases." Alexei's voice softened as he spoke to Olga. His eyes dwelt on her face gravely as he took the glass from her hand.

The ghost of mockery touched Volgorughi's lips. He despised vodka as a peasant's drink.

Alexei approached the table to set down his empty glass. For the first time, his glance fell on the painting by Wang Wei. His glass crashed on the marble floor.

"You read Chinese, don't you?" Volgorughi spoke austerely. "Perhaps you can translate this inscription?"

Alexei put both hands wide apart on the table and leaned on them, studying the ideographs. " 'Wang Wei.' And a date. The same as our A.D. 740."

"And the rest?" insisted Volgorughi.

Alexei looked at him. "Your Excellency really wishes me to read this? Aloud?"

Alexei went on. *"At an odd moment in summer I came across this painting of a river course by Wang Wei. Under its influence I sketched a spray of peach blossom on the margin as an expression of my sympathy for the artist and his profound and mysterious work. The Words of the Emperor. Written in the Lai Ching summerhouse, 1746."*

Kiada had been frightened when he looked at that inscription. Alexei was angry. Why I did not know.

Carstairs broke the silence. "I don't see anything mysterious about a picture of a river!"

"Everything about his picture is—mysterious." Kiada glanced at Volgorughi. "May one inquire how your Excellency obtained this incomparable masterpiece?"

"From a peddler in the Chinese City." Volgorughi's

tone forbade further questions. Just then his Number One Boy announced dinner.

There was the usual confusion when we started for the ball at the Japanese Legation. Mongol ponies had to be blindfolded before they would let men in European dress mount and even then they were skittish. For this reason it was the custom for men to walk and for women to drive in hooded Pekin carts. But Sybil Carstairs always defied this convention, exclaiming, "Why should I be bumped black and blue in a springless cart just because I am a woman?" She and her husband were setting out on foot when Olga's little cart clattered into the compound driven by a Chinese groom. Kiada had gone on ahead to welcome his early guests. Volgorughi lifted Olga into the cart. She was quite helpless in a Siberian cloak of blue fox paws and clumsy Mongol socks of white felt over her dancing slippers. Her head drooped against Volgorughi's shoulder drowsily as he put her down in the cart. He drew the fur cloak around her in a gesture that seemed tenderly protective. She lifted languid eyes.

"Isn't Lady Carstairs driving with me?"

"My dear, you know she never drives in a Pekin cart. You are not afraid?" Volgorughi smiled. "You will be quite safe, Olga Kyrilovna. I promise you that."

Her answering smile wavered. Then the hood hid her face from view as the cart rattled through the gateway.

Volgorughi and Lucien walked close behind Olga's cart. Alexei and I followed more slowly. Our Chinese lantern boys ran ahead of us in the darkness to light our way like the linkmen of medieval London. Street lamps in Pekin were lighted only once a month—when the General of the Nine Gates made his rounds of inspection.

The lantern light danced down a long, empty lane winding between high, blank walls. A stinging Siberian wind threw splinters of sleet in my face. We hadn't the macadamized roads of the Treaty Ports. The frozen mud was hard and slippery as glass. I tried to keep to a ridge that ran down the middle of the road. My foot slipped and I stumbled down the slope into a foul gutter of sewage, frozen solid. The lanterns turned a corner. I was alone with the black night and the icy wind.

I groped my way along the gutter, one hand against the wall. No stars, no moon, no lighted windows, no other pedestrians. My boot met something soft that yielded and squirmed. My voice croaked a question in Mandarin: "Is this the way to the Japanese Legation?" The answer came in singsong Cantonese. I understood only one word: "Alms . . ."

Like heaven itself, I saw a distant flicker of light coming nearer. Like saints standing in the glow of their own halos I recognized Alexei and our lantern boys. "What happened?" Alexei's voice was taut. "I came back as soon as I missed you."

"Nothing. I fell. I was just asking this . . ."

Words died on my lips. Lantern light revealed the blunted lion-face, the eyeless sockets, the obscene, white stumps for hands—"mere corruption, swaddled man-wise." A leper. And I had been about to touch him.

Alexei's gaze followed mine to the beggar, hunched against the wall. "She is one of the worst I've ever seen."

"She?"

"I think it's a woman. Or, shall I say, it was a woman?" Alexei laughed harshly. "Shall we go on?"

We rounded the next corner before I recovered my voice. "These beggars aren't all as wretched as they seem, are they?"

"What put that into your head, Charley?"

"Something that happened last summer. We were in a market lane of the Chinese City—Sybil Carstairs and Olga Kyrilovna, Lucien and I. A beggar, squatting in the gutter, stared at us as if he had never seen Western men before. He looked like any other beggar—filthy, naked to the waist, with tattered blue trousers below. But his hands were toying with a little image carved in turquoise matrix. It looked old and valuable."

"He may have stolen it."

"It wasn't as simple as that," I retorted. "A man in silk rode up on a mule leading a white pony with a silver embroidered saddle. He called the beggar 'elder brother' and invited him to mount the pony. Then the two rode off together."

Alexei's black eyes glittered like jet beads in the lantern light. "Was the beggar the older of the two?"

"No. That's the queer part. The beggar was young. The man who called him 'elder brother' was old and dignified. . . . Some beggars at home have savings accounts. I suppose the same sort of thing could happen here."

Again Alexei laughed harshly. "Hold on to that idea, Charley, if it makes you feel more comfortable."

We came to a gate where lanterns clustered like a cloud of fireflies. A piano tinkled. In the compound, lantern boys were gathering outside the windows of a ballroom, tittering as they watched barbarian demons "jump" to Western music.

Characteristically, the Japanese Legation was the only European house in Pekin. Candle flames and crystal prisms. Wall mirrors and a polished parquet floor. The waltz from *Traviata*. The glitter of diamonds and gold braid. Punch *à la Romaine*.

"Where is Princess Volgorughi?" I asked Sybil Carstairs.

"Didn't she come with you and Colonel Liakoff?"

"No. Her cart followed you. We came afterward."

"Perhaps she's in the supper-room." Sybil whirled off with little Kiada.

Volgorughi was standing in the doorway of the supper-room with Lucien and Carstairs. "She'll be here in a moment," Carstairs was saying.

Alexei spoke over my shoulder. "Charley and I have just arrived. We did not pass her Excellency's cart on the way."

"Perhaps she turned back," said Lucien.

"In that case she would have passed us," returned Alexei. "Who was with her?"

Volgorughi's voice came out in a hoarse whisper. "Her groom and lantern boy. Both Chinese. But Kiada and the Carstairses were just ahead of her; Monsieur de l'Orges and I, just behind her."

"Not all the way," amended Lucien. "We took a wrong turning and got separated from each other in the dark. That was when we lost sight of her."

"My fault." Volgorughi's mouth twisted bitterly. "I was leading the way. And it was I who told her she would be—safe."

Again we breasted the wind to follow lanterns skimming before us like will o' the wisps. Vainly we strained our eyes through glancing lights and broken shadows. We met no one. We saw nothing. Not even a footprint or wheel rut on that frozen ground. Once something moaned in the void beyond the lights. It was only the leper.

At the gate of the Russian Legation, the Cossack guard sprang to attention. Volgorughi rapped out a few words in Russian. I knew enough to understand the man's reply. "The *baryna* has not returned, Excellency. There has been no sign of her or her cart."

Volgorughi was shouting. Voices, footfalls, lights filled the compound. Alexei struck his forehead with his clenched hand. "Fool that I am! The leper!"

He walked so fast I could hardly keep up with him. The lantern boys were running. A Cossack came striding after us. Alexei halted at the top of the ridge. The leper had not moved. He spoke sharply in Mandarin. "Have you seen a cart?" No answer. "When she asked me for alms, she spoke Cantonese," I told him. He repeated his question in Cantonese. Both Volgorughi and Alexei spoke the southern dialects. All the rest of us were content to stammer Mandarin.

Still no answer. The Cossack stepped down into the gutter. His great boot prodded the shapeless thing that lay there. It toppled sidewise.

Alexei moved down the slope. "Lights!" The lanterns shuddered and came nearer. The handle of a knife protruded from the leper's left breast.

Alexei forced himself to drop on one knee beside the obscene corpse. He studied it intently, without touching it.

"Murdered. . . .There are many knives like that in the Chinese City. Anyone might have used it—Chinese or European." He rose, brushing his knee with his gloved hand.

"Why?" I ventured.

"She couldn't see." His voice was judicious. "She must have heard—something."

"But what?"

Alexei's Asiatic face was inscrutable in the light from the paper lanterns.

Police? Extraterritorial law courts? That was Treaty Port stuff. Like pidgin English. We had only a few legation guards. No gunboats. No telegraph. No railway. The flying machine was a crank's daydream. Even cranks hadn't dreamed of a wireless telegraphy. . . . Dawn came. We were still searching. Olga Kyrilovna, her cart and pony, her groom and lantern boy, had all vanished without a trace as if they had never existed.

As character witnesses, the Chinese were baffling. "The Princess's groom was a Manchu of good character," Volgorughi's Number One Boy told us. "But her lantern boy was a Cantonese with a great crime on his conscience. He caused his mother's death when he was born, which the Ancients always considered Unfilial."

At noon some of us met in the smoking-room of the Pekin Club. "It's curious there's been no demand for ransom," I said.

"Bandits? Within the city walls?" Carstairs was skeptical. "Russia has never hesitated to use *agents provocateurs*. They say she's going to build a railway across Siberia. I don't believe it's practical. But you never can tell what those mad Russians will do. She'll need Manchuria. And she'll need a pretext for taking it. Why not the abduction of the Russian Minister's wife?"

Kiada shook his head. "Princess Volgorughi will not be found until 'The River' is restored to its companion pictures, 'The Lake,' 'The Sea,' and 'The Cloud.' "

"What do you mean?"

Kiada answered me patiently as an adult explaining the

obvious to a backward child. "It is known that Wang Wei painted this series of pictures entitled 'Four Forms of Water.' Volgorughi has only one of them 'The River.' The separation of one painting from others in a series divinely inspired is displeasing to the artist."

"But Wang Wei has been dead more than a thousand years!"

"It is always dangerous to displease those who have Passed Above. An artist as steeped in ancient mysteries as the pious Wang Wei has power over men long after he has become a Guest On High. Wang Wei will shape the course of our lives into any pattern he pleases in order to bring those four paintings together again. I knew this last night when I first saw 'The River' and—I was afraid."

"I wonder how Volgorughi did get that painting?" mused Carstairs. "I hope he didn't forget the little formality of payment."

"He's not a thief!" I protested.

"No. But he's a collector. All collectors are mad. Especially Russian collectors. It's like gambling or opium."

Lucien smiled unpleasantly. "Art! Ghosts! Politics! Why go so far afield? Olga Kyrilovna was a young bride. And Volgorughi is—old. Such marriages are arranged by families, we all know. Women, as Balzac said, are the dupes of the social system. When they consent to marriage, they have not enough experience to know what they are consenting to. Olga Kyrilovna found herself in a trap. She has escaped, as young wives have escaped from time immemorial, by taking a lover. Now they've run off together. *Sabine a tout donné, sa beauté de colombe, et son amour . . .*"

"Monsieur de l'Orges."

We all started. Alexei was standing in the doorway. His eyes commanded the room. "What you say is impossible. Do I make myself clear?"

"Of course, Alexei. I—I was only joking." Lucien sounded piteous.

But Alexei had no pity. "A difference of taste in jokes has broken many friendships. . . . Charley, will you come back to the Russian Legation with me?"

The Tartar general's audience hall had never seemed more shabby. Volgorughi sat staring at the garish wall of red and gilt. He was wearing an overcoat, carrying hat and gloves.

"News, Excellency?" queried Alexei.

Volgorughi shook his head without looking up. "I've been to the *Tsungli Yamên.*" He spoke like a somnambulist. "The usual thing. Green tea. Melon seeds. A cold stone pavilion. Mandarins who giggle behind satin sleeves. I asked for an audience with the Emperor himself. It was offered—on the usual terms. I had to refuse—as usual. By the time a gunboat gets to the mouth of the Peiho, they may agree to open another seaport to Russian trade by way of reparation, but—I shall never see Olga Kyrilovna again. Sometimes I think our governments keep us here in the hope that something will happen to give them a pretext for sending troops into China. . . ."

We all felt that. The *Tsungli Yamên,* or Foreign Office, calmly assumed that our legations were vassal missions to the Emperor, like those from Tibet. The Emperor would not receive us unless we acknowledged his sovereignty by kow-towing, the forehead to strike the floor audibly nine times. Even if we had wished to go through this interesting performance for the sake of peace and trade, our governments would not let us compromise their sovereignty. But they kept us there, where we had no official standing, where our very existence was doubted. "It may be there are as many countries in the West as England, France, Germany and Russia," one mandarin had informed me. "But the others you mention—Austria, Sweden, Spain and America—they are all lies invented to intimidate the Chinese."

Alexei was not a man to give up easily. "Excellency, I shall find her."

Volgorughi lifted his head. "How?"

Alexei shouted. The study door opened. An old man in workman's dress came in with a young Chinese. I knew the old man as Antoine Billot, one of the Swiss clockmakers who were the only Western tradesmen allowed in Pekin.

"Charley," said Alexei, "tell Antoine about the fingering piece you saw in the hands of a beggar last summer."

"It was turquoise matrix, carved to represent two nude figures embracing. The vein of brown in the stone colored their heads and spotted the back of the smaller figure."

"I have seen such a fingering piece," said Antoine. "In the Palace of Whirring Phoenixes. It is in that portion of the Chinese City known as the Graveyard of the Wu family, in the Lane of Azure Thunder."

"It is the Beileh Tsai Heng who lives there," put in Antoine's Chinese apprentice. "Often have we repaired his French clocks. Very fine clocks of Limoges enamel sent to the Emperor Kang Hsi by Louis XIV. The Beileh's grandmother was the Discerning Concubine of the Emperor Tao Kwang."

"An old man?" asked Alexei.

"The Beileh has not yet attained the years of serenity. Though the name Heng means 'Steadfast,' he is impetuous as a startled dragon. He memorialized the late Emperor for permission to live in a secluded portion of the Chinese City so that he could devote his leisure to ingenious arts and pleasures."

I looked at Alexei. "You think the beggar who stared at us was a servant of this Prince?"

"No. Your beggar was the Prince himself. 'Elder Brother' is the correct form for addressing a Manchu prince of the third generation."

"It is the latest fad among our young princes of Pekin," explained the apprentice, "to haunt the highways and taverns dressed as beggars, sharing the sad life of the people for a few hours. They vie with each other to see which can look the most dirty and disreputable. But each one has some little habit of luxury that he cannot give up, even for the sake of disguise. A favorite ring, a precious fan, an antique fingering piece. That is how you can tell them from the real beggars."

Alexei turned to me. "When a taste for the exquisite

becomes so refined that it recoils upon itself and turns into its opposite—a taste for the ugly—we call that decadence. Prince Heng is decadent—bored, curious, irresponsible, ever in search of a new sensation." Alexei turned back to the apprentice. "Could the Beileh be tempted with money?"

"Who could offer him anything he does not already possess?" intoned the young Chinese. "His revered father amassed one hundred thousand myriad snow-white taels of silver from unofficial sources during his benevolent reign as Governor of Kwantung. In the Palace of Whirring Phoenixes even the wash bowls and spitting basins are curiously wrought of fine jade and pure gold, for this prince loves everything that is rare and strange."

Alexei hesitated before his next question. "Does the Beileh possess any valuable paintings?"

"His paintings are few but priceless. Four landscape scrolls from the divine brush of the illustrious Wang Wei."

Volgorughi started to his feet. "What's this?"

"You may go, Antoine." Alexei waited until the door had closed. "Isn't it obvious, sir? Your Wang Wei scroll was stolen."

Volgorughi sank back in his char. "But—I bought it. From a peddler in the Chinese City. I didn't ask his name."

"How could a nameless peddler acquire such a painting from such a prince honestly?" argued Alexei. "Your peddler was a thief or a receiver. Such paintings have religious as well as artistic value to the Chinese. They are heirlooms, never sold even by private families who need the money. Last night the moment I saw the marginal note written by the Emperor Ch'ien Lung I knew the picture must have been stolen from the Imperial Collection. I was disturbed because I knew that meant trouble for us if it were known you had the painting. That's why I didn't want to read the inscription aloud. It's easy to see what happened. The thief was captured and tortured until he told Heng you had the painting. Heng saw Olga Kyrilovna with Charley and Lucien in the Chinese City last summer. He must have heard then that she was your wife. When he found you had the painting, he ordered her abduction. Now he is holding her as hostage for the return of the painting. All this cannot be coincidence."

Volgorughi buried his face in his hands. "What can we do?"

"With your permission, Excellency, I shall go into the Chinese City tonight and return the painting to Heng. I shall bring back Olga Kyrilovna—if she is still alive."

Volgorughi rose, shoulders bent, chin sunk on his chest. "I shall go with you, Alexei Andreitch."

"Your Excellency forgets that special circumstances make it possible for me to go into the Chinese City after dark when no other European can do so with safety. Alone I have some chance of success. With you to protect, it would be impossible."

"You will need a Cossack escort."

"That would strip the legation of guards. And it would antagonize Heng. Olga Kyrilovna might be harmed before I could reach her. I prefer to go alone."

Volgorughi sighed. "Report to me as soon as you get back. . . . You are waiting for something?"

"The painting, Excellency."

Volgorughi walked with a shuffling step into the study. He came back with the scroll in its case. "Take it. I never want to see it again."

At the door I looked back. Volgorughi was slumped in his seat, a figure of utter loneliness and despair.

Alexei glanced at me as we crossed the compound. "Something is puzzling you, Charley. What is it?"

"If this Beileh Heng is holding Olga Kyrilovna as a hostage for the painting, he wants you to know that he has abducted her. He has nothing to conceal. Then why was the leper murdered if not to conceal something?"

Alexei led the way into a room of his own furnished with military severity. "I'm glad Volgorughi didn't think of that question, Charley. It has been troubling me too."

"And the answer?"

"Perhaps I shall find it in the Palace of Whirring Phoenixes. Perhaps it will lead me back to one of the men who dined with us yesterday evening. Except for the Carstairses, we were all separated from each other at one time or another in those dark streets—even you and I. . . ."

Alexei was opening a cedar chest. He took out a magnificent robe of wadded satin in prismatic blues and greens. When he had slipped it on he turned to face me. The Tartar cast of his oblique eyes and sallow skin was more pronounced than I had ever realized. Had I passed him wearing this costume in the Chinese City, I should have taken him for a Manchu or a Mongol.

He smiled. "Now will you believe I have the blood of Temudjin Genghis Khan in my veins?"

"You've done this before!"

His smile grew sardonic. "Do you understand why I am the only European who can go into the Chinese City after dark?"

My response was utterly illogical. "Alexei, take me with you tonight!"

He studied my face. "You were fond of Olga Kyrilovna, weren't you?"

"Is there no way?" I begged.

"Only one way. And it's safe. You could wear the overalls of a workman and carry the tools of a clockmaker. And stay close to me, ostensibly your Chinese employer."

"If Antoine Billot will lend me his clothes and tools . . ."

"That can be arranged." Alexei was fitting a jeweled nail shield over his little finger.

"Well? Is there any other objection?"

"Only this." He looked up at me intently. His pale face and black eyes were striking against the kingfisher blues and greens of his satin robe. "We are going to find something ugly at the core of this business, Charley. You are younger than I and—will you forgive me if I say you are rather innocent? Your idea of life in Pekin is a series of dances and dinners, race meetings outside the walls in spring, charades at the English Legation in winter, snipe-shooting at Hai Ten in the fall. Your government doesn't maintain an Intelligence Service here. So you can have no idea of the struggle that goes on under the surface of this pleasant social life. Imperialist ambitions and intrigues, the alliance between politics and trade, even the opium trade —what do you know of all that? Sometimes I think you don't even know much about the amusements men like Lucien find in the Chinese City. . . . Life is only pleasant on the surface, Charley. And now we're going below the surface. Respectability is as artificial as the clothes we wear. What it hides is as ugly as our naked bodies and animal functions. Whatever happens tonight, I want you to remember this: under every suit of clothes, broadcloth or rags, there is the same sort of animal."

"What are you hinting at?"

"There are various possibilities. You said Heng stared at your party as if he had never seen Western men before. Are you sure he wasn't staring at Olga Kyrilovna as if he had never seen a Western woman before?"

"But our women are physically repulsive to Chinese!"

"In most cases. But the Chinese are not animated types. They are individuals, as we are. Taste is subjective and arbitrary. Individual taste can be eccentric. Isn't it possible that there are among them, as among us, men who have romantic fancies for the exotic? Or sensual fancies for the experimental? I cannot get those words of Antoine's apprentice out of my mind: *this prince loves everything that is rare and strange. . . .*"

A red sun was dipping behind the Western Hills when we passed out a southern gate of the Tartar City. In a moment all nine gates would swing shut and we would be locked out of our legations until tomorrow's dawn. It was not a pleasant feeling. I had seen the head of a consul rot on a pike in the sun. That was what happened to barbarian demons who went where they were not wanted outside the Treaty Ports.

The Chinese City was a wilderness of twisting lanes, shops, taverns, theatres, tea-houses, opium-dens and brothels. Long ago conquering Manchu Tartars had driven conquered Chinese outside the walls of Pekin proper, or the Tartar City, this sprawling suburb where the conquered catered to the corruption of the conqueror. The Chinese City came to life at nightfall when the Tartar City slept behind its walls. Here and there yellow light shone through blue dusk from a broken gateway. Now and then we caught the chink of porcelain cups or the whine of a *yuehkin* guitar.

Alexei seemed to know every turn of the way. At last I saw why he was Russian Military Attaché at Pekin. Who else would learn so much about China and its people as this bold adventurer who could pass for a Manchu in Chinese robes? When we were snipe-shooting together, he seemed to know the Peichih-li Plain as if he carried a military map of the district in his head. Years afterward, when the Tsar's men took Port Arthur, everyone learned about Russian Intelligence in China. I learned that evening. And I found myself looking at Alexei in his Chinese dress as if he had suddenly become a stranger. What did I know of this man whom I had met so casually at legation parties? Was he ruthless enough to stab a beggar already dying of leprosy? Had he had any reason for doing so?

We turned into a narrower lane—a mere crack between high walls. Alexei whispered, "The Lane of Azure Thunder."

A green-tiled roof above the dun-colored wall proclaimed the dwelling of a prince. Alexei paused before a vermilion gate. He spoke Cantonese to the gatekeeper. I understood only two words—"Wang Wei." There were some moments of waiting. Then the gate creaked open and we were ushered through that drab wall into a wonderland of fantastic parks and lacquered pavilions blooming with all the colors of Sung porcelain.

I was unprepared for the splendor of the audience hall. The old palaces we rented for legations were melancholy places, decaying and abandoned by their owners. But here rose, green and gold rioted against a background of dull ebony panels, tortured by a cunning chisel into grotesquely writing shapes. There were hangings of salmon satin embroidered with threads of gold and pale green, images of birds and flowers carved in jade and coral and malachite. The slender rafters were painted a poisonously bright jade-green and on them tiny lotus buds were carved and gilded. There was a rich rustle of satin and the Beileh Heng walked slowly into the room.

Could this stately figure be the same fellow I had last seen squatting in the gutter, half naked in the rags of a beggar? He moved with the deliberate grace of the grave religious dancers in the Confucian temples. His robe was lustrous purple—the "myrtle-red" prescribed for princes of the third generation by the Board of Rites. It swung below the paler mandarin jacket in sculptured folds, stiff with a sable lining revealed by two slits at either side. Watered in the satin were the Eight Famous Horses of the Emperor Mu Wang galloping over the Waves of Eternity. His cuffs were curved like horseshoes in honor of the cavalry that set the Manchu Tartars on the throne. Had that cavalry ridden west instead of south, Alexei himself might have owed allegiance to this prince. Though one was Chinese and one Russian, both were Tartar.

Heng's boots of purple satin looked Russian. So did his round cap faced with a band of sable. His skin was a dull ivory, not as yellow as the southern Chinese. His cheeks were lean; his glance searching and hungry. He looked like a pure-bred descendant of the "wolf-eyed, lantern-jawed Manchus" of the Chinese chronicles. A conqueror who would take whatever he wanted, but who had learned from the conquered Chinese to want only the precious and fanciful. . . .

Something else caught my eye. There was no mistake. This was the beggar. For pale against his purple robe gleamed the fingering piece of turquoise matrix which his thin, neurotic fingers caressed incessantly.

No ceremonial tea was served. We were being received as enemies during a truce. But Alexei bowed profoundly and spoke with all the roundabout extravagance of mandarin politeness.

"An obscure design of Destiny has brought the property of your Highness, a venerable landscape scroll painted by the devout Wang Wei, into the custody of the Russian Minister. Though I appear Chinese in this garb, know that I am Russian and my minister has sent me in all haste and humility to restore this inestimable masterpiece to its rightful owner."

Heng's eyes were fixed on a point above our heads, for, Chinese or barbarian, we were inferiors, unworthy of his gaze. His lips scarcely moved. "When you have produced the scroll, I shall know whether you speak truth or falsehood."

"All your Highness's words are unspotted pearls of perpetual wisdom." Alexei stripped the embroidered case from the jade roller. Like a living thing, the painted silk slipped out of his grasp and unwound itself at the Beileh's feet.

Once again a fairy stream of lapis, jade and turquoise hues unrolled before my enchanted eyes. Kiada was right. I could hear the wind sing in the rushes and the wail of the wild geese, faint and far, a vibration trembling on the outer edge of the physical threshold for sound.

The hand that held the fingering piece was suddenly still. Only the Beileh's eyeballs moved, following the course of Wang Wei's river from its bubbling spring to its foam-flecked sea. Under his cultivated stolidity, I saw fear and, more strangely, sorrow.

At last he spoke. "This painting I inherited from my august ancestor, the ever glorious Emperor Ch'ien Lung, who left his words and seal upon the margin. How has it come into your possession?"

Alexei bowed again. "I shall be grateful for an opportunity to answer that question if your Highness will first condescend to explain to my mean intelligence how the scroll came to leave the Palace of Whirring Phoenixes?"

"Outside barbarian, you are treading on a tiger's tail when you speak with such insolence to an Imperial Clansman. I try to make allowances for you because you come of an inferior race, the Hairy Ones, without manners or music, unversed in the Six Fine Arts and the Five Classics. Know then that it is not your place to ask questions or mine to answer them. You may follow me, at a distance of nine paces, for I have something to show you."

He looked neither to right nor left as he walked soberly through the audience hall, his hands tucked inside his sleeves. At the door he lifted one hand to loosen the clasp of his mandarin jacket, and it slid from his shoulders. Before it had time to touch the ground, an officer of the Coral Button sprang out of the shadows to catch it reverently. The Beileh did not appear conscious of this officer's presence. Yet he had let the jacket fall without an instant's hesitation. He knew that wherever he went at any time there would always be someone ready to catch anything he let fall before it was soiled or damaged.

We followed him into a garden, black and white in the moonlight. We passed a pool spanned by a crescent bridge. Its arc of stone matched the arc of its reflection in the ice-coated water, completing a circle that was half reality, half illusion. We came to another pavilion, its roof curling up at each corner, light filtering through its doorway. Again we heard the shrill plaint of a guitar. We rounded a devil-screen of gold lacquer and the thin sound ended on a high, feline note.

I blinked against a blaze of lights. Like a flight of particolored butterflies, a crowd of girls fluttered away from us, tottering on tiny, mutilated feet. One who sat apart from the rest rose with dignity. A Manchu princess, as I saw by her unbound feet and undaunted eyes. Her hair was piled high in the lacquered coils of the Black Cloud Coiffure. She wore hairpins, earrings, bracelets and tall heels of acid-green jade. Her gown of seagreen silk was sewn with silver thread worked in the Pekin stitch to represent the Silver-Crested Love Birds of Conjugal Peace. But when she turned her face, I saw the sour lines and sagging pouches of middle age.

Princess Heng's gaze slid over us with subtle contempt

and came to rest upon the Beileh with irony. "My pleasure in receiving you is boundless and would find suitable expression in appropriate compliments were the occasion more auspicious. As it is, I pray you will forgive me if I do not linger in the fragrant groves of polite dalliance, but merely inquire why your Highness has seen fit to introduce two male strangers, one a barbarian, into the sanctity of the Inner Chamber?"

Heng answered impassively. "Even the Holy Duke of Yen neglected the forms of courtesy when he was pursued by a tiger."

A glint of malice sparkled in the eyes of the Beileh's Principal Old Woman. "Your Highness finds his present situation equivalent to being pursued by a tiger? To my inadequate understanding that appears the natural consequence of departing from established custom by attempting to introduce a barbarian woman into the Inner Chamber."

Heng sighed. "If the presence of these far-traveled strangers distresses you and my Small Old Women you have permission to retire."

Princess Heng's jade bangles clashed with the chilly ring of ice in a glass as she moved toward the door. The Small Old Women, all girls in their teens, shimmered and rustled after the Manchu princess, who despised them both as concubines and as Chinese.

Heng led us through another door.

"Olga!"

The passion in Alexei's voice was a shock to me. In my presence he had always addressed her as "Excellency" or "Princess." She might have been asleep as she lay there on her blue fox cloak, her eyes closed, her pale face at peace, her slight hands relaxed in the folds of her white tulle skirt. But the touch of her hands was ice and faintly from her parted lips came the sweet sickish odor of opium.

Alexei turned on Heng. "If you had not stolen her, she would not have died!"

"Stolen?" It was the first word that had pierced Heng's

reserve. "Imperial Clansmen do not steal women. I saw this far-traveled woman in a market lane of the Chinese City last summer. I coveted her. But I did not steal her. I offered money for her, decently and honorably, in accord with precepts of morality laid down by the Ancients. Money was refused. Months passed. I could not forget the woman with faded eyes. I offered one of my most precious possessions. It was accepted. The painting was her price. But the other did not keep his side of the bargain. For she was dead when I lifted her out of her cart."

The lights were spinning before my eyes. "Alexei, what is this? Volgorughi would not . . ."

Alexei's look stopped me.

"You . . ." Words tumbled from my lips. "There was a lover. And you were he. And Volgorughi found out. And he watched you together and bided his time, nursing his hatred and planning his revenge like a work of art. And finally he punished you both cruelly by selling her to Heng. Volgorughi knew that Olga would drive alone last night. Volgorughi had lived so long in the East that he had absorbed the Eastern idea of women as well as the Eastern taste in painting. The opium must have been in the sherry he gave her. She was already drowsy when he lifted her into the cart. No doubt he had planned to give her only a soporific dose that would facilitate her abduction. But at the last moment he commuted her sentence to death and let her have the full, lethal dose. He gave her good-bye tenderly because he knew he would never see her again. He promised her she would be safe because death is, in one sense, safety—the negation of pain, fear and struggle. . . .

"There was no peddler who sold him the painting. That was his only lie. He didn't prevent your coming here tonight because he wanted you to know. That was your punishment. And he saw that you could make no use of your knowledge now. Who will believe that Olga Kyrilovna, dead of a Chinese poison in the Chinese City, was killed by her own husband? Some Chinese will be suspected—Heng himself, or his jealous wife, or the men who carry out his orders. No European would take

Heng's story seriously unless it were supported by at least one disinterested witness. That was why the leper had to die last night, while Volgorughi was separated from Lucien by a wrong turning that was Volgorughi's fault. The leper must have overheard some word of warning or instruction from Volgorughi to Olga's lantern boy that revealed the whole secret. That word was spoken in Cantonese. Olga's lantern boy was Cantonese. Volgorughi spoke that dialect. The leper knew no other tongue. And Lucien, the only person who walked with Volgorughi, was as ignorant of Cantonese as all the rest of us, save you."

Heng spoke sadly in his own tongue. "The treachery of the Russian Minister in sending this woman to me dead deserves vengeance. But one thing induces me to spare him. He did not act by his own volition. He was a blind tool in the skillful hand of the merciless Wang Wei. Through this woman's death 'The River' has been restored to its companion pictures, 'The Lake,' 'The Sea,' and 'The Cloud.' And I, who separated the pictures so impiously, have had my own share of suffering as a punishment. . . ."

. . . Yes, I'll have another brandy. One more glass. Olga? She was buried in the little Russian Orthodox cemetery at Pekin. Volgorughi was recalled. The breath of scandal clung to his name the rest of his life. The Boxer Uprising finally gave the West its pretext for sending troops into China. That purple-satin epicurean, the Beileh Heng, was forced to clean sewers by German troops during the occupation and committed suicide from mortification. The gay young bloods of Pekin who had amused themselves by playing beggars found themselves beggars in earnest when the looting was over. Railways brought Western businessmen to Pekin and before long it was as modern as Chicago.

Alexei? He became attentive to the wife of the new French Minister, a woman with dyed hair who kept a Pekinese sleeve dog in her bedroom. I discovered the distraction that can be found in study of the early Chinese poets. When I left the service, I lost track of Alexei. During the Russian Revolution, I often wondered if he were still living. Did he join the Reds, as some Cossack officers did? Or was he one of the Whites who settled in Harbin or Port Arthur? He would have been a very old man then, but I think he could have managed. He spoke so many Chinese dialects. . . .

The scroll? Any good reference book will tell you that there are no Wang Wei scrolls in existence today, though there are some admirable copies. One, by Chao Méng Fu, in the British Museum, shows the course of a river. Scholars have described this copy in almost the same words I have used tonight to describe the original. But they are not the same. I went to see the copy. I was disappointed. I could no longer hear the song of the wind in the rushes or the wail of the wild geese. Was the change in the painting? Or in me?

# 1880

# Decision

## by Bill Pronzini

*A brief glimpse of married life in the old west—perhaps closer to reality than the version usually portrayed by the movies and television.*

THE DESERT SUN was a red blister in the blue of the sky when I reached the small valley. It lay nestled between jagged, wind-eroded bluffs, and crouched against the dull-rust stone at the upper end was a pole-and-sod cabin and two weathered outbuildings.

Even from where I sat my weary gelding on an outcropping of rock high above the valley floor, I could see that whoever lived there was not having an easy time of it. The shimmering desert heat had parched and withered the corn and the other vegetables in the cultivated patch along one side, and the spare buildings looked to be crumbling.

There were no horses or other livestock in the open corral near the cabin, no sign of life anywhere. It had the look of having been abandoned, but I knew that was not the case. I had seen wisps of chimney smoke rising into the fiery sky less than an hour earlier. That was what had drawn me off the main trail.

I had left Las Cruces in New Mexico Territory five days ago, with everything I owned—a few changes of clothes, some personal items, a spare Colt sixgun—packed into two sets of saddlebags. I had ridden steadily since, and I was bone-tired. Still several days out of Tucson, where I had been offered a job on one of the big ranches in the area, I was beginning to wonder if maybe I was a damned fool for not taking the train, or even a stage, west across the badlands.

Things had been fine up until last night. That was when the fullest of my waterbags had sprung a leak and all the water I had gotten from a spring just across the Arizona line seeped out into the dry dust.

I had precious little left, and even though I knew there had to be a settlement somewhere in the area—I hadn't passed near one in two days—I didn't want to be caught in the desert without water. When I had seen the chimney smoke, I had begun to feel a little better.

As I sat the chestnut, peering down into the valley, I hoped that the people down there had enough water to spare. I could see their well, set under a plank lean-to in the dusty yard before the cabin; they would have had to go pretty deep to hit an underground stream in this country, and if it was only a pocket they would be constantly low.

I took off my deep-crowned Stetson and rubbed the back of my hand across parched lips.

The trail leading down into the valley was steep and switchbacked, and it took me almost twenty minutes to reach the hard-packed floor. I rode slow, and kept my hands well up in plain sight. I had the idea that desert settlers, being as isolated as they were, might be a little leery of a lean-faced, dust-caked stranger.

I drew rein when I reached the yard immediately fronting the cabin. It was quiet there in the valley, and I could make out no sign of movement, hear no sound, from any of the buildings.

Beyond the vegetable patch, a sagging utility shed stood

with a padlock on its door; the only other structure was a long, pole-sided lean-to at the rear of the empty corral. In back of the shed, several rows of cactus grew like silent sentinels in the hot, dry soil.

I looked at the well, running the tip of my tongue across the dryness of my mouth, and then I eased the chestnut a few steps into the yard. I called out, "Hello! Anybody about?"

"What do you want here?" a woman's voice said after a moment of silence from inside the cabin. It was a young voice, rich and warm, and yet dulled by something that I couldn't identify. The door was closed, and the single window was curtained in monk's cloth; but I sensed that the woman was standing by the window, watching me through the folds.

"Don't be alarmed, ma'am," I said. "I was wondering if you could spare a little water. I'm near out, and I've got a long ride to Tucson."

There was no answer. I began to get this vague feeling of something being wrong, and I shifted uncomfortably in the saddle. "Ma'am?"

"We're having trouble with the well," she said finally. "I can't let you have much."

"I'll be pleased to pay for whatever you can spare."

"You won't need to pay."

"That's kind of you, ma'am."

"You can come down if you like."

I smiled and swung out of the saddle. The door opened a crack, but she didn't step out.

"My name is Jennifer Todd," she said from inside. "My . . . husband . . . and I own this farm."

I said, "Mine's Boone Stratton. It's a pleasure, Mrs. Todd."

"Yes, a pleasure," she said, and she opened the door and stepped out into the hot, bright glare of the sun.

My smile vanished, and I stared at her open-mouthed. She was young—no more than twenty—and honey-haired and full-breasted, with a waist no thicker than a big man's thigh; she had soft blue eyes and a heart-shaped face.

But it wasn't any of this that caused me to stare as I did. It was the blue-black bruises on both sides of her face, the deep cut above her right eye, the swollen, mottled surface of her upper lip, her right temple. Someone had beaten her, not long ago, and that someone had been merciless.

"Damnation!" I said. "Who did that to you, Mrs. Todd?"

"My husband," she said, and the bitterness was thick and hot in her voice. "This morning, just before he left for Powder Creek."

"Why?"

"He was hung over," she said simply. "Pulque hung over. Jase is mean when he's sober, and meaner when he's drunk, but when he's bad hung over he's the devil's own child."

"He's done this to you before?"

"More times than I can count in the past year."

"Maybe I got no right to say this, but why don't you leave him? Mrs. Todd, a man who'd do a thing like this to a woman wouldn't hesitate to kill her if he was riled enough."

"I tried to leave him," she said. "I tried it three times. He came after me each time and brought me back here and beat me half crazy. A work animal's got sense to obey if it's whipped enough times."

I could feel anger boiling through my blood. "A man like that ought to be shot dead!"

A small, fleeting smile touched her bruised mouth, and something flickered in the pain-dulled recesses of her eyes. She stood tall and erect, and you could tell that her spirit wasn't broken just yet; it was cowering, but it was still alive.

She said, "If I had a gun, Mr. Stratton, I'd do just that thing. I'd shoot him. But there's only one rifle and one pistol hereabouts, and Jase carries them with him all during the day. At night, he locks them up in the shed yonder."

I looked at her, and she smiled that fleeting smile

again. "I don't know what's the matter with me, telling you all my troubles, Mr. Stratton. You got some of your own, riding alone across this desert."

I stared hard at her, and a foolish thought got itself into my head. Before I could think of it, I said, "Look, Mrs. Todd, maybe I could—"

"No," she said, "no, it wouldn't work." She had read my mind.

I said, "Why not?"

"Jase would come after us and he would find us and he would bring me back, just the way he did those other three times."

"I might have something to say about that."

"He'd kill you, Mr. Stratton."

"Maybe he would and maybe he wouldn't."

"He'd kill you," she said again. Her voice was soft and flat. "I know him and you don't. I couldn't stand to have a man's death on my conscience."

"Well, there must be some way I can help."

"There's nothing," she said. "It's something I have to cope with myself, Mr. Stratton."

I just stood there, feeling suddenly awkward and uneasy.

She said, "Won't you come inside? I have some stew on the fire, and I'd like you to take the noon meal with me. And you needn't worry about Jase. He won't be home till long about dark."

I couldn't find a way to refuse her. I said, "I thank you, Mrs. Todd. I'd be proud."

The interior of the cabin was cool and dark, and smelled of spiced jackrabbit stew and boiling coffee. The few pieces of furniture were hand-hewn, but whoever made them—likely her husband—had done a poor job; none of it looked as if it would last much longer. But the two rooms that I saw were clean and neatly straightened, and you could see that she'd tried to make a home out of what she had.

"There's water in that basin by the sink," she told me, "if you want to wash up. I'll fetch some cool water from the well for drinking, and I'll see to your horse."

I started to protest, but she had already turned and was moving to the door, walking in a stiff, slow way that brought compassion into my throat. She went out and closed the door softly behind her.

I turned and went to the basin and washed myself with a cake of strong yellow soap. There was a rag towel hanging on a peg set into the wall, and I used that to dry off. Then I went to the table and sat down, and the door opened and Jennifer Todd came back inside. She smiled at me with a swollen mouth, and brushed a wisp of honey-colored hair from her forehead.

She was carrying a large gourd filled with well water, and she crossed to hand it to me. I drank deeply, gratefully. She watched for a moment, and then turned to the blackened hearth. From a spit rod suspended above a banked fire made with ocotillo limbs, she unhooked a heavy iron kettle and spooned stew onto two tin plates. She set the plates on the table, poured coffee, laid out a pan of fresh corn bread.

We ate mostly in silence. I tried to find things to say to her, but she seemed talked out. She had said all she was going to about her husband, her life here on the badlands. She turned what little conversation there was around to me.

When I had finished eating, I pushed my empty plate away and turned a couple of things over in my mind.

I said, "Mrs. Todd, you've been more than kind to share your food and your water with me, and I can't help feeling that there must be something I can do for you. I mean, maybe if I just stayed around here until that husband of yours gets home, had a little talk with him—"

"No, Mr. Stratton," she said. "If Jase came home and found a strange man here, he wouldn't wait to ask who you are or why you're here. He'd just kill you—and then maybe he'd kill me. It's better for both of us if you leave, if you pretend you'd never even stopped here."

"I can't help feeling I'd be deserting you," I said.

"I'll be able to handle things," she told me. "You really

needn't worry."

Again I wanted to press it, but this was business between a man and his wife.

Legally, even morally, I had no right to come between them. If she'd asked me for help, that would have been another matter altogether.

I then tried to offer her some money for the food and the water. But she wouldn't have any of it. She was too proud to take payment for hospitality.

We went outside, and she insisted that I fill my water bags from the well before riding out. I lowered the wooden bucket on the windlass, and filled each of the bags half full only, because I was beginning to feel guilty about not doing something for her—anything—in return. Then I mounted the freshened chestnut.

"Good-bye, Mr. Stratton," she said. "Take care."

"And you, Mrs. Todd," I answered solemnly.

I rode slowly out of the yard, onto the trail toward the sawtoothed stone bluff down which I had ridden earlier. After I had gone a couple of hundred yards, I turned to look over my shoulder. She was still standing there by the well, looking after me, her hands down at her sides and that honey hair blowing gently in the faint afternoon breeze.

I reached the base of the bluff and climbed the switchbacked trail to the outcropping of rock on which I had paused before. This time, when I turned to look back, the dusty yard was empty and the cabin door was closed. I swung the chestnut toward the main trail.

As I rode, I began to feel a mounting sense of uneasiness. Why had she talked so freely to me about her husband, about what he was, what had happened between the two of them? Most women would have wanted to hide a thing like that.

There was one answer, and when I heard in my mind some words she had spoken I knew it was the right one: *"I'll fetch some cool water from the well for drinking, and I'll see to your horse...."*

I drew sharp rein and dropped quickly out of the saddle. My fingers fumbled at the straps on the saddlebags, pulled them open, groped inside.

My spare Colt was missing.

And along with it, three or four cartridges.

I stood there, leaning against the chestnut's lathered flank, and I knew exactly what she had begun planning when she saw me ride up, and what she was planning tonight when her husband came home from Powder Creek and tried to lay hand to her again. And yet, I couldn't raise anger for what she'd done. I felt, strangely, no emotion at all.

I swung into leather again, sitting there, looking up at the falling sun on the edge of the western sky. I thought: *You've got to turn back. She's going to use your gun, just as sure as that sun up there is about to set. You've got to turn back, try to stop her before it's too late.*

And then I thought: *But it's more self-defense than anything else, because she's not a killer, deep down where it counts. And with him dead, she would be free—no more beatings, no more humiliation. She's young, and she's strong, and she could make a new beginning somewhere else.*

I knew that there was only one thing for me to do. And I did it.

I kept on riding west.

# 1892

# The
# Other Hangman

## by John Dickson Carr

*John Dickson Carr, master of the modern locked-room mystery, is also the author of a score of fine detective novels set mainly in England during the past several centuries. Here is one of his relatively rare ventures into the American past, a story about which Ellery Queen has written, "This is perhaps John Dickson Carr's finest short story—which makes it one of the finest crime-suspense short stories written in our time." What more can I add?*

WHY DO THEY ELECTROCUTE 'em instead of hanging 'em in Pennsylvania? What (said my old friend, Judge Murchison, dexterously hooking the spittoon closer with his foot) do they teach you in these new-fangled schools, anyway? Because that, son, was a murder case! It turned the Supreme Court whiskers grey to find a final ruling, and for thirty years it's been argued about by lawyers in the back room of every saloon from here to the Pacific coast. It happened right here in this county— when they hanged Fred Joliffe for the murder of Randall Fraser.

It was in '92 or '93; anyway, it was the year they put

the first telephone in the courthouse, and you could talk as far as Pittsburgh except when the wires blew down. Considering it was the county seat, we were mighty proud of our town (population 3,500). The hustlers were always bragging about how thriving and growing our town was, and we had just got to the point of enthusiasm where every ten years we were certain the census-taker must have forgotten half our population. Old Mark Sturgis, who owned the *Bugle Gazette* then, carried on something awful in an editorial when they printed in the almanac that we had a population of only 3,263. We were all pretty riled about it.

We were proud of plenty of other things, too. We had good reason to brag about the McClellan House, which was the finest hotel in the county; and I mind when you could get room and board, with apple pie for breakfast every morning, for two a week. We were proud of our old county families, that came over the mountains when Braddock's army was scalped by the Indians in 1775, and settled down in log huts to dry their wounds. But most of all we were proud of our legal batteries.

Son, it was a grand assembly! Mind, I won't say that all of 'em were long on knowledge of the Statute Books; but they knew their Blackstone and their Greenleaf on Evidence, and they were powerful speakers. And there were some—the topnotchers, full of graces and book-knowledge and dignity—who were hell on the exact letter of the law. Scotch-Irish Presbyterians, all of us, who loved a good debate and a bottle o' whiskey. There was Charley Connell, a Harvard graduate and the district attorney, who had fine hands, and wore a fine high collar, and made such pathetic addresses to the jury that people flocked for miles around to hear him; though he mostly lost his cases. There was Judge Hunt, who prided himself on his resemblance to Abe Lincoln, and in consequence always wore a frock coat and an elegant plug hat. Why, there was your own grandfather, who had over two hundred books in his library, and people used to go up nights to borrow volumes of the encyclopedia.

You know the big stone courthouse at the top of the street, with the flowers round it, and the jail adjoining? People went there as they'd go to a picture show nowadays; it was a lot better, too. Well, from there it was only two minutes' walk across the meadow to Jim Riley's saloon. All the legal cronies gathered there—in the back room of course, where Jim had an elegant brass spittoon and a picture of George Washington on the wall to make it dignified. You could see the footpath worn across the grass until they built over that meadow. Besides the usual crowd, there was Bob Moran, the sheriff, a fine, strapping big fellow, but very nervous about doing his duty strictly. And there was poor old Nabors, a big, quiet, reddish-eyed fellow, who'd been a doctor before he took to drink. He was always broke, and he had two daughters—one of 'em consumptive—and Jim Riley pitied him so much that he gave him all he wanted to drink for nothing. Those were fine, happy days, with a power of eloquence and theorizing and solving the problems of the nation in that back room, until our wives came to fetch us home.

Then Randall Fraser was murdered and there was hell to pay.

Now if it had been anybody else but Fred Joliffe who killed him, naturally we wouldn't have convicted. You can't do it, son, not in a little community. It's all very well to talk about the power and grandeur of justice, and sounds fine in a speech. But here's somebody you've seen walking the streets about his business every day for years; and you know when his kids were born, and saw him crying when one of 'em died; and you remember how he loaned you ten dollars when you needed it. . . . Well, you can't take that person out in the cold light of day and string him up by the neck until he's dead. You'd always be seeing the look on his face afterwards. And you'd find excuses for him no matter what he did.

But with Fred Joliffe it was different. Fred Joliffe was the worst and nastiest customer we ever had, with the possible exception of Randall Fraser himself. Ever see a copperhead curled up on a flat stone? And a copperhead's worse than a rattlesnake—that won't strike unless you step on it, and gives warning before it does. Fred Joliffe had the same brownish color and sliding movements. You always remembered his cart through town—he had some sort of rag-and-bone business, you understand—you'd see him sitting up there, a skinny little man in a brown coat, peeping round the side of his nose to find something for gossip. And grinning.

It wasn't merely the things he said about people behind their backs. Or to their faces, for that matter, because he relied on the fact that he was too small to be thrashed. He was a slick customer. It was believed that he wrote those anonymous letters that caused . . . but never mind that. Anyhow, I can tell you this little smirk did drive Will Farmer crazy one time, and Will did beat him within an inch of his life. Will's livery stable was burned down one night about a month later with eleven horses inside, but nothing could ever be proved. He was too smart for us.

That brings me to Fred Joliffe's only companion—I don't mean friend. Randall Fraser had a harness-and-saddle store in Market Street, a dusty place with a big dummy horse in the window. I reckon the only thing in the world Randall liked was that dummy horse, which was a dappled mare with vicious-looking glass eyes. He used to keep its mane combed. Randall was a big man with a fine mustache, and a horseshoe pin in his tie, and sporty checked clothes. He was buttery polite, and mean as sin. He thought a dirty trick or a swindle was the funniest joke he ever heard. But the women liked him—a lot of them, it's no use denying, sneaked in at the back door of that harness store. Randall itched to tell it at the barber shop, to show what fools they were and how virile he was, but he had to be careful. He and Fred Joliffe did a lot of drinking together.

Then the news came. It was in October, I think, and I heard it in the morning when I was putting on my hat to go down to the office. Old Withers was the town constable then. He got up early in the morning, although there was no need for it, and when he was going down Market Street in the mist about five o'clock he saw the gas still burning in the back room of Randall's store. The front door was wide open. Withers went in and found Randall lying on a pile of harness in his shirt-sleeves, his forehead and face bashed in with a wedging-mallet. There wasn't much left of the face, but you could recognize him by his mustache and his horseshoe pin.

I was in my office when somebody yelled up from the street that they found Fred Joliffe drunk and asleep in the flour mill, with blood on his hands and an empty bottle of Randall Fraser's whiskey in his pocket. He was still in bad shape, and couldn't walk or understand what was going on, when the sheriff—that was Bob Moran I told you about—came to take him to the lock-up. Bob had to drive him in his own rag-and-bone cart. I saw them drive up Market Street in the rain, Fred lying in the back of the cart all white with flour, and rolling and cursing. People were very quiet. They were pleased, but they couldn't show it.

That is, all except Will Farmer, who had owned the livery stable that was burnt down.

"Now they'll hang him," says Will. "Now, by God, they'll hang him."

It's a funny thing, son, I didn't realize the force of that until I heard Judge Hunt pronounce sentence after the trial. They appointed me to defend him, because I was a young man without any particular practice, and somebody had to do it. The evidence was all over town before I got a chance to speak with Fred. You could see he was done for. A scissors-grinder who lived across the street (I forget his name now) had seen Fred go into Randall's place about eleven o'clock. An old couple who lived up over the store had heard 'em drinking and yelling downstairs. At near on midnight they'd heard a noise like a fight and a fall—but they knew better than to interfere. Finally, a couple of farmers driving home from town at midnight had seen Fred stumble out of the front door, slapping his clothes and wiping his hands on his coat like a man with delirium tremens.

I went to see Fred at the jail. He was sober, although he jerked a good deal. Those pale eyes of his were as poisonous as ever. I can still see him sitting on the bunk in his cell, sucking a brown paper cigarette, wriggling his neck, and jeering at me. He wouldn't tell me anything, because he said I would go and tell the judge if he did.

"Hang me?" he says, and wrinkled his nose and jeered again. "Hang me? Don't you worry about that, mister. Them so-and-so's will never hang me. They're too much afraid of me, them so-and-so's are. Eh, mister?"

And the fool couldn't get it through his head right up until the sentence. He strutted away in court making remarks, and threatening to tell what he knew about people, and calling the judge by his first name. He wore a new dickey shirt-front he bought to look spruce in.

I was surprised how quietly everybody took it. The people who came to the trial didn't whisper or shove; they just sat still as death and looked at him. All you could hear was a kind of breathing. It's funny about a courtroom, son. It has its own particular smell, which won't bother you unless you get to thinking about what it means, but you notice worn places and cracks in the walls more than you would anywhere else. You would hear Charley Connell's voice for the prosecution, a little thin sound in a big room, and Charley's footsteps creaking. You would hear a cough in the audience, or a woman's dress rustle, or the gas-jets whistling. It was dark in the rainy season, so they lit the gas-jets by two o'clock in the afternoon.

The only defense I could make was that Fred had been too drunk to be responsible, and remembered nothing of that night (which he admitted was true). But, in addition to being no defense in law, it was a terrible frost besides. My own voice sounded wrong. I remember that six of the jury had whiskers, and six hadn't and Judge Hunt, up on the bench with the flag draped on the wall behind his head, looked more like Abe Lincoln than ever. Even Fred Joliffe began to notice. He kept twitching round to look at the people, a little uneasy-like. Once he stuck out his neck at the jury and screeched: "Say something, cantcha? Do something, cantcha?"

They did.

When the foreman of the jury said, "Guilty of murder in the first degree," there was just a little noise from those people. Not a cheer or anything like that. It hissed out all together, only once, like breath released, but it was terrible to hear. It didn't hit Fred until Judge Hunt was halfway through pronouncing sentence. Fred stood looking round with a wild, half-witted expression until he heard Judge Hunt say, "And may God have mercy on your soul." Then he burst out, kind of pleading and kidding as though this was carrying the joke too far. He said, "Listen now, you don't mean that, do you? You can't fool me. You're only Jerry Hunt. I know who you are. You can't do that to me." All of a sudden he began pounding the table and screaming, "You ain't really a-going to hang me, are you?"

But we were.

The date of the execution was fixed for the twelfth of November. The order was all signed. ". . . within the precincts of the said county jail, between the hours of eight and nine A.M., the said Frederick Joliffe shall be hanged by the neck until he is dead; an executioner to be commissioned by the sheriff for this purpose, and the sentence to be carried out in the presence of a qualified medical practitioner; the body to be interred. . . ." And the rest of it. Everybody was nervous. There hadn't been a hanging since any of that crowd had been in office, and nobody knew how to go about it exactly. Old Doc Macdonald, the coroner, was to be there and of course they got hold of Reverend Phelps the preacher and Bob Moran's wife was going to cook pancakes and sausage for the last breakfast. Maybe you think that's fool talk. But think for a minute of taking somebody you've known all your life, and binding his arms one cold morning, and walking him out in your own back yard to crack his neck on a rope—all religious and legal, with not a soul to interfere. Then you begin to get scared of the powers of life and death, and the thin partition between.

Bob Moran was scared white for fear things wouldn't go off properly. He had appointed big, slow-moving, tipsy Ed Nabors as hangman. This was party because Ed Nabors needed the fifty dollars and partly because Bob had a vague idea that an ex-medical man would be better able to manage an execution. Ed had sworn to keep sober. Bob Moran said he wouldn't get a dime unless he was sober, but you couldn't always tell.

Nabors seemed in earnest. He had studied up the matter of scientific hanging in an old book he borrowed from your grandfather, and he and the carpenter had knocked together a big, shaky-looking contraption in the jail yard. It worked all right in practice, with sacks of meal. The trap went down with a boom that brought your heart up in your throat. But once they allowed for too much spring in the rope, and it tore a sack apart. Then old Doc Macdonald chipped in about that fellow John Lee, in England —and it nearly finished Bob Moran.

That was late on the night before the execution. We were sitting round the lamp in Bob's office, trying to play stud poker. There were tops and skipping-ropes, all kinds of toys, all over that office. Bob let his kids play in there —which he shouldn't have done, because the door out of it led to a corridor of cells with Fred Joliffe in the last one. Of course the few other prisoners, disorderlies and chicken-thieves and the like, had been moved upstairs. Somebody had told Bob that the scent of an execution affects 'em like a cage of wild animals. Whoever it was, he was right. We could hear 'em shifting and stamping over our heads, and one colored boy singing hymns all night long.

Well, it was raining hard on the thin roof. Maybe that was what put Doc Macdonald in mind of it. Doc was a cynical old devil. When he saw that Bob couldn't sit still, and would throw in his hand without even looking at the buried card, Doc says:

"Yes, I hope it'll go off all right. But you want to be careful about that rain. Did you read about that fellow they tried to hang in England—and the rain had swelled the boards so's the trap wouldn't fall? They stuck him on it three times, but still it wouldn't work."

Ed Nabors slammed his hand down on the table. I reckon he felt bad enough as it was, because one of his daughters had run away and left him, and the other was dying of consumption. But he was twitchy and reddish about the eyes. He hadn't had a drink for two days, although there was a bottle on the table. He says:

"You shut up or I'll kill you. Damn you, Macdonald," he says, and grabs the edge of the table. "I tell you nothing can go wrong. I'll go out and test the thing again, if you'll let me put the rope round your neck."

And Bob Moran says, "What do you want to talk like that for anyway, Doc. Ain't it bad enough as it is?" he says. "Now you've got me worrying about something else," he says. "I went down there a while ago to look at him, and he said the funniest thing I ever heard Fred Joliffe say. He's crazy. He giggled and said God wouldn't let them so-and-so's hang him. It was terrible, hearing Fred Joliffe talk like that. What time is it, somebody?"

It was cold that night. I dozed off in a chair, hearing the rain, and that animal-cage shuffling upstairs. The colored boy was singing that part of the hymn about while the nearer waters roll, while the tempest still is high.

They woke me about half past eight to say that Judge Hunt and all the witnesses were out in the jail yard, and they were ready to start the march. Then I realized that they were really going to hang him after all. I had to join behind the procession as I was sworn, but I didn't see Fred Joliffe's face and I didn't want to see it. They had given him a good wash, and a clean flannel shirt that they tucked under at the neck. He stumbled coming out of the cell, and started to go in the wrong direction, but Bob Moran and the constable each had him by one arm. It was a cold, dark, windy morning. His hands were tied behind.

The preacher was saying something I couldn't catch, and everything went off smoothly enough until they got halfway across the jail yard. It's a pretty big yard. I didn't look at the contraption in the middle, but at the witnesses standing over against the wall with their hats off. But Fred Joliffe did look at it, and went down flat on his knees. They hauled him up again. I heard them keep on walking, and go up the steps, which were creaky.

I didn't look at the contraption until I heard a thumping sound, and we all knew something was wrong.

Fred Joliffe was not standing on the trap, nor was the bag pulled over his head, although his legs were strapped. He stood with his eyes closed and his face toward the pink sky. Ed Nabors was clinging with both hands to the rope, twirling round a little and stamping on the trap. It didn't budge. Just as I heard Ed crying something about the rain having swelled the boards, Judge Hunt ran past me to the foot of the contraption.

Bob Moran started cursing pretty obscenely. "Put him on and try it, anyway," he says, and grabs Fred's arm. "Stick that bag over his head and give the thing a chance."

"In His name," says the preacher pretty steadily, "you'll not do it if I can help it."

Bob ran over like a crazy man and jumped on the trap with both feet. It was stuck fast. Then Bob turned round and pulled an Ivor-Johnson .45 out of his hip pocket. Judge Hunt got in front of Fred, whose lips were moving a little.

"He'll have the law, and nothing but the law," says Judge Hunt. "Put that gun away, you lunatic, and take him back to the cell until you can make the thing work. Easy with him, now."

To this day I don't think Fred Joliffe had realized what happened. I believe he only had his belief confirmed that they never meant to hang him after all. When he found himself going down the steps again, he opened his eyes. His face looked shrunken and dazed-like, but all of a sudden it came to him in a blaze.

"I knew them so-and-so's would never hang me," says he. His throat was so dry he couldn't spit at Judge Hunt, as he tried to do, but he marched straight and giggling across the yard. "I knew them so-and-so's would never hang me," he says.

We all had to sit down a minute, and we had to give Ed Nabors a drink. Bob made him hurry up, although we didn't say much, and he was leaving to fix the trap again when the courthouse janitor came bustling into Bob's office.

"Call," says he, "on the new machine over there. Telephone."

"Lemme out of here!" yells Bob. "I can't listen to no telephone calls now. Come out and give us a hand."

"But it's from Harrisburg," says the janitor. "It's from the Governor's office. You got to go."

"Stay here, Bob," says Judge Hunt. He beckons to me. "Stay here, and I'll answer it," he says. We looked at each other in a queer way when we went across the Bridge of Sighs. The courthouse clock was striking nine, and I could look down into the yard and see people hammering at the trap. After Judge Hunt had listened to that telephone call he had a hard time putting the receiver back on the hook.

"I always believed in Providence, in a way," says he, "but I never thought it was so person-like. Fred Joliffe is innocent. We're to call off this business," says he, "and wait for a messenger from the Governor. He's got the evidence of a woman . . . Anyway, we'll hear it later."

Now, I'm not much of a hand at describing mental states, so I can't tell you exactly what we felt then. Most of all was a fever and horror for fear they had already whisked Fred out and strung him up. But when we looked down into the yard from the Bridge of Sighs we saw Ed Nabors and the carpenter arguing over a crosscut saw on the trap itself, and the blessed morning light coming up in glory to show us we could knock that ugly contraption to pieces and burn it.

The corridor downstairs was deserted. Judge Hunt had got his wind back, and, being one of those stern elocutionists who like to make complimentary remarks about God, he was going on something powerful. He sobered up when he saw that the door to Fred Joliffe's cell was open.

"Even Joliffe," says the judge, "deserves to get this news first."

But Fred never did get the news, unless his ghost was listening. I told you he was very small and light. His heels were a good eighteen inches off the floor as he hung by the neck from an iron peg in the wall of the cell. He was hanging from a noose made in a child's skipping-rope; blackfaced dead already, with the whites of his eyes showing in slits, and his heels swinging over a kicked-away stool.

No, son, we didn't think it was suicide for long. For a little while we were stunned, half crazy, naturally. It was like thinking about your troubles at three o'clock in the morning.

But you see, Fred's hands were still tied behind him. There was a bump on the back of his head, from a hammer that lay beside the stool. Somebody had walked in there with the hammer concealed behind his back, had stunned Fred when he wasn't looking, had run a slipknot in that skipping-rope, and jerked him up a-flapping to strangle there. It was the creepiest part of the business, when we'd got that through our heads, and we all began loudly to tell each other where we'd been during the confusion. Nobody had noticed much. I was scared green.

When we gathered round the table in Bob's office, Judge Hunt took hold of his nerve with both hands. He looked at Bob Moran, at Ed Nabors, at Doc Macdonald, and at me. One of us was the other hangman.

"This is a bad business, gentlemen," says he, clearing his throat a couple of times like a nervous orator before he starts. "What I want to know is, who under sanity would strangle a man when he thought we intended to do it anyway, on a gallows?"

Then Doc Macdonald turned nasty. "Well," says he, "if it comes to that, you might inquire where that skipping-rope came from to begin with."

"I don't get you," says Bob Moran, bewildered-like.

"Oh, don't you," says Doc, and sticks out his whiskers. "Well, then, who was so dead set on this execution going through as scheduled that he wanted to use a gun when the trap wouldn't drop?"

Bob made a noise as though he'd been hit in the stomach. He stood looking at Doc for a minute, with his hands hanging down—and then he went for him. He had Doc back across the table, banging his head on the edge, when people began to crowd into the room at the yells. Funny, too; the first one in was the jail carpenter, who was pretty sore at not being told that the hanging had been called off.

"What do you want to start fighting for?" he says, fretful-like. He was bigger than Bob, and had him off Doc with a couple of heaves. "Why didn't you tell me what was going on? They say there ain't going to be any hanging. Is that right?"

Judge Hunt nodded, and the carpenter—Barney Hicks, that's who it was; I remember now—Barney Hicks looked pretty peevish, and says:

"All right, all right, but you hadn't ought to go fighting all over the joint like that." Then he looks at Ed Nabors. "What I want is my hammer. Where's my hammer, Ed? I been looking all over the place for it. What did you do with it?"

Ed Nabors sits up, pours himself four fingers of rye, and swallows it.

"Beg pardon, Barney," says he in the coolest voice I ever heard. "I must have left it in the cell," he says, "when I hanged Fred Joliffe."

Talk about silences! It was like one of those silences when the magician at the Opera House fires a gun and six doves fly out of an empty box. I couldn't believe it. But I remember Ed Nabors sitting big in the corner by the barred window, and his shiny black coat and string tie. His hands were on his knees, and he was looking from one to the other of us, smiling a little. He looked as old as the prophets then, and he'd got enough liquor to keep the nerve from twitching beside his eye. So he just sat there, very quietly, shifting the plug of tobacco around in his cheek, and smiling.

"Judge," he says in a reflective way, "you got a call from the Governor at Harrisburg, didn't you? Uh-huh. I knew what it would be. A woman had come forward, hadn't she, to confess Fred Joliffe was innocent and she had killed Randall Fraser? Uh-huh. The woman was my daughter. Jessie couldn't face telling it here, you see. That was why she ran away from me and went to the Governor. She'd have kept quiet if you hadn't convicted Fred."

"But why? . . ." shouts the judge. "Why? . . ."

"It was like this," Ed goes on in that slow way of his. "She'd been on pretty intimate terms with Randall Fraser, Jessie had. And both Randall and Fred were having a whooping lot of fun threatening to tell the whole town about it. She was pretty near crazy, I think. And, you see, on the night of the murder Fred Joliffe was too drunk to remember anything that happened. He thought he had killed Randall, I suppose, when he woke up and found Randall dead and blood on his hands.

"It's all got to come out now, I suppose," says he, nodding. "What did happen was that the three of 'em were in that back room, which Fred didn't remember. He and Randall had a fight while they were baiting Jesse. Fred whacked him hard enough with that mallet to lay him out, but all the blood he got was from a big splash over Randall's eye. Jessie . . . Well, Jessie finished the job when Fred ran away, that's all."

"But, you damned fool," cries Bob Moran, and begins

to pound the table, "why did you have to go and kill Fred when Jessie had confessed?"

"You fellows wouldn't have convicted Jessie, would you?" says Ed, blinking at us. "No. But, if Fred had lived after her confession, you'd have had to, boys. That was how I figured it out. Once Fred learned what did happen, that he wasn't guilty and she was, he'd never have let up until he'd carried that case to the Superior Court out of your hands. He'd have screamed all over the state until they either had to hang her or send her up for life. I couldn't stand that. As I say, that was how I figured it out, although my brain's not so clear these days. So," says he, nodding and leaning over to take aim at the cuspidor, "when I heard about that telephone call, I went into Fred's cell and finished my job."

"But don't you understand," says Judge Hunt, in the way you'd reason with a lunatic, "that Bob Moran will have to arrest you for murder, and . . ."

It was the peacefulness of Ed's expression that scared us then. He got up from his chair, and dusted his shiny black coat, and smiled at us.

"Oh no," says he very clearly. "That's what you don't understand. You can't do a single damned thing to me. You can't even arrest me."

"He's bughouse," says Bob Moran.

"Am I?" says Ed affably. "Listen to me. I've committed what you might call a perfect murder, because I've done it legally. . . . Judge, what time did you talk to the Governor's office, and get the order for the execution to be called off? Be careful now."

And I said, with the whole idea of the business suddenly hitting me:

"It was maybe five minutes past nine, wasn't it, Judge? I remember the courthouse clock striking."

"I remember it too," says Ed Nabors. "And Doc Macdonald will tell you Fred Joliffe was dead before ever that clock struck nine. I have in my pocket," says he, unbuttoning his coat, "a court order which authorizes me to kill Fred Joliffe, by means of hanging by the neck—which I did—between the hours of eight and nine in the morning —which I also did. And I did it in full legal style before the order was countermanded. Well?"

Judge Hunt took off his stovepipe hat and wiped his face with a bandana. We all looked at him.

"You can't get away with this," says the judge, and grabs the sheriff's order off the table. "You can't trifle with the law in that way. And you can't execute sentence alone. Look here! 'In the presence of a qualified medical practitioner.' What do you say to that?"

"Well, I can produce my medical diploma," says Ed, nodding again. "I may be a booze hoister, and mighty unreliable, but they haven't struck me off the register yet. . . . You lawyers are hell on the wording of the law," says he admiringly, "and it's the wording that's done for you this time. Until you get the law altered with some fancy words, there's nothing in that document to say that the doctor and the hangman can't be the same person."

After a while Bob Moran turned around to the judge with a funny expression on his face. It might have been a grin.

"This ain't according to morals," says he. "A fine citizen like Fred shouldn't get murdered like that. It's awful. Something's got to be done about it. As you said yourself this morning, Judge, he ought to have the law and nothing but law. Is Ed right, Judge?"

"Frankly, I don't know," says Judge Hunt, wiping his face again. "But, so far as I know, he is. What are you doing, Robert?"

"I'm writing him out a check for fifty dollars," says Bob Moran, surprised-like. "We got to have it all nice and legal, haven't we?"

# 1897
# A Note on American Literature by My Uncle, Monroe Sanderson

## by Henry Slesar

*A small, unclassifiable gem of a story, harking back to those days when classic novels were written for monthly magazine serialization prior to book publication.*

I WAS A BOY of twelve and my Uncle, Monroe Sanderson well into his fifties when the unfortunate illness of his wife Theodora brought about the extraordinary encounter with the great American novelist, Langworthe Bailey (1871-1940). Fortunately, the details of that historic meeting were recorded by my Uncle himself in a letter to my father, Andrew Sanderson, but it was only recently that this document came to light.

As background, a brief biography of my Uncle may be in order. He was born of poor parents in Brockton, Mass., in 1842, and attained his position of eminence despite a lack of formal schooling. In 1866, he entered the retailing profession and soon began operation of a small chain of stores, his success enabling him to amass a considerable fortune. It is pertinent to note that Literature probably ranked last among his interests, and he often stated, somewhat boastfully, that he never read anything but sales reports and stock market tables.

Perhaps it was his preoccupation with business that delayed his interest in Marriage for so long. He had already celebrated his fifty-fourth birthday when he announced his betrothal to Theodora Kimberly, a young lady of good family and notable attractiveness. The fact that almost a quarter of a century separated their birthdates was of some concern to the family, but Miss Kimberly's quiet demeanor soon put all fears to rest. I still recall with pleasure a surrey ride in the company of this charming person, whose creamy complexion and shapely figure could be appreciated even by a lad of twelve. My Uncle was the happiest of mortals, and therefore all the more distressed by the sudden onslaught of her mysterious and dangerous malady. But at this point, my Uncle's own words may be more enlightening.

May 12, 1897

Dear Andrew:

Now that this dreadful episode is concluded, I feel able to take pen in hand and recount for you the extraordinary circumstances of the past few weeks.

As you know, Theodora's health became impaired at the beginning of this winter, and Dr. L—— recommended a journey to a warmer clime. Despite the deleterious effect upon the business, I took a month's leave and accompanied Theo on a southern excursion. She seemed to improve, but upon her return, the condition, described by Dr. L—— as acute internal fatigue, worsened considerably.

Strangely enough, it was our dear Mother who provided the insight which eventually explained Theo's unusual condition. Mother suggested that perhaps Theo was the victim of a brain fever induced by her incessant reading. Theo is addicted to what she calls Modern Literature, and indeed, this is one of the few subjects upon which my wife and I stand divided. How anyone can become absorbed in wholly imaginary events is beyond me, and yet

Theo's happiest days are those on which a periodical called *McLary's Monthly Magazine* arrives.

At the time Mother made this intelligent surmise, *McLary's* was publishing a six-part serialization entitled *Constance of Carib Farm,* by an Author whose name, Langworthe Bailey, meant nothing to me but is, I am assured, considered to be luminous in the firmament of American literature. The fact that the first installment coincided with the beginning of Theo's illness did not strike me as peculiar. However, it was upon the arrival of Part Two, shortly after our return north, that the color once more drained from Theo's cheeks and the sparkle dimmed in her eyes. When the third installment came, Theo spent the entire day in her room, weeping copious tears.

Suspecting now a possible connection between *Constance of Carib Farm* and my wife's ailment, I made an attempt to read the text of Mr. Bailey's opus, but found the chore far too tedious. I managed, however, to obtain a synopsis of the story from Miss Pricepacker, my secretary, who was also a subscriber to *McLary's Monthly*.

Miss Pricepacker informed me that *Constance* concerned a young woman who lived in a small impoverished farm community whose people lived by a code of strict morality. Unfortunately, the heroine rebelled against her environment, and became involved with a scoundrel who took advantage of her innocence. For the sake of her honor, Constance's parents forced her to marry a wealthy merchant who was considerably her senior. Constance agreed, but her heart broke as she pronounced the vows of marital fidelity to a Man She Did Not Love.

This, so far, was the story of *Constance of Carib Farm,* and obviously Theo had been so moved by this plight of this imaginary woman that she had actually become ill in sympathy. When I informed Dr. L—— of my discovery, he agreed completely, but not with my desire to halt the arrival of that troublesome magazine, fearing that Theo might become hysterical if denied knowledge of the outcome of Constance's problems.

It was Part Five which caused me the greatest alarm. When Theo completed that section of Mr. Bailey's drama, she immediately contracted a fever. Dr. L—— could offer no explanation of this new development, but Miss Price-packer could. For the author of *Constance of Carib Farm*, not content with the woes of his heroine, had now placed her on her deathbed.

One evening, Dr. L—— took me aside and said, "Mr. Sanderson, I have consulted my medical histories, and have found a case very similar to your wife's. Do you know of an English Author named Samuel Richardson?"

I said I did not; that Authors, English, American, or Esquimeaux, were all anathema to me.

"Well, Samuel Richardson was the Author of several well-known works. One was *Pamela*, and another was *Clarissa*, sometimes mistakenly referred to as *Clarissa Harlowe*. This story, too, was told in installments, and this heroine, too, was about to expire when a gentleman called upon the Author, Mr. Richardson, with an earnest plea that she be spared. It seems that this gentleman had a daughter, a young lady who had followed the adventures of Clarissa directly to the deathbed, and the Doctors had assured the grieving father that if Clarissa Harlowe died, his daughter would succumb, too. Unfortunately, Mr. Richardson would not distort his Art for the sake of any real-life contingency. Clarissa Harlowe was allowed to die. And so, I am afraid, did that poor gentleman's unlucky daughter."

"Good heavens!" I said, as Dr. L—— completed this shocking narrative. "Are you telling me that the fate of this—Constance may be the fate of my Theo?"

"I am afraid there is that possibility," Dr. L—— replied with a sigh. "Of course, you may seek out this Langworthe Bailey and present your case to him. But I warn you that the Artistic Conscience is a hard taskmaster, and you must not expect too much of him."

I did not, as Dr. L—— advised, expect too much, but a meeting was arranged by Mr. C—— of the Merchants' & Seamen's Bank who handled Mr. Bailey's finances. It took place in a rather dismal hotel room on Lower Broadway, but Mr. Bailey himself was a cheerful, youngish gentleman who laughed heartily and rather frequently, I thought, considering the mournful tenor of his literary work. He listened patiently to the problem as I outlined it, and when I concluded, he shook his head with both commiseration and regret.

"I'm awfully sorry, old man," he said, "but the outcome of *Constance* is a foregone conclusion; my publishers had a detailed synopsis months ago. As a matter of fact, you're not the only one who'd rather Constance lived; *McLary's Magazine* feels exactly the same way. Happy ending and all that rot."

"And why not?" I said eagerly. "Why not a Happy Ending, Mr. Bailey? Must life always be so grim a proposition?"

However, my pleas fell on deaf ears. The best I could extract from him was a promise that he would be a guest in my home, and see for himself the damage he would be inflicting. I felt sure that the sight of Theo's suffering would make him think twice of pursuing his dreadful course.

It was over a week before Langworthe Bailey made good his promise, and the necessities of the situation demanded that he pay that visit under a false flag. It would never do to introduce Theo to the Author of *Constance,* so Mr. Bailey chose the pseudonym of Richard Brackett. Theo was not well-disposed to the idea of company, but Mr. Bailey, or rather Brackett, proved so charming a guest, with so many droll stories to tell, that I actually heard Theo laugh again.

At the end of the evening, I drew the Author aside and inquired about his opinion. "You are a fortunate man, Mr. Sanderson," he said. "Your wife is most delightful." "But a very ill woman," I said, "and one over whom you exercise the power of life or death." "Really, Mr. Sanderson," he said, "I believe you have a greater gift for melodrama than I." I scorned this attempt at flattery, and implored him to return soon.

Langworthe Bailey did return, the very next afternoon, and before long he became a regular caller at my home. I began at last to detect that he was moved by Theo's condition, and by the fate that awaited her unless he chose to rescue her from the brink. Still, I could not be sure.

Then it happened. One afternoon, seated in my office, I heard a cry from Miss Pricepacker, and when I went to inquire, I saw a copy of *McLary's Monthly* on her desk. My heart leaped into my throat as I realized that Part Six of *Constance of Carib Farm* had finally appeared.

"Tell me the worst," I said with a shudder. "The truth, Miss Pricepacker! Has poor Constance—gone to her reward?"

"No!" my secretary cried joyously, with tears of happiness in her eyes. "She is well, Mr. Sanderson, completely well!"

I rushed from the office upon hearing this intelligence, and found Theo in her bedroom, looking flushed and yet not feverish, the opened copy of *McLary's Monthly* on her lap. As I embraced her, I silently thanked that noble man of Literature who had sacrificed his Art in order to restore my beloved wife to me.

As you can see, my Uncle was extremely grateful to Langworthe Bailey, and the noted author became a regular caller at his home, still, of course, bearing the pseudonym of Richard Brackett. It is this pseudonym, perhaps, which explains why Langworthe Bailey's biographers never knew of his friendship with the Sanderson family or recognized how my Uncle Monroe, although a mere storekeeper, had a profound effect upon an important American novel.

As previously stated, Uncle Monroe never read fiction of any kind, and this proved to be a blessing. For as students of American literature know, in the final scenes of *Constance of Carib Farm,* the despairing young heroine is suddenly confronted with Hope in the form of a handsome young man named Richard Brackett. He becomes her lover, and her aged husband, unaware of the reason for his wife's renewed joy of living, lives out his own years in contentment. Apparently, my Uncle Monroe contributed a bit more to American letters than he realized.

# 1901

# The Ripper of Storyville

## by Edward D. Hoch

*New Orleans at the turn of the century . . . . This story of mine was a favorite of the late Cornell Woolrich, which is why I have included it here.*

BEN SNOW MET Archer Kinsman in a little Texas town near the Gulf Coast. It had been a year of wandering for Ben, and with the coming of winter he'd headed south ahead of the snow and cold. Here, near the Mexican border, there was still a scent of the old west in the air, still a blending of horseflesh and longhorns and gunsmoke. It was Ben's sort of town—at least till Archer Kinsman found him there.

Kinsman was old, not so much in years as in appearance. He was a man with one foot in the grave, and the fancy carriage, the pearl-handled pistols, the expensive cigars would not keep him out of it. He found Ben in the back room of the Rio Cafe, and settled down across the table from him with an air of troubled haste. "You're Ben Snow, aren't you?"

"That's right," Ben said, taking in the trappings of

wealth, the ashen complexion that aged the hard lines of the face.

"I'd like to hire you for a job," the man said. "I'm Archer Kinsman. You may have heard the name."

"Sorry. I'm a stranger in these parts." Whatever he wanted, it would probably be good for a free drink at the very least.

"But your fame has preceeded you, Mr. Snow." And there was the knowing smile again, that look which had followed him across the west.

"You want to hire a gun?"

"I want to hire the fastest gun in New Mexico."

"Wrong state, Mr. Kinsman. This is Texas."

"But you're from New Mexico, aren't you?"

Ben sighed and drained the bottom of his beer glass. "Yes. I'm from New Mexico."

"Let me buy you a beer." He signalled to the bartender out front. "I've heard stories, you know. About your little adventure in Mexico, and the others. You're quite a man."

"Let's be frank, Mr. Kinsman. You've heard stories that I'm Billy the Kid, not dead after nearly twenty years but very much alive, wandering the West with a fast gun for hire. The stories aren't true."

Kinsman brushed it aside. "Of course not—didn't believe them for an instant! But you're still the man I want to hire. There is absolutely no killing involved. In fact quite the opposite. I want you to bring my daughter back from New Orleans."

"Then why do you need a fast gun?"

"I need a man who can protect himself against some tough customers. My daughter . . . well, perhaps I should tell you the whole story." He passed a handkerchief across his face, and his skin was as white as the cloth. "There were the three of us—my wife, my daughter Bess, and myself. We lived up north a ways. After years of nothing I'd managed to get together enough money to buy a small ranch, and things were looking pretty good. But I suppose I wasn't a very good father. I certainly wasn't a very good husband. One night I found my wife in bed with my foreman. I shot him, of course, but she jumped in front of my gun and they both died. Bess was eighteen when it happened, and I guess it was an awful shock to her. I never knew whether she blamed me or her mother more, but I suppose we were both destroyed that night in her eyes. Anyway, she left the ranch—walked out on me—and I haven't laid eyes on her in six years."

Though his eyes had blurred a bit in the telling, it was still more than obvious that Archer Kinsman was carved out of stone. His wife and daughter had gone, and for all his words the fact didn't really upset him. The only thing that interested Ben was why, after those six years, he was suddenly taking some action. "You say she's in New Orleans?"

Kinsman nodded. "At first she wrote to me occasionally. Not so much to reassure me as to add to my torment, I think. She'd drifted along the coast to New Orleans and became . . . well, a common prostitute. I think that's the worst thing a father can say about his daughter, but damn it there's no other halfway polite name for it. She wrote me that she was following in her mother's footsteps, and it was a letter near tore my heart out. I went looking for her a few years ago, got as far as that section—Storyville, they call it now—and I turned right around and came back home. I guess I was afraid of what I might find. God—the white girls and the black ones are together, in the same houses!"

"And you want me to go there, to find her?"

He nodded again. "I'll pay you well to bring her back to me, Snow. I know you're a man can do it."

"Why is it so important, after six years?"

His hand shook as he reached for his drink. "Look at me, just look at me! There's death in these eyes, on this face. I've been to the best doctors in the state and they all tell me the same thing. A blood disease of some sort. No cure, no hope. I'll be a dead man in a month, two months, three months at most. It's an awful thing to know you're going to die."

"Everyone has to die, Mr. Kinsman."

"But do you really believe that? Don't you think, deep down inside, that you might be the exception?"

"I might have when I was younger," Ben admitted. "I think every youth has dreams of immortality." And then suddenly, hardly knowing he'd spoken the words, or why, he added, "I'll get your daughter for you, Mr. Kinsman. I'll bring her back."

"God, I want to see her worse than anything else in the world. To see her before I die. I've written her, sent her a hundred dollars every Christmas, and on her birthday. . . . I'm a rich man now, Mr. Snow. It was almost as if complete success followed on the tragedy of my life. A year after she left me, a year after I killed my wife, oil was discovered on my land. Imagine—damned black stuff that kills off the grazing land! And yet it's made me a millionaire. I'd kept it a secret for a long time, not daring to tell Bess when I wrote her, fearing that she'd come back just for the money. But last month I told her, because with death staring me in the face that was her money, all of it."

"Did she answer your letter?"

"No. As I said, at first she wrote fairly regularly. Lately, during the past two years, I've hardly had a word from her. A simple *Thanks* scrawled on a post card in response to my Christmas gift. And a cheap greeting card for my birthday. At least she still remembers that. But nothing, not a word, when I told her she might soon have a million dollars."

"Do you have her address?"

"No. I write to General Delivery and she picks them up there. I have a picture, a photograph, taken when she was fifteen, if that's any help."

Ben studied the photograph, and saw a girl with long blonde hair. A pretty girl who might now be beautiful. In the picture she still clung to the wisp of innocence about the eyes, but that would be gone now. The face would be changed. And the body.

And the mind.

"All right," Ben sighed. "But you still haven't explained it all. Why me? Why not just a lawyer to bring her back?"

"I don't know. I suppose it's the murders that have added to my anxiety."

"Murders?" The word sent a familiar chill down Ben's spine.

"I imagined you'd read about it in the papers."

"I rarely read papers."

"Three weeks ago one of these women was killed in Storyville. Slashed to death with a knife. Last week there was another identical killing. Some of the papers have hinted there'll be more. They think it's him."

"Him? Who?"

"That English fellow. What was his name? Jack the Ripper. . . ."

Storyville had come into being in the heart of New Orleans only a few years earlier, in '97, as a result of a city ordinance sponsored by Alderman Story. Although prostitution had been legal in the city since before the Civil War, this was the first attempt to limit it to a specific section of the city. It was a large hunk of the area, too —bounded by Iberville Street, St. Louis, North Basin, and North Robertson Street. In it were to be found the houses, saloons and casinos which made up the dark side of New Orleans life. Street after street, here was the Arlington Palace, the New Mahogany Hall, the Poodle Dog Cafe, Pete Lala's Cafe, and more. White and Negro, working together, playing together. The houses themselves ranged from marbled, elevator-equipped palaces like the New Mahogany to tiny one-room "cribs" just off the street. It was a city in itself, and over it all hung the muted beat of a new music, muffled only by the closed doors and shuttered windows now that winter had shuffled south.

Ben Snow heard the music on his first afternoon in Storyville, as he wandered down Basin Street on the flimsy trail of the girl named Bess Kinsman. He wore his gun under his coat—not the tiny Derringer he sometimes carried but the old .45 he hardly knew the heft of any more. New Orleans was eastern, but it was still .45 country. At least this week. It was four days since he'd left Kinsman in Texas, long enough for another girl to have died horribly in the shady back alleys of Storyville. The morning paper had told him all there was to know: her name was "Sadie Stride, Negro," about thirty years of age. She'd been found face down in a shallow fountain in front of one of the more elaborate houses. There was no doubt that the same knifer had killed all three girls.

*Ripper Prowls Storyville!* one paper screamed. And maybe he was. Ben didn't really care at that point, so long as he kept his knife off one girl named Bess Kinsman. But the heavy gun felt good at his side.

"Bess Kinsman."

"Bess Kinsman? Don't know her. Nearly six hundred girls in the district this winter. Look, go over to the Arlington Annex and buy a *Blue Book* for a quarter. If she's a Storyville girl she's listed in there."

"Thanks. What's that music they're playing, anyway?"

"That there's called jazz sometimes. It's real music."

At the saloon called the Arlington Annex there was a single black piano player, and he too was running through the rhythm and beat of it. The customers, a mixture of races, seemed to have caught the feeling of the music. A dark girl at the bar was moving her body a bit in time to it, and one couple was doing a fast dance in the back. Ben followed instructions and purchased a *Blue Book* for twenty-five cents, then sat down at a table to study it with growing amazement.

Here, in carefully alphabetized lists, were the women of Storyville—white, octoroon (though only a half-dozen of these), and "Negro." There were ads for the bars too, and for some of the available musicians. They were piano players for the most part, colored almost exclusively, and several prided themselves on their ability to play jazz. But just then Ben was more interested in the listing of girls. *Kinsman, Bess*—there it was, as big and bold as life. All right, Bess, we've found you.

He walked the three dusky blocks to the address that had followed her name, not really knowing whether he'd find a mansion or a crib. The place, when he reached it, was somewhat between the two extremes, a pale gray house that needed painting. It was not the typical New Orleans place, with scrolling ironwork on the second-floor balcony. No, this one looked more to Ben's inexperienced eye as if it might originally have been built by a northerner—perhaps one of the post-war wave that swept over the disaster of the southland.

"I'm looking for Bess Kinsman," he told the colored girl who answered the door.

"Sorry. We don't open till seven."

"I'm here on business. But not your kind, exactly. I want to talk to her."

"She ain't here. I'll call Countess Lulu for you."

Ben shrugged and stood waiting on the doorstep, trying to conjure up a mental portrait of the woman named Countess Lulu. He would have been way off—she was white, somewhere past forty, with a look of quiet dignity which must have accounted for the name. At one time she might have been heavier than she was now, for the flesh of her face seemed strangely folded in spots, aging her certainly beyond her years.

"Yes? You are looking for one of my girls?"

Ben nodded, removing his hat because it seemed the thing to do. "That's right, Bess Kinsman."

"You police? About the Ripper?"

"No, nothing like that. I just want to speak with Bess. I'll pay for her time, if that's what's bothering you."

Countess Lulu seemed uncertain. "She's out right now. But if you want to wait . . . ."

"I'd like to. Thanks." He followed her into a parlor hung with drab velvet drapes that seemed designed to shut out every vestige of light or sound. There was only one person in the parlor, a huge pale-skinned man chewing on an ugly damp cigar.

"This here's Piggy, our piano player. Every house has

to have jazz these days to be any good."

Piggy munched on the cigar and mumbled a half-hearted greeting. He was slumped over a battered upright piano, almost embracing it with a sleepy sort of desire. It might just then have been a woman in his arms.

"Has she been with you long?"

"Ever since I came to Storyville. Nearly two years now. Fine girl, and very popular with the customers."

"Does she ever talk about her father? About her life back in Texas?"

"Sometimes. Not often. The girls don't live much in the past."

Ben was carefully rolling a cigarette. "Are you from New Orleans?"

Countess Lulu shook her head. "Tampa, Havana, Mexico City. I move around. Right now this is the place to be."

"Is New Orleans that sinful a city?"

She gave a vague shrug. "Prostitution's been legal here for almost fifty years. And during the Civil War a northern commander actually issued an order that any southern lady insulting a Yankee soldier in New Orleans could be treated as a common prostitute. Things like that have done little to uplift the city's standing. Men come to New Orleans expecting a wide-open city, and we give it to them. Wait until the Mardi Gras tomorrow night and you'll really see something!"

Ben had heard about the pre-Lenten festival, when all of the city swarmed into Storyville to forget the staid life of the other fifty-one weeks. Often with masks hiding their faces, the wealthy ran wild among the poor in a near-orgy of drunken revelry. He hadn't realized the time was almost upon them, but it was mid-February and Lent would begin on Wednesday.

"Perhaps I'll stay over for it," Ben told her. Behind him, Piggy gave a chuckle at the piano and started running through a tune Ben didn't know.

"We'd put you up here if we had an extra room," Lulu offered. "Sometimes between girls we're near empty.

Girls move around a lot. Here today, gone tomorrow. I came to town just after one of the houses burned down, and I was lucky to latch onto some loose ones. Well . . . I think this is Bess now." She'd risen as the front door opened and closed. Two girls and a man entered, and he knew at once which of the ladies was the one he sought.

Her hair was the blonde of the photograph, and if the face was different it was only the difference that aging and hardness could bring. She would be about twenty-four now, nine years older than the picture he carried in his pocket.

"Hello, Bess."

She eyed him with a hard, suspicious look. "Do I know you?"

"I'm a friend of your father. He sent me to find you."

She glanced uncertainly at the two who had entered with her—a handsome dark-haired girl with a look of the South about her, and an alert young man with a chipped front tooth and a thin black mustache. The girl was already going on up the stairs. "I gotta change my clothes, Bess. I'll be in my room if you want me."

"O.K., Dotty. Now, mister, we can talk in here." She motioned back toward the parlor.

"I was thinking of someplace more private."

"For five silver dollars you can come up to my room. The price includes a shot of whiskey."

Ben hesitated only a moment. "Fair enough. Does your friend here come along?"

The man with the mustache grunted and Bess said, "I'll see you later, Hugo. Business before pleasure, you know."

She led the way upstairs carefully quilted with thick carpeting, down a narrow hallway lit by the uneven flickering of gas lamps. And Ben followed with a growing feeling of uncertainty. A simple job was becoming more complex all the time. As he entered the room she indicated, he knew the door across the hall had opened a bit, knew the girl named Dotty was watching through the crack.

"Nice room you have," he told her when she'd closed

the door.

"It'll do. Now what do you want?"

He walked over and carefully sat down on the bed. "I thought I told you. Your father sent me."

"What does he want after all these years?"

"I think you know. He wants you home, back in Texas. He's dying."

"I got his letter," she admitted.

"Will you come back with me?"

The expression on her face was difficult to read. It might have been hesitation, it might have been fear. But she answered, "I can't. It's been too long."

"He still loves you."

"Did he tell you why I left? Did he tell you what happened?"

Ben nodded. "He told me."

"And you think I can go back? To the man who murdered my mother?"

"The man is your father. He's dying."

She lit a cigarette. It was the first time Ben had ever seen a woman smoke. "I can't go back. That's all there is to it."

"He's a wealthy man, Bess. A millionaire. And it's all going to be yours. Couldn't you even go back for a million dollars?"

"You don't understand," she said. "You don't know what I've been through, what I've become." He knew, but he didn't say it. Somehow the words didn't fit her face.

"These killings have your father worried. You must be able to understand that much, at least."

"I live here for six years, lead this kind of a life, and he worries now that I might get killed!"

Ben sighed and got to his feet. He could see that further conversation would be useless. "All right. Perhaps I'll see you again. I plan to be around for a few days." Then, as an afterthought, "Who were the people you came in with?"

"I don't see that it's any of your business, Mr. . . . ?"

"Snow."

". . . Snow, but I'll tell you anyway. Dotty has the room across the hall. I've known her for five years, almost since I first came here. Hugo is a good friend. I might even marry him someday, though I'm sure my father would never approve. Satisfied?"

"Satisfied," he said with a smile. "See you around. And think about it, huh? He really cares about you."

"Goodbye, Mr. Snow."

"Aren't you forgetting the five dollars?"

"I was being nasty. Forgive me." For the first time there seemed something beneath the hard outer shell. He smiled as he went out the door.

Downstairs, Piggy was playing the piano and a couple of colored youths had drifted in off the street to listen. Countess Lulu was nowhere to be seen. Ben went outside into the twilight and started aimlessly down the avenue. Already, around him, the sounds of night were swelling up, strange sounds. Happy, vibrant sounds, but still strange.

Ben saw the man before he was near enough to speak. He came out of the gaslit gloom with a steady, certain pace, and his hands were deep in the pockets of a great-coat oddly warm for the climate, even in February. The man smiled slightly and stopped dead in Ben's path. "Don't go for that gun," he said quietly. "I mean no harm."

"Who are you?"

"Police. Detective Inspector Jonathan Withers, at your service, sir."

"Oh?"

"You're a stranger in the area. A stranger in the midst of a rash of murders needs questioning. Agreed?"

"Agreed." The man was obviously English, but with a touch of the South in his speech. He would have been there a number of years.

Inspector Withers smiled. "We're getting along fine. Now I've already had some reports on you. Name, Ben Snow. Correct?"

"Correct. I was hired by a Texas oilman to find his daughter and bring her back home, which I am attempting to do." He went on to sketch in some brief details of his visit and the day's movements around Storyville.

Withers nodded and seemed satisfied. "Come in here. I'll buy you a beer. We have more to talk about." And a few minutes later, over their drinks, he leaned forward and asked, "Have you ever heard of Jack the Ripper?"

"A little. A mass murderer over in London a few years back."

Withers nodded. "In 1888, to be exact. He killed seven women, all prostitutes, and he's never been apprehended. There was a story he'd come to the United States, killed a couple of women up in New Jersey."

"You're English," Ben said, giving words to the obvious.

Inspector Withers smiled thinly. "I was a London bobby in 1888. I suppose in one way or another I've been on the trail of the Ripper ever since."

"You think this is the same man?"

"The crimes are amazingly similar. Prostitutes, struck down in the streets and alleys of the red-light district, horribly hacked with a knife. And of course if I'm right there'll be more killings. He'll get his courage up and go inside again, as he did in London. Right into their rooms."

"Who were these three women?"

The detective counted them off on his fingers. "First, a few weeks back, was a reformed prostitute named Jane Swann. She sang at one of the bars. Killed in an alley. Then, just the other night, Sadie Stride, dead in a fountain a few blocks from here. The Ripper's fifth victim, by the way, was named Elizabeth Stride. Maybe just a coincidence, maybe not."

"Could it be something else? Could there be a racial angle?"

Inspector Withers shook his head. "The first two were white, the latest one colored. We've found no connection among them except for the fact they were all prostitutes at one time. Of course, it's difficult to go back very far—so many people coming and going all the time."

The beat of a jazz piano rose and fell at intervals, like the piquant pounding of some distant surf. "You don't really think I'm involved?" Ben asked.

"Probably not. At least I know you're not Jack the Ripper. There are some reports, though . . ."

"That I might be Billy the Kid? One's as ridiculous as the other."

"You carry a gun under your coat."

"Don't you think it's a good idea, with a mad killer at large?"

Inspector Withers shrugged. "I naturally take the attitude that the police are able to provide sufficient protection."

"Did they provide it for the Stride girl the other night?"

The detective stood up, signifying the conversation was ended without an answer to Ben's final question. "I'll be in touch with you," he said. "If you learn anything, I can always be found."

Ben watched him leave and then ordered another beer. He sat for a time listening to the piano, watching the city of night awaken, stretch, and go off to live. Finally, as he knew he would, he found himself wandering back to the house three blocks from Basin. It was alight now, with all the sad joys of darkness, loud with the music and the laughter that signaled a kind of escape to the world of Storyville. It had been escape, at least, for Bess Kinsman.

Countess Lulu was at the door. "Decided to come back as a customer?"

"Not exactly. I wanted to see Bess again."

"Cost you cash this time. To me."

He handed her the money and started upstairs. The place was quiet for the moment, then he noticed that Piggy was away from his beloved piano. A black man passed him on the stairs, looking away, hurrying to be out of the place. Ben knocked on her door and entered when she gave the word. If she was surprised to see him again she made no sign of it, but only sat waiting on the bed in an air of innocence that must have started with Eve.

"Hello again, Bess."

"You're back soon."

"I was wondering if you'd thought about it. Going back to Texas."

"I've thought about it."

The hardness was there, in her eyes, on her lips. This would not be the same girl Archer Kinsman had driven away, six years earlier. "And?"

"I told you my answer earlier. I haven't changed my mind."

Hardness, even with that innocence which still clung like a devil. She had to be an amazing actress, but which mood was the act? "I was hoping . . ."

He never finished the sentence. A scream had started, raising like the wail of the damned, to be cut off as suddenly as it began. Bess Kinsman was on her feet in an instant. "It's Dotty, across the hall!"

They were into the hall, pounding on the door, forcing the lock, because somehow the sudden silence was more terrifying than the scream. Countess Lulu had appeared from somewhere, and Piggy, and the other girls, and on their faces was written the single fearful thought. And the door shivered and splintered under Ben's shoulder and they were looking in on it.

At first it didn't seem so bad. At first she looked almost alive, sitting on the floor with her back to the wall looking at the great red gash where her stomach had been. Then, as they watched, her head started to fall to one side and they saw the thin red razor line on her throat.

It was then that Bess screamed . . . .

Inspector Withers was unhappy. He paced the downstairs parlor like a caged tiger, waiting while his men completed the task in the upper room. "A fourth one," he said, "and the day before Mardi Gras. Can you imagine what that madman will do tomorrow, when he's free to wander masked and unnoticed?"

Ben had settled onto Piggy's piano bench, listening,

watching, his hand never far from his gun. He had met many murderers before, but this one, so near and yet so unseen, had unnerved even him. "How did he get in?"

Withers shrugged. "Through the window, across the roof. It would seem that the choice of Dotty Ringsome as the victim was dictated simply by the location of her room and the fact that she was alone at the time."

But Ben was thinking. "Her scream was cut off so quickly, though. She didn't start screaming when she saw him coming through the window. He must have actually had the knife in her stomach before she yelled. Then he silenced her with a slash at her throat. Wouldn't this indicate it was someone she knew? Someone she trusted?"

"She might have been dozing on the bed with her eyes closed."

"I suppose so," Ben conceded.

He waited for a time longer, answering questions about what little he knew, watching while everyone in the house underwent the inquisition by Withers and his men. Finally, some time after midnight, they allowed him to leave. He walked the few blocks to the Arlington Palace and found there a room for the night.

Sleep came quickly, but he kept his gun under the pillow, close at hand. His last thought was that somehow he had to get Kinsman's daughter out of that place. The evil that had struck down four girls was very close to her . . . .

In the morning he found the Storyville blocks strangely transformed, wearing in the midst of their hidden terror the colorful streamers and gay trappings of carnival time. It was Mardi Gras, the day before Lent, and already there was a scattering of masked, costumed figures in the streets. Down the block a newsboy shouted the latest on the Ripper murders, but even this went unnoticed or unadmitted on a day set aside for gaity.

The Arlington Annex adjoined the hotel lobby and in the mornings provided a reasonable place to eat breakfast. A bartender was polishing glasses and one of the girls brought Ben a plate of bacon and eggs with an early-morning air of bustle. At this hour the only other customer was a vaguely familiar young man with a mustache and a chipped tooth. It took Ben only a moment to place him —Bess's friend, Hugo.

"Hello, there," he offered through a mouthful of food.

"Snow, isn't it?"

"That's right, Ben Snow."

"I'm Hugo Dadier. I hear Bess's old man hired you."

"I guess that's right. He wants her back in Texas."

Dadier had remained standing at the bar. Now he walked over to Ben's table. "I've known Bess from almost her first day in New Orleans. I like to think I can take care of her."

"Can you protect her against the Ripper? Can you get her away from this kind of life she's leading? Can you give her a million dollars?"

"I can try," Dadier said, the eternal answer of the eternal young man, even here among the sins of Storyville.

"Do you think you're right for her. What are you—a pimp, a drug peddler, maybe?"

"Bess and I are two of a kind. We understand each other."

"I'll bet. You should take an ad for her in the *Blue Book*. It might help her business." The remark angered Dadier, but before he could reply Ben had a thought. "Say, do they keep back issues of the *Blue Book* here?"

"I don't know," Dadier said with a shrug, controlling his anger. "Ask the bartender, not me."

Ben walked over to the long polished bar and interrupted the glass-wiping task. "Back issues of the *Blue Book*— do you have any?"

The bartender eyed him oddly. "What good are back issues? The current one's got all the girls listed. The girls not listed aren't around any more."

"I just wanted to see some."

"Didn't start publishing it till '95."

"All right. Do you have them from '95 on?"

"Guess I could find you a set, back in the office. Just a

minute." Ben waited and presently the bartender returned, bearing five dog-eared copies of past *Blue Books.* "You can look at 'em here, but I gotta have them back."

"Fine."

Hugo Dadier had resumed his position at the bar as Ben sat down and began paging through the first of the booklets, not knowing exactly what he was seeking, yet feeling somehow that he would find it here. The books had grown in size with each passing year, and in '97 they had proudly proclaimed the official birth of the Storyville district. Gradually the ads for piano players had begun to appear, though the word "jazz" was not yet used in them.

But right now Ben was more interested in the names. He scanned the lists, making an occasional note, and found what he wanted in a sudden flash of brilliance. The book was two years old, but it seemed to be there. Perhaps, just perhaps, the key to the Ripper murders.

"You seen Inspector Withers around this morning?" he called out to the bartender.

"Not yet. He usually comes by about noon, but today's Mardi Gras."

"I know."

Ben stuffed one of the *Blue Books* into his pocket and made for the door. "Say, I told you I had to have those back!" the bartender called after him, but he was already into the street, swallowed up by a constantly growing crowd of masked, painted revelers.

It took Ben two hours to track down Withers, and when he found him the Englishman was helping to break up a crowd that had gathered outside of one of the houses on North Robertson. A girl, obviously drunk or drugged, had climbed out on the roof in a brief beaded costume and was attempting to do a French cancan, much to the delight of the crowd below.

"Well," he said, finally noticing Ben in the midst of them, "enjoying the show?"

"I've been looking for you. Can we talk?"

Inspector Withers studied his set face for a moment, then motioned down the street. "At the station house.

Come on."

Over a cigarette-stained table in an almost bare office, Ben produced the two-year-old *Blue Book*. He saw the spark of interest in the detective's eyes at once, and he said, "I think I'm on to something, but I need a bit of your knowledge of the district."

"Go on."

"This book lists the girls, with their current addresses, as you know. Well, two years ago all of the dead girls were living at the same address."

"The hell! Let me see that!"

"They were all at Pearl's Pleasure Palace. Now you tell me the rest of it, Inspector."

Withers frowned, then leaned back in his chair. "Of course! I know one or two of them had worked at Pearl's, but after two years I'd forgotten about the others. Pearl's is the place that burned down."

"How many girls were there?"

"At the time of the fire? She had six, I think."

"No piano player?"

Withers shook his head. "Not then. That's a recent addition to these places."

"All right." Ben picked up the book again. "Here are the names I found: Sadie Stride . . ."

"The Ripper's third victim."

"Jane Swann . . ."

"The first victim. She got out of the business right after the fire."

"Laura O'Toole . . ."

"Forget her. She was killed in the fire."

"Mary Quinn . . ."

"The second victim."

"Dotty Ringsome . . ."

"Victim number four, just last night. As you know."

"And Pearl herself?"

Withers frowned at the memory. "Pearl was a middle-aged bum, a heavy drinker. Some even said her drinking caused the fire that night. Last year she killed a man with a broken bottle and fled to South America. She's still there, living in Brazil."

Ben sighed at the list before him. He turned the page and stared down at the final name he'd checked. "The sixth girl in Pearl's house . . ."

"And the Ripper's next victim, if you're correct."

". . . was Bess Kinsman."

The Inspector's face hardened. "Come on," he said. . . .

But it wasn't to be that easy. The streets now in late afternoon were crowded with the noise and color of carnival, filled to overflowing with masked men and painted women who had forgotten or never cared about the Ripper who had already killed four girls. They were out for pleasure, a physical representation of the "pursuit of happiness" the Constitution guaranteed. The Constitution—no, Ben remembered, it was the Declaration of Independence—had put it nicely, but they hadn't said anything in there about murderers. There was no law saying people had to suddenly turn off the happiness just because there was a killer in their midst.

He watched the costumes passing in front of Countess Lulu's house, noting especially one fellow dressed as a policeman. It looked like Piggy, but he couldn't be sure. He couldn't be sure of anything just then.

Withers came out of the house, his eyes sweeping the passing crowds. "Well, she's all right. So far, at least. I'll send an officer down to keep an eye out."

"Make sure he doesn't wear a mask. There's a phony cop out in the crowd."

Withers spotted him and started edging through the crowd. In a moment he was gone, swallowed up in the colorful flow. But Ben stood his ground in front of Countess Lulu's. He knew Archer Kinsman wouldn't be paying much for a dead daughter. A jazz band of sorts went by, the first he'd seen, led by a trumpet-blowing black man dressed like the devil. And as the evening's early shadows began to lengthen in the street he went inside to see how things were.

"What a night!" Lulu was chirping. "Every girl's busy and there are three birds waiting!"

"Where's your music?"

"Piggy's drunk, parading out there someplace." She left him and vanished through a hall doorway.

He stayed a few moments, watching the costumed men who waited in the parlor. Then the thought of it all began to sicken him and he turned away, heading back to the street. His hand was on the doorknob when he heard something crash to the floor above his head. Somebody screamed—it might have been Bess Kinsman.

Ben took the stairs three at a time, his hand already brushing aside the coat to get his gun free. Her door was locked but as he rattled the knob she screamed out again. *"Ben, help! It's the Ripper!"*

His shoulder hit the flimsy door, remembering Dotty Ringsome's door the night before, remembering what he'd found there. But Bess Kinsman was very much alive, struggling with a masked figure dressed in a checkered harlequin costume. His right hand clutched a curving knife that flickered with reflected light as they struggled by the bed. *"Shoot him, Ben! He's killing me!"*

But her body was between Ben's gun and the masked killer. As he moved in on the struggling figures the knife plunged downward, slashing at Bess's stomach, darkening her pink housecoat with a sudden spatter of blood. She screamed once more and toppled to the floor, and as Ben caught her falling figure the Ripper hurled himself at the bedroom's sole window, smashing through it in a headlong dive to the roof below.

Ben tore away the housecoat and tried to stop the flow of blood with his handkerchief. Then, as others crowded into the room behind him, he went out the window after the costumed figure.

The roof slanted upward from the window, then ended suddenly with a five-foot gap before the adjoining house. Ben took the leap without thinking twice, landing clawing at the slippery slate. Above him, against the blue night sky, the harlequin costume paused in flight to hurl a shingle of slate down at his gripping fingers. He felt the bits of rock nick his cheek, then he was up, stripping the impeding coat from his shoulders, checking the feel of the gun still in his holster as he climbed. Ahead, the enemy had swung down, hand over hand, to cling flylike to the ornate iron railing of the housefront.

Ben followed, feeling the rusty metal underhand, seeing now the very eyes of the enemy inches away, close enough almost to reach. And the knife blade dull now with darkness, moving like a cobra as the killer hung with one hand clinging. The blade shot out, slashing, as Ben lost his footing and hung by his fingers above the street twenty feet below. And now the slasher moved in for the kill and the sweep of the knife came closer. Dangling, Ben risked one hand, dropping it to the holster at his side, pulling the gun free, firing as he hung swinging in the air against the iron grillworked balcony.

It was not the best shot of his life, but it sufficed. The masked figure shuddered as the bullet tore into his side and relaxed his grip on the metal. He fell slowly, like a deflated balloon, and landed on the paving below with a sick thud of finality.

Ben climbed down and fought his way through the gathering crowd. He bent to the bloody, broken figure and ripped away the mask. It was the face of Bess's friend, Hugo Dadier. . . .

The following day was Ash Wednesday, the beginning of Lent, and even in Storyville there were those who went to church this day. But for Inspector Withers and Ben Snow there were other things to be done. At the hospital they found Bess Kinsman resting comfortably in a narrow white bed. She was smiling, even though she'd been told a few hours earlier the identity of her attacker.

"It's hard to believe, I know," she told them, "but at times there was a bit of strangeness about him. To think that he killed those four girls so horribly . . ."

"There is no doubt he did it," Withers said. "The knife was the type used in all the killings. Of course he's too young to have been Jack the Ripper, but he must have been just as insane."

"Perhaps not," Ben said quietly. "Or at least not quite as insane as he might seem."

Bess turned to him with difficulty. "You know why he did it? Why he killed the others and tried to kill me?"

"I think so." He turned away from her. "I imagine it will all come out at the trial."

"The trial!" she said, startled. "But he's dead!"

"Not his trial—yours. Inspector Withers is here to arrest you as an accessory in those four murders."

"But . . . but that's crazy! He tried to kill me too! Why would I want those girls dead?" She was sitting up in the bed, her face as white as the sheets.

Ben sighed, feeling tired and a bit lonely. "You wanted them dead because your name is Laura O'Toole. You wanted them dead because the real Bess Kinsman was killed in a fire two years ago. . . ."

"You were clever," he went on, "very clever. In fact, you made no real mistakes. But I was curious as to why you, of all people, hadn't mentioned the connection among the four murder victims. The police and most everyone else might have forgotten they were all at Pearl's Pleasure Palace at the time of the fire, but certainly you would have remembered. And then of course there was the attempt on your life last night. When I found that the Ripper was your friend Hugo Dadier I was baffled for a moment. He of all people would never have attacked you last night, because he was actually at the Arlington while I was looking over back copies of the *Blue Book*. He knew I had found the connecting link between the victims, and he knew I would be expecting an attack on you. Also, of course, he was in a position where he could have killed you at any time—so why risk everything with his half-hearted attempt of last evening, at the very time I was expecting it and guarding the house? The answer of course was that the attack was a fake. He never meant to kill you, but he had to attempt it last night solely because he did know I was expecting it. Otherwise I might begin to suspect you."

"You call this a fake?" she shouted from the bed. "My stomach ripped open with a knife?"

"I think in that last instant you had an idea all your own. I think you decided Hugo had served his purpose in killing the girls. So you shouted for me to shoot him, which wasn't in the plan. He saw your double-cross and jabbed a little deeper than he'd planned. Of course I was on my guard as soon as you called my name through the closed door—it meant you'd been watching me enter the house."

"And why in hell did I do all this?" She was not the same girl any more. The hard, cold calculation had taken over completely now.

"Well, those four girls were at Pearl's when it burned down, so I asked myself what they might know that made their deaths so important. And I remembered something. I remembered that Bess Kinsman's long letters to her father stopped about two years ago. That's when it came to me. Bess was the one who died in the fire, and you were the other girl—Laura O'Toole. You must have looked enough alike to fool occasional customers and casual acquaintances, but the other girls in the house would have known you took Bess's place after the fire."

"Why? Do you know that too, smart guy?"

"Why? Well, I imagine in the beginning it was only for that hundred dollars her father sent her every Christmas and birthday. Of course you would have known about it, and with Bess Kinsman dead in the fire you must have seen how easy it would be to change places with her. It meant two hundred dollars a year, and you were reasonably certain her father would never try to visit her here. The four girls knew about the switch, of course, and Pearl, and your friend Hugo. But people come and go so fast in Storyville, it was easy to fool the rest. Countess Lulu, for example, didn't show up till just after the fire— so to her you were always Bess Kinsman and no one else."

"So why did I decide to kill the girls after two years?"

"They hadn't minded a little two-hundred-a-year rack-et, but when you got that letter last month saying Bess's father was dying, telling you for the first time he was worth a million dollars in oil lands, you knew you had to remove the witnesses to your impersonation. Those girls would want their cut—a big cut—to keep quiet. Pearl was already far away in South America, and would never return with a murder rap waiting for her, so you had only the four to remove. Hugo did it for you, not knowing you'd take the first opportunity to dispose of him too. And of course the Jack the Ripper idea made a natural cover-up for the true motive."

"That's a good story," she said, calmer now. "You think you can prove it?"

"The murders started a week after you got Kinsman's letter about the million-dollar inheritance. It's not evidence, but it's a fact of the kind juries like to hear."

Inspector Withers interrupted her. "We can easily prove you're not Bess Kinsman—by handwriting, among other things. And now that we know what we're looking for, I'm sure we'll turn up other witnesses who knew both you girls. If necessary we can bring Archer Kinsman here to meet you."

"If he lives that long," she challenged.

Ben sighed and ran his hand along the white railing of the bed. "That was my first clue of something wrong—the fact that you wouldn't go back to Texas to your dying father. The fact that Bess had kept writing to him at first implied she still cared a little for him, yet you refused to go back, even with a million dollars waiting for you. You couldn't, of course, because though you look a little like a picture of Bess at fifteen, you'd never fool her father. You had to gamble on getting the money anyway, knowing old Kinsman had no other relatives. I imagine you would have produced Lulu and scores of other recent friends to convince the lawyers you really were Bess, once Kinsman was dead."

"I'm not saying a word," she mumbled. "We'll see what a jury says."

"Yes, we will," Withers agreed. "We might not convict

you of the murders, but the fraud charges and your general character will put you away for a good many years."

When Ben left the room she had started to cry. The hardness was dissolving, and he wouldn't have been surprised if Withers obtained a full confession before too many days.

But for Ben now there was only remaining the short trip back to Texas, back to the waiting Archer Kinsman with the sort of story he'd hate to tell any father. He almost wished, deep in his heart, that death would beat him to Kinsman's side. That would be the simplest way. . . .

# 1915

# Proposal Perilous

## by Morris Hershman

*Paris during World War I, and a brief encounter between two people.*

MISS HARRIET KING OF PHILADELPHIA, Pennsylvania, U.S.A., in Paris on urgent business, had received her first proposal of marriage from a man she'd known a very short time. She had not clasped her hands together joyfully, accepted him on the spot, or done any of the million things a young girl would have done.

Miss King was not a young girl. Though her friends valiantly insisted that you'd never think it to look at her, Miss King was fifty-three years of age.

Her first proposal! Even now, as her patent-leather oxfords thudded harshly on the sidewalk of a typical Parisian boulevard, she experienced the same chill of doubt she'd had when he asked her. She realized once more that she would have to tell him—inside of an hour now, for the decision had been promised today—that she was fond of Henri (dearest Henri) but she had thought it over carefully and decided not to marry him.

If she'd been twenty-three instead of fifty-three, Miss King's decision would have been the same. After all, she wasn't tied down. In what she sometimes thought of as her shockingly restricted circle, not one marriage that she knew of had turned out quite well for both the man and the woman involved.

As she grew older, the idea of losing her freedom and going to the bed of a virtual stranger appalled her. She ought to have known somehow that a man like Henri wouldn't feel the same way she did about marriage, but the proposal had taken her completely unawares.

"Give me a little time," she had pleaded, running her hands through her hair in desperation."

*"Ma petite 'arriette, when?"*

"A week, Henri. You'll know in a week."

Even though it was now October of 1915, and things were not shaping up too well for France and her chief ally, England, Miss King had come to Paris because she was afraid not of the Germans but of her conscience. An elderly aunt of hers who'd never cared much for Harriet during her lifetime had requested in her will that "my beloved niece, Harriet" come to France "in order to act as one of my executors."

When the old woman passed away in the early part of July, Harriet had spoken to her brother about going. Aided by innumerable aunts and uncles, they all talked it over among themselves and decided for her that if she, Harriet, did refuse to go, she'd always regret the injustice to a dearly loved relative. Harriet, therefore, booked passage on the first available liner.

And she had met Henri. He was a dealer in used furniture, which he was buying on speculation. He claimed that the price of used furniture would skyrocket just as soon as the war was over, next year perhaps, because the factories, geared as they were to munitions making, would find it long and costly to convert to peacetime production.

Short and stout, with large black eyebrows and a fine beard which he industriously pomaded three times a week, Henri conformed in every way to the average tourists's conception of the *petit bourgeois*. He had an economical turn of mind as well and he'd once shown her a pocket-sized memorandum book in which he noted his daily expenses in a handwriting so small that his words fitted comfortably between the ruled lines.

And in a few short days, Henri had proposed.

"So far as money is concerned, *ma petite,* I have the business, which even now is bringing me a substantial income. There are no children from previous marriages to arouse antagonism on one side or the other. God be thanked, there are no in-laws! Since we are both middle-aged people, you will not have to endure the chasing around after young girls on my part. At this time I want most of all a devoted helpmate."

He had a charming villa out of town where they could live together. From the enthusiastic descriptions he gave, Miss King would have had no difficulty in finding her way through the house and garden with her eyes closed.

And she was going to refuse him. Though she might never have another chance at a husband, she was going to refuse him. . . .

Usually, Miss King traveled with a Baedeker in her pocketbook and noted her surroundings carefully, as if she expected to come across a stray monument on the very next block. She was indefatigable. Nothing daunted her. Having paid out good money for a trip, Miss King didn't want the time to be wasted. But the problem of what exact words to use in telling Henri of her decision preyed on her mind to such an extent that she'd hardly seen where she was going.

Turning off the boulevard into a pitch-black side street, however, Miss King became aware of her surroundings for the first time. With the night everything had taken on a brownish tinge along the narrow thoroughfare, so that walking on it was like walking in a bottle of beer.

Her eyes rested casually on a shop window in front of which a group of small boys crouched, playing marbles, and halted apprehensively before a row of semi-private houses.

She wished she knew in which one of those houses Henri lodged. He'd written the number down for her on the back of an envelope, nearly forgetting it himself because he stayed there so infrequently when he came to Paris; and she had put it away somewhere and promptly lost it. The house was on this street, beyond question—but was it Number 51 or 67 that Miss King wanted?

She had just made up her mind to ask the concierge of each house when she saw Henri himself peering out anxiously from an upstairs window. He caught sight of her in a moment. He waved boyishly, his head vanished and the window was closed after him.

The house she'd been looking for, Number 67, was no better and no worse than any of the others. A thin, T-shaped gravel path bisected a small garden that obviously hadn't been cared for in years, but the house itself had been repainted a few months ago and it looked comfortable.

Once inside, Miss King walked up a flight of stairs and knocked at his door.

Henri had dressed rapidly and was in a state of high excitement as he welcomed her with bows and apologies. "You insist upon coming to see this room. *Voila!* I 'ope you are not too disappointed."

"I'm not at all disappointed," she answered in French. Next to the uncurtained window she had seen downstairs, Miss King was confronted with a large mahogany chest of drawers. At her right was an old-fashioned four-poster bed, at her left a gramophone and a small table piled with magazines. Stiff-backed chairs had been placed in every corner and Miss King sat down on the nearest one. Henri sat down with a flourish. "I am charmed by it all, Monsieur—"

"I should like you to call me Henri," he interposed.

There was a silence. Henri leaned forward attentively.

"Henri, I have considered your proposal"—half-forgotten words Miss King had not even thought of since the turn of the century came back to her—"and while I am deeply sensible of the honor, I am unable to—"

His eyes widened. *"Voyons, ma petite.'arriette—"*

"It would never work out, Henri. The whole arrangement is impossible. You and I belong to different worlds. You have a business here and your friends and your home. Everything I have is in America."

He nodded.

"Don't forget that I am fifty-three years old, Henri, and a creature of habit. I don't really want to give up those habits. A great many things that I'm used to I couldn't possibly give up for any man. You see, it's not as if we could either of us go ahead and sacrifice all for love."

"But why not?" he pleaded. "I am willing to."

She interrupted him again. "Take into consideration the fact that France is at war now, Henri. The Germans may conceivably enter Paris at any time, tomorrow or the day after. My family will be worried to death about me."

"Your family?"

"My brothers, Henri. I live with them and they have control of my income, small though it is. For sentimental reasons alone, I wouldn't want to be married without their approval."

"I had not realized," he said after a pause, "that it would be so difficult."

They gazed at each other for a moment.

"Perhaps I had better go now," said Miss King, when she felt that the silence was becoming intolerable. She was a little shocked to hear him agree.

"I do not see why we have to prolong it myself." Sighing audibly, he pushed back his chair and stood up. "Too, my concierge is a very inquisitive woman."

He went to the door with her. Miss King reflected that he would probably never know just how eased she was by his calm acceptance of the news. She was a little tired, too, since it was all over and done with.

Framed in the doorway at the head of the stairs, it occurred to Miss King that she would remember this day as long as she remembered anything. In a weary or disgruntled state of mind, she would tell herself that it was no more than she deserved. *Why didn't you stay in France with Henri? He loved you. He wanted you.* As long as she remembered anything she would remember this.

If there had been someone for her to talk it over with—if they'd both been younger! Fifty-three—fifty-three.

Henri took her hand, kissing it gravely.

"Shall we go downstairs together?"

"Thank you, but it's only one flight."

"There's no reason for me to inquire"—he was obviously holding his breath—"I don't suppose you've changed your mind?"

"No."

"Then we have only to say good-bye and it is over."

"Good-bye, Henri, I'll always remember you."

A door opened somewhere on the ground level and the inquisitive concierge Henri had complained of peered up the badly lighted staircase at them, her arms akimbo.

Very formally Henri said, "Good-bye, Mademoiselle King."

Very formally she echoed, "Good-bye—good-bye, Monsieur Landru." . . .

Some five years later, in a wide rambling stone cottage on the outskirts of Philadelphia, Miss Harriet King sat frowning distractedly at her needlework.

At precisely three-fifteen the door opened. One of her brothers came in, holding a rumpled newspaper under his arm. Laying aside what she earnestly hoped to make a scarf out of in less than a week, Miss King glanced at the headlines. The black print stared at her.

## PARIS BLUEBEARD ARRESTED
## LANDRU CHARGED WITH FOUR MURDERS

She drew in her breath sharply. For a moment, the newspaper crinkled and shuddered in her trembling hands. She remembered suddenly the vital importance of controlling herself and made a tight little ball of her fingers.

She heard her brother's voice coming from a great distance. "Can you imagine it, Harriet?" His voice seemed to drip with pure scorn. "This Landru used to marry friendless women and kill 'em for whatever they had."

"It's terrible," Miss King said, hardly recognizing her own voice, so aged and coarse was it. "Simply terrible."

"You were on the other side a few years back, as I recall." Her brother cleared his throat embarrassedly. "Could have run into him for all you know. It's fortunate that you had—ahem!—the family to get home to—hm! Yes. I hate to think what might have happened otherwise."

When her brother had left, closing the door behind him with an ear-splitting thud, Harriet King stared at the newspaper for a long time.

She picked up her needlework again. *He loved you—He wanted you.*

"I wonder," she thought, looking down with bitter resentment at the clacking needles in her hand. "I wonder just how fortunate I've been."

# 1919

# All the Way Home

## by Jaime Sandaval

*A nostalgic remembrance of farm life in rural America just after World War I, and of one terrible night in a boy's life.*

THE HIRED MAN drove me back to the farm from the cemetery. Becky's funeral had taken a lot out of me, although at my age I should be used to them. I came back from my father's funeral in a horse and buggy, from my mother's in an old tin lizzie, and from Becky's in a many-horsed thunderbolt. I've lived too long.

My father's farm—my farm—is on a spit of land jutting out into Lake Superior. It's a good farm. With a little help from the cows, it has taken care of us through the long years. But now there's no one I can even leave it to—I'm the last of the Harwoods.

What really hurts is knowing how Becky must have wondered—all the years after my mother died—why I never asked her to marry me. She never let on, of course, and there was nothing I could say, or do. Not since that terrible night on Wild Swan Point so many years ago. . . .

There used to be an old, abandoned wooden lighthouse at the end of the causeway leading out to the point. It hasn't been there for a long time, but at sunset when the west wind blows and the clouds are dark on the lake, I can sit by the window and look down the road, and once again a light seems to shine from a window high up in the old lighthouse.

When I was twelve years old the light shone because my father had fixed up a room in the lighthouse for Miss Abby Hunter, up near the top where she wanted to be. My mother didn't like it when Miss Abby came back to live in our neighborhood again. Before she'd left, Miss Abby had taught school and lived on the Brainard farm about a mile from us. I once heard my mother say that some people were no better than they should be. My father heard her say it, too, and it made him angry. He told my mother she was a fool to believe all the gossip she heard.

We were at the supper table in the big farm kitchen, and there were rusks and wild strawberry jam. I wanted another rusk, but when I looked up and saw my father's face after he'd spoken, I was afraid to ask for it. My father was a big, strong, solid-looking man, with red cheeks and pale blue eyes and a quick temper that scared me sometimes. But he never scared my mother. She spoke right up to him, especially after Miss Abby came to live at the lighthouse.

I liked Miss Abby. She lent me books, but after my mother found out I had to hide them. Miss Abby always looked dressed up, with a ribbon in her blonde hair. She was small, and quick-moving, and pretty. When she was teaching, she never seemed much older than the bigger kids in school.

The lighthouse was a strange place to want to live in. It was old, so old it hadn't been used as a lighthouse for many years. There wasn't anything in the cobwebbed space at the bottom but a lot of bad-smelling oil drums. I never saw the room my father fixed up for Miss Abby at the top of the spiraling wooden staircase. She never invited me to see it, and I didn't know how to ask.

I came back to the farm one morning after collecting the eggs and taking the cows down to the pasture by the lake where we had a dock and where my father's sailboat was tied up during the summer. The dock was near the barn and the road, too, so I hadn't far to go. In the spring and fall my father used to go out with his nets and catch lake trout, perch, and pike.

He met me at our gate, saying he wanted to talk to me. As soon as I saw he wasn't angry any more, it made me feel important. "Tommy," he said, "twice a week I want you to carry a pail of milk down to Miss Abby at the lighthouse. You can milk Daisy after supper and get down and back before dark. Make it Sunday and Wednesday nights. And let's keep it a secret—just between the two of us." He put his finger to his lips and winked.

It sounded fine to me. I had no brothers or sisters, and I got so lonesome sometimes I welcomed the chance to talk to anyone. My mother was always busy in the kitchen after supper, and I knew she wouldn't miss me. Mom was a tall, stout woman with black hair and snapping black eyes. She was almost pretty when she smiled, but she hardly ever smiled after Miss Abby came to live at the lighthouse. I heard my father tell her once she'd better learn to control her tongue. My mother got red in the face. Her eyes glared, and she left the room.

I could hardly wait to milk Daisy the first night and be on my way down to Wild Swan Point. For the milk-carrying my father got me a special pail with a tight lid. It didn't spill even when I ran. When I reached the point, the sun was going down behind the lighthouse, and Miss Abby was sitting outside. She looked like a doll in her fluffy dress against the dirty wooden wall of the lighthouse.

She greeted me warmly and asked me to sit down while she put the milk away. I could see she was making a woodpile inside the big door. There was lots of driftwood around, and I carried some inside and stacked it. When

Miss Abby came down, she thanked me. It was dark when I reached home, and I turned and looked back down the road and saw the high-up lighted window, like a small and lonely star against the night.

One Sunday afternoon in August the Brainards stopped by. They had a boy a year older than me. His name was Nate, and I didn't like him. He was bigger than me, and he was always picking a fight. Mrs. Brainard began saying how queer it was for Miss Abby to come back and live in the old lighthouse, and Nate sat grinning in his chair across the room from me. Finally he motioned with his head, and we went outside.

He headed for the outhouse. Ours was the best one in the neighborhood. It was painted green, and had a kind of small porch with mosquito netting all around, and a wild cucumber vine grew across the top. Nate stayed a long time, and when he came out he had a piece of chalk in his hand.

"What you been doing with the chalk?" I asked him.

"Go on in and see," he said.

I went in. One look was enough. All down one wall he'd written my father's name and Miss Abby's, and other things. He was all doubled up laughing when I charged out the door. I got him down, and we rolled on the ground, hitting and scratching and biting.

All of a sudden I was swung up off Nate into the air. "Can't you damn kids get along?" my father hollered in my ear. Nate sat up, looking scared. He glanced at the open outhouse door, and then away. My father looked at him, set me down, and went inside. Nate jumped up and streaked for the gate. My father burst out in time to see him vault the fence into the road.

"I'll make his tail smoke when I get my hands on him," he said. His lips were a thin hard line. He turned to me, and I stopped rubbing the eye that had got in the way of Nate's elbow. "Sorry, Tommy. Now run get me something to—" He broke off as my mother turned the corner and walked up to us.

Nobody said a word. My mother stared at each of us in

turn. Two red spots blazed on her pale cheeks. My father was still standing in the open door. My mother went to push by him. He half raised an arm to stop her, then lowered it. She went inside.

I got out of there. I knew they'd say terrible things to each other. I went in the back door to the kitchen, and in the small mirror over the sink tried to see if my eye looked as bad as it felt. It was getting dark outside, and I was late with the chores. I went out to the barn and started on the cows. After a while my father came in and sat down on a stool and went to work without saying a word, his face grim in the lantern light.

I filled the special pail for Miss Abby and left the barn. I walked down the path to the road-gate, and I had just reached for the latch when my mother spoke to me from the darkness to one side. "Where are you going?" she asked me. I nearly dropped the pail. She didn't wait for me to answer. She took the pail from me, and without a word walked back with it to the barn.

I didn't know what to do. They didn't come out. I went back to the kitchen and waited for what seemed like a long time. I was hungry, but didn't want to be the only one eating. My mother came in, finally. She didn't speak. She walked as though her eyes weren't seeing. She went right through the kitchen and on upstairs. Outside I could hear my father washing up at the pump, and then he walked down the path.

I remembered the writing on the outhouse wall, and I wet a rag at the pump and went down to the barn for the lantern. The first step I took inside I saw the gaping stall in the line of placidly chewing cows. Daisy's stall was empty. Daisy was gone, and my father was gone, too. My stomach felt cold.

I went back to the silent kitchen after finishing up out back. I lighted the lamp and put it on the table by the window. I must have fallen asleep with my head beside the lamp, because the parlor clock struck ten and woke me up. There wasn't a sound in the whole house.

I went upstairs to bed, but I couldn't fall sleep again. I

thought about my mother and my father, and the way it used to be before Miss Abby came back. I wondered what would happen now, when my mother found out that Daisy was gone.

I didn't want to come downstairs in the morning at all. The big bedroom door was open when I passed it, and I felt better. Maybe everything would be all right. Downstairs my mother was at the stove and my father was at the table, eating, but they didn't say anything, even to me, and it wasn't all right.

I stayed away from the house all morning. In the afternoon I went down to the corn crib and got out *Tom Sawyer* that Miss Abby had lent me. I kept it hidden there so my mother wouldn't know. I went down the path to read under the big elm beside the road. The sun was shining, but clouds were forming in the west and it was getting cooler.

I'd reached Chapter Five and almost forgotten where I was when someone said hello. I looked up and saw Joe Macy, the Rural Free Delivery mailman from Indian Bay. He was standing by our box at the gate with a letter in his hand. "Give this to your pa," he said to me. "He'll be glad of the chance to take it to the point."

I knew what it was even before I got up and took it from him. It was addressed to Miss Abby. Joe Macy grinned at me, a snaggle-toothed grin. "Me, I aim to get on home before it storms," he said.

I stood there wishing I was bigger. I'd have taken the grin right off his ugly face. Over in the west the cloudbanks were larger, and it was beginning to blow.

I wanted to hide the letter, but I was afraid to. I put *Tom Sawyer* back in the corn crib, and took the letter to the kitchen. My mother was working the churn and my father was oiling a trap. They had their backs to each other. My father put down the trap as if glad to have something else to do and took the letter from me. He turned it over and over in his big hands.

"Where'd this come from?" he asked me in a queer voice.

"Joe brought it to the gate just now," I said. "He said you could take it to Miss Abby so he'd get home before the storm."

"No!" my mother screamed. It was so close I ducked. I hadn't heard her come up behind me. "No, no! You're not going down there! Are you trying to drive me out of my mind, Tom?"

"Don't tell me in my own house what I'm not going to do, woman!" he shouted at her. He looked at me, and shoved the letter in his pocket. "It will keep," he said in a calmer tone. "I've got to go out and get in the nets before the storm tears them up."

He left the house. My mother sank down in a chair and began to moan and rock herself from side to side. I don't think she knew I was still there. I couldn't stand it. I went outside, too. It was almost dark, and blowing hard—much too hard for my father to be heading out in the boat to pull in his nets.

I started to run for the dock, but, when I turned the corner of the barn I stopped. I could see the dock from there, and silhouetted against the lake and the low-flying clouds I could see the boat's stubby mast. My father hadn't gone out on the lake. I knew where he'd gone.

In another five minutes it was so dark I couldn't even see the dock, let alone the boat. I went into the barn to get out of the wind. Daisy's empty stall reminded me of things all over again. Through a crack in the door left by a broken hinge I could look down the road and see the light high up in the lighthouse on Wild Swan Point.

I couldn't stay in the barn. I couldn't go back to the house. Out on the path the wind tore at me. I reached the road and started to run. Down the causeway I could hear big waves breaking against the rocky shore. I got to the lighthouse and sat down on the bench outside the big door to catch my breath. I began to be chilled in the wind, and I went to the door to go inside.

In the dark I couldn't find the latch at first, but when I did the door opened easily and didn't creak or groan as it had when I was delivering the milk. Someone had oiled the hinges. It was quiet inside, away from the soughing of the wind and the crashing of the waves. It was pitch-black, except for a single crack of light up at the top of the spiral staircase.

I felt around, looking for something to sit on. I almost yelled out loud when I bumped into something big and warm. It took me a second to realize it was Daisy, tethered inside out of the storm. She butted me with her head the way she always did when she wanted to be milked. I was afraid she would moo, so I got away from her.

I ran into the railing at the foot of the stairs, and I looked up again to the crack of light at the top. It seemed the most natural thing in the world to climb those stairs, one hand on the railing, the other on the wall. When I stood at the top outside the door, I could hear Miss Abby's voice. That high up I could hear the wind again, but I could hear her, too.

"—got to stop arguing with me, Tom," she was saying. "You saw the letter. They can't keep the child any longer. I've got to go and get her and bring her back here with me."

"No!" my father said sharply. "It's—it's no place for a child, Abby. We'll think of something. Give me a few days."

"The letter said right now, Tom. I'm going tomorrow. You can think of something when I'm back."

"Good God, Abby, do you realize what you're doing to me?" My father's voice sounded as it did the time he hit his hand with the maul. "It's impossible, I tell you! I can't—"

"You can and you will. I've been patient long enough. Look at me, Tom. Are you going to say you can't find a way? That I should go and not come back?"

"No!"

Miss Abby's silvery laugh broke the silence that set in after my father's hoarse exclamation. She murmured something I couldn't make out, and then neither of them spoke again. The light under the edge of the door went out suddenly. I crept back down the winding stairs in the darkness and let myself out the big door at the bottom. All I could think of was what was going to become of us.

Outside it was lighter. The moon showed fitfully through the racing clouds. The wind was higher than ever, and the waves smashed solidly on the rocks. I started back to the house. I was too cold and too tired to stand around.

Two-thirds of the way back over the causeway, I heard dislodged pebbles on the path ahead of me. Without even thinking, I plunged down into the rocks, and hid. Above me a cloaked shadow passed by, on the way to the lighthouse. I knew it was my mother even before the moon came out again for a second and showed me plainly. She was bent forward against the wind, talking to herself. When she passed, I got up out of the rocks and ran all the way home.

When I got there, I couldn't go inside. I couldn't stop thinking of my mother and father and Miss Abby at the lighthouse, and the dreadful things they'd say to each other. Nothing would ever be the same for any of us again.

I struggled against the wind down to the barn. I knew the animal heat of the cows always kept it warm. I took down a pitchfork and piled fresh hay into a corner of Daisy's empty stall. I must have gone to sleep there, because it seemed like a long time later that I heard a bell ringing. At first I thought it was in a dream, and then it got louder and louder.

I jumped up and ran to the barn door. The floor shook from the thunder of horses' hooves as the four-horse team from Indian Bay skittered down the road with the old fire pumper. Its iron bell was clanging steadily.

I whirled to look at the house. It was safely dark. I turned to look toward the point, but I think I knew before I looked. I could hear it before I could see it: the whole lighthouse was ablaze—great roaring sheets of flame were blowing out from the top hundreds of feet over the lake.

I just stood there. My mother had intended to kill Miss Abby, but without knowing it she had killed my father, too. She thought he was out in the boat. What would she do to herself when she found out he wasn't?

I ran down to the dock. Flat on my stomach on the rough planking, I clawed at the hard knots in my father's snubbing rope at the other end of which the boat pitched violently in the black choppy water. My fingernails were broken when I finally got it untied. I had a knife in my pocket, but I couldn't leave a cut rope end. The boat lurched away into the darkness of the lake, and I got up and ran back to the house. I was in bed when they came with the news about the lighthouse.

No one but me ever knew what happened on Wild Swan Point that terrible night. The lighthouse burned flat, with a fire so fierce no one could get near it. The oil drums at the bottom burned for two days, and it was two more before they could sift the ashes. They found human bones mixed with Daisy's, not too many of either, and the human ones were buried as Miss Abby's. It never occurred to anybody that someone else could have been in the lighthouse.

On the third day a trawler found my father's boat a couple of miles out on the lake. They towed it into our dock. My mother had never left the dock the whole three days except for a couple of hours at a time. The lakemen told her gently that at the height of the storm my father must have been washed over the side.

When everything was done that had to be done, my mother hired a man to help with the farm. I did what I could, too. For a month my mother's eyes were sunk deep into her head. The only person she talked to was me, but nights I could hear her praying behind her closed bedroom door.

She didn't show any signs of getting better, and I didn't know what to do. She didn't eat hardly anything at all. I was sitting out on the front steps one afternoon when a man came down the road with a battered satchel in his hand, leading a little girl by the other hand. "Mrs. Harwood live here?" he called in from the gate.

I nodded. I couldn't have said anything. I was looking

at the little girl. She was about three years old, with the bluest of eyes. There was no ribbon in her yellow hair.

They came up the path, and the man took off his hat and mopped his forehead. "Quite a way from Indian Bay," he said, and knocked on the door. I could feel my heart beating while I waited for my mother to answer the door. When she did, she looked out at the man inquiringly, but when she saw the little girl her features froze.

"Mrs. Harwood home?" the man asked.

"I'm Mrs. Harwood," my mother said.

"Oh." He looked taken aback. "Well, then, is the other Mrs. Harwood home?"

"I'm the only—" my mother began, and wrenched her gaze from the blue eyes and yellow hair. "Come along inside," she said curtly to the man. They went in and closed the door.

I patted the step beside me. "Come on and sit down here," I invited the little girl. "What's your name?"

"Becky." That was all she said. She sat down beside me with a tired sigh. Her little white shoes were all over road dust, and her thin features were pinched with weariness.

"I'm Tom," I told her. Even my mother had stopped calling me Tommy lately.

We sat in silence. I wasn't looking directly at her, but I heard her start to cry. She put her head down on her knees so that I shouldn't see her face. I didn't know what to do, so I put my arm around her.

My mother and the man were inside the house a long time. When they came out, the man had his hat on and was putting something in his pocket. He went down the path and up the road without saying another word. Twice he stopped to turn and look back at us, but my mother paid him no mind. "Come along dear," she said to Becky, and held out her hand to her. "It's time to get the cows milked, Tom," she said to me in the same breath.

From the tone of her voice I knew everything was going to be all right.

And for fifteen years it was, until my mother died of cancer. She didn't have an easy time. It didn't seem as though she wanted one. She never set foot in a church after that night on Wild Swan Point, and she wouldn't let the minister in the house, but she made Becky and me go to Sunday school every week.

There were a lot of good years afterward, too, except that I had to sit and watch Becky patiently waiting for me to ask her to marry me. I sent her away to school, over her protests. She came back to the farm. My housekeeper complained for years about the waste of money on the unnecessary young hired men I insisted on having around the place. Becky never seemed to see them in any way that mattered.

There wasn't any answer I could find, then or ever.

Now Becky's gone too, and there's just me.

But it won't be for long.

# 1926

# Belgrade 1926

## *by Eric Ambler*

*A complete episode from Eric Ambler's classic espionage novel, A COFFIN FOR DIMITRIOS, recapturing the shadowy world of Balkan intrigue between the wars.*

MEN HAVE LEARNED to distrust their imaginations. It is, therefore, strange to them when they chance to discover that a world conceived in the imagination, outside experience, does exist in fact. The afternoon which Latimer spent at the Villa Acacias, listening to Wladyslaw Grodek, he recalls as, in that sense, one of the strangest of his life. In a letter to the Greek, Marukakis, which he began that evening, while the whole thing was still fresh in his mind, he placed it on record.

Geneva.
*Saturday.*

My Dear Marukakis,

I remember that I promised to write to you to let you know if I discovered anything more about Dimitrios. I wonder if you will be as surprised as I am that I have actually done so. Discovered something, I mean; for I intended to write to you in any case to thank you again for the help you gave me in Sofia.

When I left you there, I was bound, you may remember, for Belgrade. Why, then, am I writing from Geneva?

I was afraid that you would ask that question.

My dear fellow, I wish that I knew the whole answer. I know part of it. The man who employed Dimitrios in Belgrade in 1926, lives just outside Geneva. I can even explain how I got into touch with him. I was introduced. But just why I was introduced and just what the man who introduced us hopes to get out of it I cannot imagine. I shall, I hope, discover those things eventually. Meanwhile, let me say that if you find this mystery irritating, I find it no less so.

Did you ever believe in the existence of the "master" spy? Until today I most certainly did not. Now I do. The reason for this is that I have spent the greater part of today talking to one.

He is a tall, broad-shouldered man of about sixty, with thinning grey hair still tinged with the original straw color. He has a clear complexion, bright blue eyes and steady hands—obviously, a man with few vices who has taken good care of himself. He lives in an expensive lakeside villa with two servants and a chauffeur for the Rolls. No wife in evidence. He looks like a man quietly enjoying the well-earned fruits of a blameless and worthy career. He professes to be engaged, for recreational purposes, in writing a life of St. Stephen. His nationality, I understand, was originally Polish. I may not tell you his name, so I shall call him, in the best spy-story tradition, "G."

G. was a "master" spy (he has retired now, of course) in the same sense that the printer my publisher uses is a "master" printer. He was an employer of spy labor. His work was mainly (though not entirely) administrative in character.

Now I know that a lot of nonsense is talked and written about spies and espionage, but let me try to put the question to you as G. put it to me.

He began by quoting Napoleon as saying that in war the basic element of all successful strategy was surprise.

G. is, I should say, a confirmed Napoleon-quoter. No doubt Napoleon did say that or something like it. I am quite sure he wasn't the first military leader to do so. Alexander, Caesar, Genghis Khan and Frederick of Prussia all had the same idea. In 1918 Foch thought of it, too. But to return to G.

G. says that "the experiences of the 1914-18 conflict" showed that in a future war (that sounds so beautifully distant, doesn't it?) the mobility and striking power of modern armies and navies and the existence of air forces would render the element of surprise more important than ever; so important, in fact, that it was possible that the people who got in with a surprise attack first might win the war. It was more than ever necessary to guard against surprise, to guard against it, moreover, before the war had started.

Now, there are roughly twenty-seven independent states in Europe. Each has an army and an air force and most have some sort of navy as well. For its own security, each of those armies, air forces, and navies must know what each corresponding force in each of the other twenty-six countries is doing—what its strength is, what its efficiency is, what secret preparations it is making. That means spies —armies of them.

In 1926, G. was employed by Italy; and in the spring of that year he set up house in Belgrade.

Relations between Yugoslavia and Italy were strained at the time. The Italian seizure of Fiume was still as fresh in Yugoslav minds as the bombardment of Corfu; there were rumors, too (not unfounded as it was learned later in the year) that Mussolini contemplated occupying Albania.

Italy, on her side, was suspicious of Yugoslavia. Fiume was held under Yugoslav guns. A Yugoslav Albania alongside the Straits of Otranto was an unthinkable proposition. An independent Albania was tolerable only as long as it was under a predominantly Italian influence. It might be desirable to make certain of things. But the Yugoslavs might put up a fight. Reports from Italian agents in Belgrade indicated that in the event of war Yugoslavia intended to protect her seaboard by bottling herself up in the Adriatic with minefields laid just north of the Straits of Otranto.

I don't know much about these things, but apparently one does not have to lay a couple of hundred miles' worth of mines to make a two-hundred-miles-wide corridor of sea impassable. One just lays one or two small fields without letting one's enemy know just where. It is necessary, then, for them to find out the positions of those minefields.

That, then, was G.'s job in Belgrade. Italian agents found out about the minefields. G., the expert spy, was commissioned to do the real work of discovering where they were to be laid, without—a most important point this —without letting the Yugoslavs find out that he had done so. If they did find out, of course, they would promptly change the positions.

In that last part of his task G. failed. The reason for this failure was Dimitrios.

It has always seemed to me that a spy's job must be an extraordinarily difficult one. What I mean is this. If I were sent to Belgrade by the British Government with orders to get hold of the details of a secret mine-laying project for the Straits of Otranto, I should not even know where to start. Supposing I knew, as G. knew, that the details were recorded by means of markings on a navigational chart of the Straits. Very well. How many copies of the chart are kept? I would not know. Where are they kept? I would not know. I might reasonably suppose that at least one copy would be kept somewhere in the Ministry of Marine; but the Ministry of Marine is a large place. Moreover, the chart will almost certainly be under lock and key. And even if, as seems unlikely, I were able to find in which room it is kept and how to get to it, how would I set about obtaining a copy of it without letting the Yugoslavs know that I had done so?

When I tell you that within a month of his arrival in Belgrade, G. had not only found out where a copy of the chart was kept, but had also made up his mind how he was going to copy that copy *without the Yugoslavs knowing,* you will see that he is entitled to describe himself as competent.

How did he do it? What ingenious maneuver, what subtle trick made it possible? I shall try to break the news gently.

Posing as a German, the representative of an optical instrument maker in Dresden, he struck up an acquaintance with a clerk in the Submarine Defence Department (which dealt with submarine nets, booms, mine-laying and mine-sweeping) of the Ministry of Marine!

Pitiful, wasn't it! The amazing thing is that he himself regards it as a very astute move. His sense of humor is quite paralyzed. When I asked him if he ever read spy stories, he said that he did not, as they always seemed to him very naive. But there is worse to come.

He struck up this acquaintance by going to the Ministry and asking the door-keeper to direct him to the Department of Supply, a perfectly normal request for an outsider to make. Having got past the door-keeper, he stopped someone in a corridor, said that he had been directed to the Submarine Defence Department and had got lost and asked to be redirected. Having got to the S.D. Department, he marched in and asked if it was the Department of Supply. They said that it was not, and out he went. He was in there not more than a minute, but in that time he had cast a quick eye over the personnel of the department, or, at all events, those of them he could see. He marked down three. That evening he waited outside the Ministry until the first of them came out. This man he followed home. Having found out his name and as much as he could about him, he repeated the process on succeeding evenings with the other two. Then he made his choice. It fell on a man named Bulic.

Now, G.'s actual methods may have lacked subtlety; but there was considerable subtlety in the way he employed them. He himself is quite oblivious of any distinction here. He is not the first successful man to misunderstand the reasons for his own success.

G.'s first piece of subtlety lay in his choice of Bulic as a tool.

Bulic was a disagreeable, conceited man of between forty and fifty, older than most of his fellow clerks and disliked by them. His wife was ten years younger than he, dissatisfied and pretty. He suffered from catarrh. He was in the habit of going to a café for a drink when he left the Ministry for the day, and it was in this café that G. made his acquaintance, by the simple process of asking him for a match, offering him a cigar, and, finally, buying him a drink.

You may imagine that a clerk in a government department dealing with highly confidential matters would naturally tend to be suspicious of café acquaintances who tried to pump him about his work. G. was ready to deal with those suspicions long before they had entered Bulic's head.

The acquaintance ripened. G. would be in the café every evening when Bulic entered. They would carry on a desultory conversation. G., as a stranger to Belgrade, would ask Bulic's advice about this and that. He would pay for Bulic's drinks. He let Bulic condescend to him. Sometimes they would play a game of chess. Bulic would win. At other times they would play four-pack bezique with other frequenters of the café. Then, one evening, G. told Bulic a story.

He had been told by a mutual acquaintance, he said, that he, Bulic, held an important post in the Ministry of Marine.

For Bulic the 'mutual acquaintance' could have been one of several men with whom they played cards and exchanged opinions and who were vaguely aware that he worked in the Ministry. He frowned and opened his mouth. He was probably about to enter a mock-modest qualification of the adjective "important." But G. swept on. As chief salesman for a highly respectable firm of optical instrument makers, he was deputed to obtain an order due to be placed by the Ministry of Marine for binoculars. He had submitted his quotation and had hopes of securing the order but, as Bulic would know, there was nothing like a friend at court in these affairs. If, therefore, the good and influential Bulic would bring pressure to bear to see that the Dresden company secured the order, Bulic would be in pocket to the tune of twenty thousand dinar.

Consider that proposition from Bulic's point of view. Here was he, an insignificant clerk, being flattered by the representative of a great German company and promised twenty thousand dinar for doing precisely nothing. As the quotation had already been submitted, there was nothing to be done there. It would stand its chance with the other quotations. If the Dresden company secured the order he would be twenty thousand dinar in pocket wihout having compromised himself in any way. If they lost it *he* would lose nothing except the respect of this stupid and misinformed German.

G. admits that Bulic did make a half-hearted effort to be honest. He mumbled something about his not being sure that his influence could help. This, G. chose to treat as an attempt to increase the bribe. Bulic protested that no such thought had been in his mind. He was lost. Within five minutes he had agreed.

In the days that followed, Bulic and G. became close friends. G. ran no risk. Bulic could not know that no quotation had been submitted by the Dresden company as all quotations received by the Department of Supply were confidential until the order was placed. If he were inquisitive enough to make inquiries, he would find, as G. had found by previous reference to the *Official Gazette,* that quotations for binoculars had actually been asked for by the Department of Supply.

G. now got to work.

Bulic, remember, had to play the part assigned to him by G., the part of influential official. G., furthermore, began to make himself very amiable by entertaining Bulic and the pretty but stupid Madame Bulic at expensive restaurants and night clubs. The pair responded like thirsty plants to rain. Could Bulic be cautious when, having had the best part of a bottle of sweet champagne, he found himself involved in an argument about Italy's overwhelming naval strength and her threat to Yugoslavia's seaboard? It was unlikely. He was a little drunk. His wife was present. For the first time in his dreary life, his judgment was being treated with the deference due to it. Besides, he had his part to play. It would not do to seem to be ignorant of what was going on behind the scenes. He began to brag. He himself had seen the very plans that in operation would immobilize Italy's fleet in the Adriatic. Naturally, he had to be discreet, but . . .

By the end of that evening G. knew that Bulic had access to a copy of the chart. He had also made up his mind that Bulic was going to get that copy for him.

He made his plans carefully. Then he looked around for a suitable man to carry them out. He needed a go-between. He found Dimitrios.

Just how G. came to hear of Dimitrios is not clear. I fancy that he was anxious not to compromise any of his old associates. One can conceive that his reticence might be understandable. Anyway, Dimitrios was recommended to him. I asked in what business the recommender was engaged, but G. became vague. It was so very long ago. But he remembered the verbal testimonial which accompanied the recommendation.

Dimitrios Talat was a Greek-speaking Turk with an "effective" passport and a reputation for being "useful" and at the same time discreet. He was also said to have had experience in "financial work of a confidential nature."

If one did not happen to know just what he was useful for and the nature of the financial work he had done, one might have supposed that the man under discussion was some sort of accountant. But there is, it seems, a jargon in these affairs. G. understood it and decided that Dimitrios was the man for the job in hand.

Dimitrios arrived in Belgrade five days later and presented himself at G.'s house just off the Knez Miletina.

G. remembers the occasion very well. Dimitrios, he says, was a man of medium height who might have been almost any age between thirty-five and fifty—he was actually thirty-seven. He was smartly dressed and . . . but I had better quote G.'s own words:

"He was chic in an expensive way, and his hair was becoming gray at the sides of his head. He had a sleek, satisfied, confident air and something about the eyes that I recognized immediately. The man was a pimp. I can always recognize it. Do not ask me how. I have a woman's instinct for these things."

So there you have it. Dimitrios had prospered. Had there been any more Madame Prevezas? We shall never know. At all events, G. detected the pimp in Dimitrios and was not displeased. A pimp, he reasoned, could be relied upon not to fool about with women to the detriment of the business in hand. Also Dimitrios was of pleasing address. I think that I had better quote G. again:

"He could wear his clothes gracefully. Also he looked intelligent. I was pleased by this because I did not care to employ riffraff from the gutters. Sometimes it was necessary but I never liked it. They did not always understand my curious temperament."

G., you see, was fussy.

Dimitrios had not wasted his time. He could now speak both German and French with reasonable accuracy. He said:

"I came as soon as I received your letter. I was busy in Bucharest but I was glad to get your letter as I had heard of you."

G. explained carefully and with circumspection (it did not do to give too much away to a prospective employee) what he wanted done. Dimitrios listened unemotionally. When G. had finished, he asked how much he was to be paid.

"Thirty thousand dinar," said G.

"Fifty thousand," said Dimitrios, "and I would prefer

to have it in Swiss francs."

They compromised on forty thousand to be paid in Swiss francs. Dimitrios smiled and shrugged his agreement.

It was the man's eyes when he smiled, says G., that first made him distrust his new employee.

I found that odd. Could it be that there was honor among scoundrels, that G., being the man he was and knowing (up to a point) the sort of man Dimitrios was, would yet need a smile to awaken distrust? Incredible. But there was no doubt that he remembered those eyes very vividly. Preveza remembered them, too, didn't she? "Brown, anxious eyes that made you think of a doctor's eyes when he is doing something to you that hurts." That was it, wasn't it? My theory is that it was not until Dimitrios smiled that G. realized the quality of the man whose services he had bought. "He had the appearance of being tame but when you looked into his brown eyes you saw that he had none of the feelings that make ordinary men soft, that he was always dangerous." Preveza again. Did G. sense the same thing? He may not have explained it to himself in that way—he is not the sort of man to set much store by feelings—but I think he may have wondered if he had made a mistake in employing Dimitrios. Their two minds were not so very dissimilar and that sort of wolf prefers to hunt alone. At all events, G. decided to keep a wary eye on Dimitrios.

Meanwhile, Bulic was finding life more pleasant than it had ever been before. He was being entertained at rich places. His wife, warmed by unfamiliar luxury, no longer looked at him with contempt and distaste in her eyes. With the money they saved on the meals provided by the stupid German she could drink her favorite cognac; and when she drank she became friendly and agreeable. In a week's time, moreover, he might become the possessor of twenty thousand dinar. There was a chance. He felt very well, he said one night, and added that cheap food was bad for his catarrh. That was the nearest he came to forgetting to play his part.

The order for the binoculars was given to a Czech firm. The *Official Gazette,* in which the fact was announced, was published at noon. At one minute past noon, G. had a copy and was on his way to an engraver on whose bench lay a half-finished copper die. By six o'clock he was waiting opposite the entrance to the Ministry. Soon after six, Bulic appeared. He had seen the *Official Gazette.* A copy was under his arm. His dejection was visible from where G. stood. G. began to follow him.

Ordinarily, Bulic would have crossed the road before many minutes had passed, to get to his café. Tonight he hesitated and then walked straight on. He was not anxious to meet the man from Dresden.

G. turned down a side street and hailed a taxi. Within two minutes his taxi had made a detour and was approaching Bulic. Suddenly, he signaled to the driver to stop, bounded out on to the pavement and embraced Bulic delightedly. Before the bewildered clerk could protest, he was bundled into the taxi and G. was pouring congratulations and thanks into his ear and pressing a check for twenty thousand dinar into his hand.

"But I thought you'd lost the order," mumbles Bulic at last.

G. laughs as if at a huge joke. "Lost it!" And then he "understands." "Of course! I forgot to tell you. The quotation was submitted through a Czech subsidiary of ours. Look, does this explain it?" He thrusts one of the newly printed cards into Bulic's hand. "I don't use this card often. Most people know that these Czechs are owned by our company in Dresden." He brushes the matter aside. "But we must have a drink immediately. Driver!"

That night they celebrated. His first bewilderment over, Bulic took full advantage of the situation. He became drunk. He began to brag of the potency of his influence in the Ministry until even G., who had every reason for satisfaction, was hard put to it to remain civil.

But toward the end of the evening, he drew Bulic aside. Estimates, he said, had been invited for rangefinders. Could he, Bulic, assist? Of course he could. And now

Bulic became cunning. Now that the value of his cooperation had been established, he had a right to expect something on account.

G. had not anticipated this, but, secretly amused, he agreed at once. Bulic received another check; this time it was for ten thousand dinar. The understanding was that he should be paid a further ten thousand when the order was placed with G.'s "employers."

Bulic was now wealthier than ever before. He had thirty thousand dinar. Two evenings later, in the supper room of a fashionable hotel, G. introduced him to a Freiherr von Kiessling. The Freiherr von Kiessling's other name was, needless to say, Dimitrios.

"You would have thought," says G., "that he had been living in such places all his life. For all I know, he may have been doing so. His manner was perfect. When I introduced Bulic as an important official in the Ministry of Marine, he condescended magnificently. With Madame Bulic he was superb. He might have been greeting a princess. But I saw the way his fingers moved across the palm of her hand as he bent to kiss the back of it."

Dimitrios had displayed himself in the supper room before G. had affected to claim acquaintance with him in order to give G. time to prepare the ground. The "Freiherr," G. told the Bulics after he had drawn their attention to Dimitrios, was a very important man. Something of a mystery, perhaps; but a very important factor in international big business. He was enormously rich and was believed to control as many as twenty-seven companies. He might be a useful man to know.

The Bulics were enchanted to be presented to him. When the "Freiherr" agreed to drink a glass of champagne at their table, they felt themselves honored indeed. In their halting German they strove to make themselves agreeable. This, Bulic must have felt, was what he had been waiting for all his life: at last he was in touch with the people who counted, the real people, the people who made men and broke them, the people who might make him. Perhaps he saw himself a director of one of the

"Freiherr's" companies, with a fine house and others dependent on him, loyal servants who would respect him as a man as well as a master. When, the next morning, he went to his stool in the Ministry, there must have been joy in his heart, joy made all the sweeter by the faint misgivings, the slight prickings of conscience which could so easily be stilled. After all, G. had received his money's worth. He, Bulic, had nothing to lose. Besides, you never knew what might come of it all. Men had taken stranger paths to fortune.

The "Freiherr" had been good enough to say that he would have supper with Herr G. and his two charming friends two evenings later.

I questioned G. about this. Would it not have been better to have struck while the iron was hot. Two days gave the Bulics time to think. "Precisely," was G.'s reply; "time to think of the good things to come, to prepare themselves for the feast, to dream." He became preternaturally solemn at the thought and then, grinning, suddenly quoted Goethe at me. *Ach! warum, ihr Götter, ist unendlich, alles, alles, endlich unser Glück nur?* G., you see, lays claim to a sense of humor.

That supper was the critical moment for him. Dimitrios got to work on Madame. It was such a pleasure to meet such pleasant people as Madame—and, of course, her husband. She—and her husband, naturally—must certainly come and stay with him in Bavaria next month. He preferred it to his Paris house and Cannes was sometimes chilly in the spring. Madame would enjoy Bavaria; and so, no doubt, would her husband. That was, if he could tear himself away from the Ministry.

Crude, simple stuff, no doubt; but the Bulics were crude, simple people. Madame lapped it up with her sweet champagne while Bulic became sulky. Then the great moment arrived.

The flower girl stopped by the table with her tray of orchids. Dimitrios turned round and, selecting the largest and most expensive bloom, handed it with a little flourish to Madame Bulic with a request that she accept it as a token of his esteem. Madame would accept it. Dimitrios drew out his wallet to pay. The next moment a thick wad of thousand-dinar notes fell from his breast pocket on to the table.

With a word of apology Dimitrios put the money back in his pocket. G., taking his cue, remarked that it was rather a lot of money to carry in one's pocket and asked if the "Freiherr" always carried as much. No, he did not. He had won the money at Alessandro's earlier in the evening and had forgotten to leave it upstairs in his room. Did Madame know Alessandro's? She did not. Both the Bulics were silent as the "Freiherr" talked on: they had never seen so much money before. In the "Freiherr's" opinion Alessandro's was the most reliable gambling place in Belgrade. It was your own luck, not the croupier's skill, that mattered at Alessandro's. Personally he was having a run of luck that evening—this with velvety eyes on Madame—and had won a little more than usual. He hesitated at that point. And then: "As you have never been in the place, I should be delighted if you would accompany me as my guests later."

Of course, they went; and, of course, they were expected and preparations had been made. Dimitrios had arranged everything. No roulette—it is difficult to cheat a man at roulette—but there was *trente et quarante*. The minimum stake was two hundred and fifty dinar.

They had drinks and watched the play for a time. Then G. decided that he would play a little. They watched him win twice. Then the "Freiherr" asked Madame if she would like to play. She looked at her husband. He said, apologetically, that he had very little money with him. But Dimitrios was ready for that. No trouble at all, Herr Bulic! He personally was well known to Alessandro. Any friend of his could be accommodated. If he should happen to lose a few dinar, Alessandro would take a check or a note.

The farce went on. Alessandro was summoned and introduced. The situation was explained to him. He raised protesting hands. Any friend of the "Freiherr" need not even ask such a thing. Besides, he had not yet played. Time to talk of such things if he had a little bad luck.

G. thinks that if Dimitrios had allowed the two to talk to one another for even a moment, they would not have played. Two hundred and fifty dinar was the minimum stake, and not even the possession of thirty thousand could overcome their consciousness of the value in terms of food and rent of two hundred and fifty. But Dimitrios did not give them a chance to exchange misgivings. Instead, as they were waiting at the table behind G.'s chair, he murmured to Bulic that if he, Bulic, had time, he, the "Freiherr," would like to talk business with him over luncheon one day that week.

It was beautifully timed. It could, I feel, have meant only one thing to Bulic: "My dear Bulic, there really is no need for you to concern yourself over a paltry few hundred dinar. I am interested in you, and that means that your fortune is made. Please do not disappoint me by showing yourself less important than you seem now."

Madame Bulic began to play.

Her first two hundred and fifty she lost on *couleur*. The second won on *inverse*. Then, Dimitrios, advising greater caution, suggested that she play *à cheval*. There was a *refait* and then a second *refait*. Ultimately she lost again.

At the end of an hour the five thousand dinar's worth of chips she had been given had gone. Dimitrios, sympathizing with her for her "bad luck," pushed across some five-hundred-dinar chips from a pile in front of him and begged that she would play with them "for luck."

The tortured Bulic may have had the idea that these were a gift, for he made only the faintest sound of protest. That they had not been a gift he was presently to discover. Madame Bulic, thoroughly miserable now and becoming a little untidy, played on. She won a little; she lost more. At half-past-two Bulic signed a promissory note to Alessandro for twelve thousand dinar. G. bought them a drink.

It is easy to picture the scene between the Bulics when at last they were alone—the recriminations, the tears, the interminable arguments—only too easy. Yet, bad as things were, the gloom was not unrelieved; for Bulic was to lunch the following day with the "Freiherr." And they were to talk business.

They did talk business. Dimitrios had been told to be encouraging. No doubt he was. Hints of big deals afoot, of opportunities for making fabulous sums for those who were in the know, talk of castles in Bavaria—it would all be there. Bulic had only to listen and let his heart beat faster. What did twelve thousand dinar matter? You had to think in millions.

All the same, it was Dimitrios who raised the subject of his guest's debt to Alessandro. He supposed that Bulic would be going along that very night to settle it. He personally would be playing again. One could not, after all, win so much without giving Alessandro a chance to lose some more. Supposing that they went along together— just the two of them. Women were bad gamblers.

When they met that night Bulic had nearly thirty-five thousand dinar in his pocket. He must have added his savings to G.'s thirty thousand. When Dimitrios reported to G.—in the early hours of the following morning—he said that Bulic had, in spite of Alessandro's protests, insisted on redeeming his promissory note before he started to play. "I pay my debts," he told Dimitrios proudly. The balance of the money he spent, with a flourish, on five-hundred-dinar chips. Tonight he was going to make a killing. He refused a drink. He meant to keep a cool head.

G. grinned at this and perhaps he was wise to do so. Pity is sometimes too uncomfortable; and I do find Bulic pitiable. You may say that he was a weak fool. So he was. But Providence is never quite as calculating as were G. and Dimitrios. It may bludgeon away at a man, but it never feels between his ribs with a knife. Bulic had no chance. They understood him and used their understanding with devilish skill. With the cards as neatly stacked against me as they were against him, I should perhaps be no less weak, no less foolish. It is a comfort to me to believe that the occasion is unlikely to arise.

Inevitably he lost. He began to play with just over forty chips. It took him two hours of winning and losing to get rid of them. Then, quite calmly, he took another twenty on credit. He said that his luck must change. The poor wretch did not even suspect that he might be being cheated. Why should be suspect? The "Freiherr" was losing even more than he was. He doubled his stakes and survived for forty minutes. He borrowed again and lost again. He had lost thirty-eight thousand dinar more than he had in the world when, white and sweating, he decided to stop.

After that it was plain sailing for Dimitrios. The following night Bulic returned. They let him win thirty thousand back. The third night he lost another fourteen thousand. On the fourth night, when he was about twenty-five thousand in debt, Alessandro asked for his money. Bulic promised to redeem his notes within a week. The first person to whom he went for help was G.

G. was sympathetic. Twenty-five thousand was a lot of money, wasn't it? Of course, any money he used in connection with orders received was his employers', and he was not empowered to do what he liked with it. But he himself could spare two hundred and fifty for a few days if it were any help. He would have liked to do more, but . . . Bulic took the two hundred and fifty.

With it G. gave him a word of advice. The "Freiherr" was the man to get him out of his difficulty. He never lent money—with him it was a question of principle, he believed—but he had a reputation for helping his friends by putting them in the way of earning quite substantial sums. Why not have a talk with him?

The "talk" between Bulic and Dimitrios took place after a dinner for which Bulic paid in the "Freiherr's" hotel sitting-room. G. was out of sight in the adjoining bedroom.

When Bulic at last got to the point, he asked about Alessandro. Would he insist on his money? What would happen if he were not paid?

Dimitrios affected surprise. There was no question, he

hoped, of Alessandro's not being paid. After all, it was on his personal recommendation that Alessandro had given credit in the first place. He would not like there to be any unpleasantness. What sort of unpleasantness? Well, Alessandro held the promissory notes and could take the matter to the police. He hoped sincerely that that would not happen.

Bulic was hoping so, too. Now, he had everything to lose, including his post at the Ministry. It might even come out that he had taken money from G. That might even mean prison. Would they believe that he had done nothing in return for those thirty thousand dinar? It was madness to expect them to do so. His only chance was to get the money from the "Freiherr"—somehow.

To his pleas for a loan Dimitrios shook his head. No. That would simply make matters worse, for then he would owe the money to a friend instead of an enemy; besides, it was a matter of principle with him. At the same time, he wanted to help. There was just one way; but would Herr Bulic feel disposed to take it? That was the question. He scarcely liked to mention the matter; but, since Herr Bulic pressed him, he knew of certain persons who were interested in obtaining some information from the Ministry of Marine that could not be obtained through the usual channels. They could probably be persuaded to pay as much as fifty thousand dinar for this information if they could rely upon its being accurate.

G. said that he attributed quite a lot of the success of his plan (he deems it successful in the same way that a surgeon deems an operation successful when the patient leaves the operating theater alive) to his careful use of figures. Every sum from the original twenty thousand dinar to the amounts of the successive debts to Alessandro (who was an Italian agent) and the final amount offered by Dimitrios was carefully calculated with an eye to its psychological value. That final fifty thousand, for example. Its appeal to Bulic was twofold. It would pay off his debt and still leave him with nearly as much as he had had before he met the "Freiherr." To the incentive of fear they added that of greed.

But Bulic did not give in immediately. When he heard exactly what the information was, he became frightened and angry. The anger was dealt with very efficiently by Dimitrios. If Bulic had begun to entertain doubts about the *bona fides* of the "Freiherr" those doubts were now made certainties; for when he shouted "dirty spy," the "Freiherr's" easy charm deserted him. Bulic was kicked in the abdomen and then, as he bent forward retching, in the face. Gasping for breath and with pain and bleeding at the mouth, he was flung into a chair while Dimitrios explained coldly that the only risk he ran was in not doing as he was told.

His instructions were simple. Bulic was to get a copy of the chart and bring it to the hotel when he left the Ministry the following evening. An hour later the chart would be returned to him to replace in the morning. That was all. He would be paid when he brought the chart. He was warned of the consequences to himself if he should decide to go to the authorities with his story, reminded of the fifty thousand that awaited him and dismissed.

He duly returned the following night with the chart folded in four under his coat. Dimitrios took the chart in to G. and returned to keep watch on Bulic while it was photographed and the negative developed. Apparently Bulic had nothing to say. When G. had finished he took the money and the chart from Dimitrios and went without a word.

G. says that in the bedroom at that moment, when he heard the door close behind Bulic and as he held the negative up to the light, he was feeling very pleased with himself. Expenses had been low; there had been no wasted effort; there had been no tiresome days; everybody, even Bulic, had done well out of the business. It only remained to hope that Bulic would restore the chart safely. There was really no reason why he should not do so. A very satisfactory affair from every point of view.

And then Dimitrios came into the room.

It was at that moment that G. realized that he had

made one mistake.

"My wages," said Dimitrios, and held out his hand.

G. met his employee's eyes and nodded. He needed a gun and he had not got one. "We'll go to my house now," he said and started towards the door.

Dimitrios shook his head deliberately. "My wages are in your pocket."

"Not your wages. Only mine."

Dimitrios produced a revolver. A smile played about his lips. "What I want is in your pocket, *mein Herr*. Put your hands behind your head."

G. obeyed. Dimitrios walked toward him. G., looking steadily into those brown anxious eyes, saw that he was in danger. Two feet in front of him Dimitrios stopped. "Please be careful, *mein Herr*."

The smile disappeared. Dimitrios stepped forward suddenly and, jamming his revolver into G.'s stomach, snatched the negative from G.'s pocket with his free hand. Then, as suddenly, he stood back. "You may go," he said.

G. went. Dimitrios, in turn, had made *his* mistake.

All that night men, hastily recruited from the criminal cafés, scoured Belgrade for Dimitrios. But Dimitrios had disappeared. G. never saw him again.

What happened to the negative? Let me give you G.'s own words:

"When the morning came and my men had failed to find him, I knew what I must do. I felt very bitter. After all my careful work it was most disappointing. But there was nothing else for it. I had known for a week that Dimitrios had got into touch with a French agent. The negative would be in that agent's hands by now. I really had no choice. A friend of mine in the German Embassy was able to oblige me. The Germans were anxious to please Belgrade at the time. What more natural than that they should pass on an item of information interesting to the Yugoslav government?"

"Do you mean," I said, "that you deliberately arranged for the Yugoslav authorities to be informed of the removal of the chart and of the fact that it had been photographed?"

"Unfortunately, it was the only thing I could do. You see, I had to render the chart worthless. It was really very foolish of Dimitrios to let me go; but he was inexperienced. He probably thought that I would blackmail Bulic into bringing the chart out again. But I realized that I would not be paid much for bringing in information already in the possession of the French. Besides, my reputation would have suffered. I was very bitter about the whole affair. The only amusing aspect of it was that the French had paid over to Dimitrios half the agreed price for the chart before they discovered that the information on it had been rendered obsolete by my little *démarche.*"

"What about Bulic?"

G. pulled a face. "Yes, I was sorry about that. I always have felt a certain responsibility toward those who work for me. He was arrested almost at once. There was no doubt as to which of the Ministry copies had been used. They were kept rolled in metal cylinders. Bulic had folded this one to bring it out of the Ministry. It was the only one with creases in it. His fingerprints did the rest. Very wisely he told the authorities all he knew about Dimitrios. As a result they sent him to prison for life instead of shooting him. I quite expected him to implicate me, but he did not. I was a little surprised. After all it was I who introduced him to Dimitrios. I wondered at the time whether it was because he was unwilling to face an additional charge of accepting bribes or because he felt grateful to me for lending him that two hundred and fifty dinar. Probably he did not connect me with the business of the chart at all. In any case, I was pleased. I still had work to do in Belgrade, and being wanted by the police, even under another name, might have complicated my life. I have never been able to bring myself to wear disguises."

I asked him one more question. Here is his answer:

"Oh, yes, I obtained the new charts as soon as they had been made. In quite a different way, of course. With so much of my money invested in the enterprise I could not return empty-handed. It is always the same: for one reason or another there are always these delays, these wastages of effort and money. You may say that I was careless in my handling of Dimitrios. That would be unjust. It was a small error of judgment on my part, that is all. I counted on his being like all the other fools in the world, on his being too greedy; I thought he would wait until he had had from me the forty thousand dinar due to him before he tried to take the photograph as well. He took me by surprise. That error of judgment cost me a lot of money."

"It cost Bulic his liberty." I am afraid I said it a trifle stuffily, for he frowned.

"My dear Monsieur Latimer," he retorted, "Bulic was a traitor and he was rewarded according to his deserts. One cannot sentimentalize over him. In war there are always casualties. Bulic was very lucky. I would certainly have used him again, and he might ultimately have been shot. As it was, he went to prison. For all I know he is still in prison. I do not wish to seem callous, but I must say that he is better off there. His liberty? Rubbish! He had none to lose. As for his wife, I have no doubt that she has done better for herself. She always gave me the impression of wanting to do so. I do not blame her. He was an objectionable man. I seem to remember that he tended to dribble as he ate. What is more, he was a nuisance. You would have thought, would you not, that on leaving Dimitrios that evening he would have gone there and then to Alessandro to pay his debt? He did not do so. When he was arrested late the following day he still had the fifty thousand dinar in his pocket. More waste. It is at times like those, my friend, that one needs one's sense of humor."

Well, my dear Marukakis, that is all. It is, I think, more than enough. For me, wandering among the ghosts of old lies, there is comfort in the thought that you might write to me and tell me that all this was worth finding out. You might. For myself, I begin to wonder. It is such a poor story, isn't it? There is no hero, no heroine; only villains and fools.

We shall, I hope, meet again very soon. *Croyez en mes meilleurs souvenirs.*

Charles Latimer

# 1929

# The Austin Murder Case

## *by Jon L. Breen*

*Jon L. Breen offers us here a cleverly written pastiche of the Philo Vance mysteries so popular in the late 1920s, complete with Vance's famous footnotes. If the crime and its solution are not to be taken with complete seriousness, they still offer an interesting sidelight on one of our unique cultural events—the death of silent movies and the advent of the talkies.*

OF ALL THE CURIOUS and inexplicable crimes that came to the attention of Philo Vance during the incumbency of his friend John F. X. Markham as District Attorney of New York County, there is wide disagreement as to which one was the most bizarre, which one permitted the greatest exploitation of his deductive powers. Perhaps because of the brevity of the investigation and the speed with which Vance was able to put his finger on the guilty person, the murder of Jack Austin, or as it was often called in the press, The Talkie Murder Case, has often been ignored in such disussions. But some feel, among them Vance himself, that his exposition of the vital clue in this case was one of the most dazzling strokes of his career.

Our connection with the Austin murder case began, as did so many of Vance's exploits, with a visit from District Attorney Markham. But this time it was not a worried Markham, puzzled over some unfathomable crime, but a more jovial District Attorney, passing along an invitation to a social engagement.

"It's a little masquerade party, Vance, at the home of Jack Austin, a week from Thursday night. He thought that you and Mr. Van Dine, both of whose works he admires very much, would like to come."

"Most ingratiatin' of you to extend the invitation, Markham old chap, but to tell you the truth I don't find the idea altogether thrillin'. I can find better things to do with my time, don't y'know, than to dress up and go to a costume party at the digs of a most annoyin' and irritatin' vaudevillian. Thanks anyway, old dear."

"Mr. Austin will be most disappointed. I dare say you're the only person in the city of New York who would turn down an invitation to Jack Austin's last party before he leaves Manhattan."

"Actu'lly leavin' ol' New York? Not altogether distressin' idea, y'know, but may I ask where he's goin'?"

"Hollywood. To make talking pictures."

Vance puffed his *Régie* and sniffed disgustedly. "If one of the talkin' cinema's first accomplishments will be to allow that chap's nasal off-key singin' to be heard by millions of people throughout the world, it's just another proof of the mistake the film industry's makin' in desertin' true cinema."[1]

"Quite so, Vance. Since you have such an enthusiasm for the silent film, though, perhaps you'll find the party more intriguing than you had at first thought."

---

[1] A devotion to the silent film was but another feature of Vance's many-faceted personality. He was the author of *Epistemological Symbolism in the Films of William S. Hart; Elmo Lincoln, the Renaissance Man;* and *Broncho Billy Anderson and Aristotelian Tragedy*—all highly regarded by film scholars.

"Might I?" rejoined Vance languidly. "And why might that be?"

"Each guest will come as his favorite movie star. I, for instance, am going as Tom Mix. Judge Peter Hawley will be there as Henry B. Walthall. Austin himself will impersonate Charlie Chaplin."

Vance turned to me. "'Pon my word, Van, it might be an inter'stin' time at that. I have always wanted to become Douglas Fairbanks for an evening, and here an unprecedented opportunity presents itself. Respectin' your desire to remain inconspicuous, we might find a less dynamic star for you to impersonate—Jack Mulhall, Donald Keith, or one of those chaps."[1]

"Sporting of you to accept, Vance!" Markham exclaimed. "I'll relay your response to Jack Austin."

A week later Vance and I made our appearance at Jack Austin's stately Manhattan mansion. The first person we met as we entered was Stitt, the Austin butler, who set the tone for the evening's proceedings with his Keystone Kop costume.[2] As soon as we entered the mansion's immense ballroom, decorated in a motion-picture soundstage motif, Jack Austin himself rushed over to greet us. His costume of battered hat, baggy pants, cane, and old shoes, together with the small mustache and ducklike walk he had affected for the occasion, gave us the sensation that it was Charlie the little tramp himself who cordially held out his hand and said, "Mr. Vance and Mr. Van Dine! How good of you to come!"

"It's wholly our pleasure, y'know, Mr. Austin," Vance

[1] We finally settled on Malcolm McGregor.

[2] Stitt's natural reticence prohibited his playing this role to its best advantage, but some of the other Kop-costumed servants, hired especially for the occasion, presumably from a casting bureau, gave a more uninhibited performance. Additionally, Austin had found a brace of serving men who bore startling resemblances to the comedy duo of Stan Laurel and Oliver Hardy.

drawled. And, as if further inspired by his surroundings, he leaped over a chair and turned a double somersault with an agility I hardly knew he possessed, as if the Doug Fairbanks Black Pirate regalia gave him an athletic ability he otherwise lacked. Austin and his guests laughed delightedly, particularly a lovely red-haired flapper-type, quite obviously designed to represent the vivacious Clara Bow, with the beauty and personality of the original.

Austin performed the introductions. "Mr. Vance, this is Miss Molly Hawley." Vance smiled and bowed to the waist in the best Fairbanksian manner. "And I am sure you are acquainted with her father, Judge Peter Hawley."

Judge Hawley, a slight, distinguished-looking man of late middle age, was known to both of us. But we hardly recognized him as the judge, he so resembled Henry B. Walthall in his greatest role, that of the Little Colonel in *The Birth of a Nation*.

It occurred to me as we met the other guests how strangely appropriate their costumes were. For example, Arletta Bingham, a society flirt with many broken hearts (and homes) in her wake, was well cast as the vamp Theda Bara. Markham, in white ten-gallon hat and flamboyant cowboy garb, made a perfect Tom Mix. Indeed, much of the same kind of personal magnetism that had made Mix a star had led the voters of New York to put Markham into office.

Sergeant Ernest Heath of the Metropolitan Police, a frequent participant in Vance's previous cases, was among those present, rather surprisingly. In Heath's case no costume was necessary, since he bore an uncanny resemblance to the humorous character actor Eugene Pallette.[1]

Broadway playboy Roger Kronert impersonated country-boy hero Charles Ray—he appeared at the party in bare feet, blue jeans, checkered shirt, and wide-

[1]The reference here, of course, to the portly Pallette of his later years. The more svelte-figured Pallette, to whose heroics in the French tale of *Intolerance* audiences of 1916 thrilled, would never have been mistaken for the good Sergeant Heath.

brimmed straw hat, a fishing pole over his shoulder.[1] The most amazing and startling figure was struck by Broadway producer George Gruen, known as "the new Flo Ziegfeld." It was appropriate that the creator of incredibly elaborate stage shows should turn up with the most elaborate disguise of all, an incredibly faithful imitation of Lon Chaney's famed Phantom-of-the-Opera makeup, which has precipitated feminine screams of terror in movie houses throughout the world. Aside from the makeup, Gruen's costume consisted of traditional evening dress and an all-enveloping black opera cape.

It was a highly successful evening, made so not only by the inventive clowning of the host but by the astonishing vigor with which Vance threw himself into his swashbuckling role, doing everything like Fairbanks short of swinging from the chandelier. Only on a few occasions, in the early part of the evening, did any discordant notes introduce themselves, but those few incidents certainly foreshadowed the tragedy that was to strike before the gay festivities ran their course. It appeared that while all of the guests were wishing Jack Austin good luck, a few of them were not really on the best of terms with their host.

It was no secret, for one thing, that Arletta Bingham was being summarily cast off by the departing Austin, and Miss Bingham was far more accustomed to rejecting than to being rejected. As the evening wore on, and drink loosened her tongue, her gay veneer began to slip away and a hidden bitterness to show itself.

"You're a big man, aren't you, Jack?" she slurred. "Going to be a big talking, singing, dancing movie-talkie-singie star. Well, ain't that swell?"

"It's such a wonderful thing!" exclaimed Molly Haw-

---

[1] In mid-evening Kronert made a startling costume change, suddenly appearing in full evening dress, thus illustrating the recent change in Ray's screen character from country boy to man-about-town. Kronert's feet remained bare, however, symbolizing the unfortunate Ray's failure to make a completely successful transformation.

ley. "To be seen by millions of people all over the world in one performance, where on the stage you can display your talent only to a few hundred at a time."

"I feel it's a great opportunity," said Austin, with feigned humility. "I hope I'm worthy of it."

George Gruen entered the discussion suddenly. He, like Miss Bingham, was beginning to wobble on his feet. "Talking pictures are just a fad, Jack! They'll never catch on with the public. They go to movies to sleep—to be stimulated, they go to the theater. And talkies will neither stimulate them like the legitimate theater nor let them rest like the movies. Jack, take my word for it, you're making a terrible mistake."

"If that is so, George, I shall come back to Broadway, and I'm sure you'll be glad to give me a job." Austin drifted away to join another group of guests, and the conversation quickly became more openly bitter.

Arletta Bingham cackled drunkenly, "Broadway forgets fast. In three or four years his name won't mean a thing. He'll be a forgotten has-been. He won't even be able to get a job."

"And you'll still be a living legend in every bed on Broadway," said Roger Kronert, raising his glass in facetious salute. The vamp snarled sullenly and took a gulp of her drink. As Kronert passed, she aimed at his bare toes with a vicious thrust of her heel and narrowly missed.

George Gruen was talking to his drink more than to those around him. "He's a welsher, that Jack Austin. He's a dirty welsher."

"Come, come, George," replied Monty Baby, a well-known Broadway agent, wearing the familiar hat, vest, and glum expression of Buster Keaton. "You let him out of his contract like a gentleman. Why spoil it now?"

"He had no right," the quasi-Opera Phantom moaned. "He's a welsher. He wants to ruin me on Broadway." It was well-known that with so many of Broadway's top stars heading west, Gruen was having trouble finding a star for his new show, reportedly a weak vehicle that would take the artistry of an Al Jolson, an Eddie Cantor, a George Jessel, or a Jack Austin to put it across. Austin's leaving the cast had been a well-publicized blow to the producer, but Gruen had been very sporting about it— at least in the theatrical pages.

Another bad moment came when one of the waiters, elaborately mustached in the manner of lead-Kop Ford Sterling, spilled a tray of drinks on Jack Austin. It was a comical incident, as the waiter's fumbling and Austin's reaction had the style of a well-planned Hollywood "sight gag." However, it soon became clear the incident was not planned and Austin was surprisingly angered by it. "You idiot!" he said between clenched teeth. "Get out of here!"

"But, Mr. Austin—" the unfortunate servant began.

"Get out of here!" Austin iterated. Then he virtually chased the serving man back toward the kitchen. Recovering his composure, he returned to his guests in the comical tramp walk.

"What a temper," said a startled Clara-Molly Bow-Hawley, who had been looking on in shock.

Another young woman, dressed in the homely garb of the perpetual-ingenue Mary Pickford, replied, "You needn't know Jack Austin long to find out about that. I know. I loved him. Once."

Shortly, the latter-mentioned lady, a New York debutante named Edna Stuyvesant, was cavorting with Vance and Austin in a manner reminiscent of the United Artists partners, Pickford, Chaplin, and Fairbanks.[1] This entertainment served to get the party back to its previous quotient of merriment, and it remained so until eleven o'clock.

At that hour, with most of the guests at the height of their enjoyment and many of them more-or-less intoxicated, it was suddenly realized that their host had not put in an appearance for some time.

"What can have happened to him?" asked Molly Hawley.

"He's dropped out of sight," Roger Kronert observed.

[1]The fourth partner, D.W. Griffith, was not represented at the party. It was hoped that Griffith himself might be present, but the motion-picture pioneer had sent his regrets at the last moment.

"I remember him steppin' into the library around nine-thirty, and I don't believe I've seen the boy since," said Vance. "I'll see if he's become ill or something." And he strode toward the door of the library, hurdling the huge punch bowl on his way. Markham, Heath, Stitt the butler, several other guests, and I followed him, though walking around the punch bowl. What we saw when Vance opened the library door was enough to bring the festivities of the evening to an abrupt halt.

Jack Austin lay dead on the floor of the library, near the fireplace. His tramp costume was covered with blood, his Chaplinesque mustache pitifully askew. He had seemingly been stabbed several times, and the apparent weapon, an ornately-chased Oriental letter opener, lay near the body.[1]

"He's done away with himself," said Roger Kronert.

"Quite impossible, old chap, judging from the placement and multiplicity of the wounds," said Vance.

"Then he's been murdered!" exclaimed Sergeant Heath.

"Deucedly penetratin', Sergeant."

"Who could have done this?" Judge Hawley whispered.

"Virtually anyone here, I should think," replied Markham grimly.

"Or an outsider," offered Heath, indicating the open window.

"It must have been a prowler," Hawley said shakily.

Vance, kneeling beside the body, had made a discovery. "I think the old boy's tryin' to tell us something, Markham. Look at what he's clutchin' in his right hand."

"A pair of cheaters!" exclaimed Heath.

"But Austin didn't wear eyeglasses," said Judge Hawley.

"You'll notice," said Vance, "that they are of the large,

---

[1] Vance had several penetrating observations to make about the origin, design, and artistic merits of the weapon. Were this a full-length novel, I would reproduce those remarks here, since they would undoubtedly be of interest to collectors. Unfortunately, the short-story form offers less latitude for the introduction of such peripheral matters.

round type affected by the motion-picture comedian Harold Lloyd. If one of the guests here tonight had come as Harold Lloyd, we might regard this as a most rewardin' clue to the miscreant's identity. However, I don't recall anyone wearin' such a costume."

Stitt, the butler, suddenly spoke up. "Harold Lloyd sent his regrets, sir. He could not come."

Vance rose. "Ah. Then there was to be a Harold Lloyd here tonight?"

"Yes, sir. Mr. Archie Belmont."

The name brought several gasps from the group. All the guests, suddenly sober, were now gathered around the body.

"Why, he hated Jack!" Arletta Bingham exclaimed.

Roger Kronert supported this contention. "He was supposed to get the part in that talkie they signed Jack Austin for. He hated Austin's guts."

"Seems a likely suspect, Vance," Markham said.

"It's possible," Vance murmured.

"Open and shut, if you ask me," said Heath. "I'll call the lab boys. Show's over now, folks," he added, dispersing the crowd. "Let's give this corpse some air."

"Vance and I will have to talk to this fellow Belmont, see what sort of alibi he has," said Markham. "You can hold the fort here, Heath. We'll want to question everyone later, so no one may leave."

Several protests came from the assembled guests.

"Save your breath, folks!" Heath said. "This is a murder investigation. It's not a party no more."

"In that case, Mr. D.A.," said Arletta Bingham tauntingly, "hadn't you better get out of that cowboy outfit before you carry this any further?"

And suddenly we all realized how absurd we looked. Markham in his Tom Mix regalia, Vance in his Black Pirate apparel, Judge Hawley in a Confederate Civil War uniform, Roger Kronert barefoot in a tuxedo, Gruen in his opera cape and hideous makeup. With all meriment vanished, we looked rather pathetic and comic and even, taken in conjuction with the brutally murdered little tramp figure, somewhat terrifying.

I shall never forget that macabre scene. With Austin's murder, Charlie Chaplin, Doug Fairbanks, Mary Pickford, and Buster Keaton had all vanished, leaving only their outward habiliments behind. All of their merry spirit was washed away by the destructive tide of violent, unanticipated death.

"Yes," said Markham, "I think we should change into street clothes. Inconveniently, Mr. Vance, Mr. Van Dine, and I all arrived in costume, but I think those of you who donned your costumes here could be allowed to change. Then, Sergeant Heath will want to take your statements. Carry on, Heath."

"But, Mr. Markham, if you leave now, you'll miss Doc Doremus."[1]

"So we will. Well, if he says anything really funny, write it down. Mr. Van Dine may be able to use it in a footnote."[2]

Stitt provided us with Belmont's address, a plush Park Avenue apartment, and soon Vance, Markham, and I were in a taxicab on our way there, glad to leave the horror of deflated dreams behind us at the now-somber Austin mansion.

"All that blood," Markham, still in the all-white uniform of a wild west "good guy," was saying, "The murderer had to be spattered with it, Vance! And so I don't see how it could be someone who was at the party. Any of them could have slipped into the library unseen, but how could they have gotten out and rejoined the party without being covered with enough blood to give them away to the other guests?"

Vance did not attempt to answer the question.

"I'm sure Belmont is our man, Vance. It appears the simple, uncomplicated product of a diseased, insane, vengeful mind. Don't you agree?"

Vance said sorrowfully, "Markham, old dear, I make it a practice not to jump to conclusions about people whose

---

[1] The Chief Medical Examiner, who had figured in several of Vance's previous cases.

[2] He said nothing worth footnoting on this occasion.

psyches I have not probed. Belmont may prove to be psychologically incapable of this murder. I will know soon enough."

Markham snorted. "If you had to present a case to a jury, Vance, you'd be more interested in hard-core evidence."

"Quite so, but I am an amateur in crime detection. Once I find a murderer, I have no taste for mountin' him in a big album like a prize postage stamp. I'm not int'rested, y'know, in your stupid courts and your silly rules of evidence. That's your department, my dear chap, and the people of New York pay you handsomely for it."

Markham grunted in reply. That was the extent of our conversation en route to Belmont's quarters.

We found Belmont at home alone. He greeted us affably enough. At first glance, it seemed unlikely he had been out that evening. He appeared to all the world like a man spending a quiet evening at home.

"We expected to see you at Jack Austin's party tonight, Mr. Belmont," said Markham.

"What a bore that would have been! He sent over a costume for me to wear—a Harold Lloyd getup. I sent my regrets. I hope I never see that ham again."

"You probably won't," remarked Markham heavily. "Have you sent the costume back?"

"No, it's still here. Why? What's this all about?"

"May we see the costume, please?"

"Yes, of course. What's happened anyway?"

"Jack Austin was murdered tonight, Mr. Belmont. He had a pair of Harold Lloyd glasses clutched in his hand when we found him."

Belmont looked up with a start. "Murdered? Say, you surely can't think that I—"

"We understand that you hated Jack Austin because he was chosen for that part in the talkie picture."

Belmont laughed. "Look, that's one of those things that happen. It would have been a great opportunity for me, but I've lost parts before. I was disappointed, but I'd hardly commit murder over it. As for hating Austin, I'll admit I was no fan of his. He was an insufferable egotist, an impossible man to work with, and an utter cad, a one-hundred percent wretch. Whoever killed him deserves a medal. But I am not the man."

"Mightn't you get that part now that he's dead?" inquired Markham.

"A possibility. But it hadn't occurred to me until you just mentioned it."

Markham's expression indicated he doubted the statement. In the meantime, Belmont had found the box the costume had come in. The familiar Harold Lloyd glasses, however, were absent.

"I don't understand it," muttered Belmont. "I must have mislaid them."

"Perhaps you mislaid them at Jack Austin's home, Mr. Belmont. Perhaps, during your struggle, he grabbed them off your very nose."

"Mr. Markham, why would I wear the Harold Lloyd costume at all, if I wasn't even going to the party? That doesn't make any sense!"

"I don't pretend to understand the mind of a cold-blooded murderer. Mr. Belmont, by the authority vested in me by the people of New York County, I arrest you for the murder of Jack Austin and remind you that anything you say may be used against you."

"Tut! Tut! Markham,"[1] said Vance softly. These were the only words he uttered while we were in Belmont's apartment. They were enough to show Markham that Vance felt the District Attorney was proceeding too hastily, and Markham seemed uneasy after the arrest was made.

Back at the Austin mansion, we found that Heath had been hard at work taking statements from the guests.

"I think they can go home now, don't you, Vance?" Markham said hopefully. "I imagine we can consider this investigation as good as closed."

"Not quite, Markham," Vance replied. "I am not convinced that Mr. Belmont is psychologically capable—"

[1]Egyptology was yet another of Vance's many so-called "dilettante" interests.

"Psychology again!" Heath exclaimed disgustedly. "Mr. Vance, I know you've done some good work in the past, but you can't take every case like it's a page out of—who's the fellow?"

"Freud, you mean? My dear Heath, a psychological approach is suitable to any problem of crime. And there are other people far more psychologically capable of committing this crime, people in this house now."

Before the discussion could continue, Stitt approached us, still ludicrously dressed as one of Mack Sennett's Keystone Kops. "Mr. Vance," he said stiffly, "I think there is something you should know."

"What is that?"

"Those glasses that Mr. Austin had in his hand are not the same pair that were sent to Mr. Belmont."

"They weren't, eh? Then there were two pairs?"

"Yes. The pair that Mr. Austin had in his hand were given him by Mr. Harold Lloyd himself. They occupied an honored place on the mantelpiece in the library."

"I see. Then they were always here, not brought in by someone from outside. That puts a pos'tively different light on matters, y'know. He grasped 'em not from the nose of his murderer, as Mr. Markham has postulated, but from the mantelpiece."

"In an effort to tell us the murderer's identity," said Markham.

"Quite so. Changes matters a bit, eh what?"

Markham appeared exasperated. "But, Vance, I honestly don't see how this development changes anything. I still would put the same interpretation on the clue, wouldn't you? That is, as an indication of the guilt of the man who was to impersonate Harold Lloyd—that is, Archie Belmont."

"No, indeed, Markham. Austin's message to us is a bit more subtle than that. In fact, I might not have been able to read it, had I not linked it with a couple of other pertinent clues."

"Do I understand you to mean, Vance," demanded

Markham, seeming near apoplexy, "that you claim to have solved this case?"

"Oh, quite, old chap."

"And Belmont is not the murderer in your redoubtable estimation?"

" 'Fraid not, old boy."

"Then who did it?" demanded Heath.

"Gather the guests in the ballroom and I'll tell you all about it," Vance promised, puffing his *Régie* nonchalantly.

Markham complied, though too upset to speak above a strangled whisper. A few moments later, Vance was telling the assembled group, "A most entertainin' comedy, y'know. I rather fancy it would make a fine picture, non-talkin' of course. Archie Belmont, who somehow mislaid his big round glasses, was accused of a crime in which his big round glasses didn't really figure at all. Amusin', what? Quite so."

Few of the tense gathering appeared very amused. In strained silence, they hung on Vance's every syllable.

"It's all extr'ordin'rily simple. Y'see. The real murderer is here, among the people in this room. A person capable of bitterness and vindictive hatred. One capable of plannin' a darin' and complicated crime."

He paused dramatically and looked at each face in turn —the pale, beautiful visage of Molly Hawley, the ashen, haggard face of Judge Hawley, her father; the handsome, uncharacteristically serious face of Roger Kronert; the scowl of George Gruen, his Lon Chaney makeup removed; the sneering, now unlovely features of Arletta Bingham; the impassive countenance of the butler, Stitt.

Which of these was guilty, we all wondered—all but the one who knew.

"The murderer was one whose costume allowed him to cover up any annoyin' blood with which he might have been spattered—cover it up with a handy black opera cape!" Suddenly, all eyes were on George Gruen, who began to rise out of his chair but thought better of it when he felt Heath's beefy hand on his shoulder. "A man who hated Jack Austin for leavin' him on the brink of financial disaster. A man who is noted on Broadway for colossally elaborate muscial production with countless chorus girls and expensive, intricate sets, a producer of—in short—*spectacles!"*

With breathtaking suddenness, Gruen produced a dagger from under his cloak and plunged it into his own heart. The drama was over.

And so ended the famous Austin murder case. To me, I confess, it is more memorable than any of Vance's other cases—and for reasons apart from Vance's great detective skill.

Though you may have difficulty in believing it, we were men, Vance and I, not mere cardboard figures. I admit here for the first time that during the course of this investigation I fell in love for the only time in my life—in love with Miss Molly Hawley, the judge's red-haired daughter. Of course, I could say nothing, for to do so would be to break one of my own rules.[1]

I could have composed long paragraphs celebrating her Titian locks, her flawless white teeth, her dimpled cheeks, but I had long ago vowed never to lose my equanimity in the manner of Dr. Watson and other narrators of detective tales who have allowed themselves such indulgences as romance.

By being true to the rules, I consigned myself to a life of loneliness. And seeing every Clara Bow movie I possibly can has not significantly abated that loneliness.

---

[1]S. S. Van Dine's "Twenty Rules for Writing Detective Stories," Rule Number 3: "There must be no love interest in the story."

# 1932

# The Legacy

## by Clayton Matthews

*A small Texas town in the early 1930s—one of a series Clayton Matthews has been writing about Sheriff Jason Little and his fellow citizens.*

M Y UNCLE LEROY was the meanest man in all of Conroe County. Everybody said so. Some even said he was the meanest man alive but as Sheriff Jason Little always pointed out when that was said in front of him, this statement was a little loose since many of those saying it had never been out of the county, so how could they know?

"Not that Leroy Collins isn't a mean man," Sheriff Jason would add with his spare grin. "I'm not downgrading him in that respect. I've told him to his face any number of times, for all the good it did."

Actually Sheriff Jason was only a deputy, the sheriff being over at the county seat, but he was the only law in our little east Texas town. His hardest chore usually was that of separating two rambunctious Saturday night drunks.

I came to live with my Uncle Leroy and Aunt Aggie

when I was just ten, after my folks were killed in an automobile accident. Aunt Aggie was my mother's sister, and it was either live with them or be sent off to an orphanage.

"I couldn't live with myself if I let Kyle be sent to an orphanage," Aunt Aggie said. "Not my sister's only child."

I don't think my uncle would have agreed to it except he thought he might get an extra farmhand for room and board. He got a bad bargain in me. I was never any good around a farm. Take just one instance. I could never learn to milk a cow. The only way I could get milk was by using the thumb and forefinger and that took forever. Uncle Leroy roared and stomped and took a strap to me, but I didn't improve, not even after four years.

Where my uncle was mean and sour, Aunt Aggie was kind, gentle as she could be. Where he was tall, lean as a cadaver, always scowling, and smelling of the barn, Aunt Aggie was slight, always had a smile for me, and smelled of freshly baked biscuits and cornbread. She wasn't what you'd call pretty, at least not when I first saw her. She was well past forty then, of course, and she looked careworn, her brown hair already streaked with gray. The things I remember best about her were her kind smile, the gentle stroke of her fingers in my hair, the soft croon of her voice.

They didn't have any children of their own. When I was old enough to look back I realized I could easily have been spoiled, since Aunt Aggie doted on me. My uncle saw to it that I wasn't. If she was especially good to me, he found a reason to use his strap. As well as being naturally mean, he was miserly. I wore clothes to school until they looked like a patchwork quilt before he'd buy me something new. Aunt Aggie made as many of my clothes as she could. The only Christmas presents I ever received were things she made for me.

It wasn't that he couldn't afford it. He had one hundred and sixty acres of rich river-bottom land and almost every square inch of it was cultivated, except for the pond and some timber around it.

The pond was one reason folks named him mean. Actually it was more a lake than a pond, large in size and quite deep. The way Sheriff Jason told it to me, Aunt Aggie's father, whose farm it had been before he died, had kept the pond stocked with fish and let anyone who wished fish there. Uncle Leroy charged folks a dollar, and anyone he caught fishing without paying the dollar he ran off with a shotgun.

Sheriff Jason had the farm to the south of us, eighty acres. He let most of it stay idle, spending a great deal of his time in town sheriffing.

Uncle Leroy despised him, calling him lazy and shiftless. "It's purely a sin the way that man runs a place. A man like Jason Little shouldn't even own a farm."

Aunt Aggie would reply, "Jason and his sister are comfortable. They want for nothing. They raised two boys on that farm after Jason's Martha died. Jason says he works hard enough to satisfy their needs."

"You always was soft for that man," Uncle Leroy grumbled. "I reckon you'd have married him if I hadn't—"

Aunt Aggie's color heightened. "Hush now! Don't go talking that old foolishness in front of Kyle."

"I like most everybody," Sheriff Jason was fond of saying, "but I can't find it in me to like Leroy Collins. He's a hard worker, I'll hand him that, and I reckon that's a virtue with many folks. The way I see it, hard work is a way some folks have of working off their meanness."

Sheriff Jason was plump and drawling, bald as an apple. He didn't have an office, so weekdays he drove the mile into town in his old Model A and spent most of the day on an upended pop box at the filling station, sucking on an old black pipe and yarning. Those men not engaged in weekday pursuits, and some who were, would drop by and visit. In those days Scattergood Baines was a favorite fictional character, certainly one of mine, and I came to think of Sheriff Jason as our town's Scattergood Baines, sitting on his pop box, dispensing wisdom, settling problems and spinning outrageous yarns.

I often stopped by the filling station on my way home from school, even knowing that I'd be late doing my chores and in danger of a whack from Uncle Leroy's strap. Most times Sheriff Jason would drive me as far as his house, which was only a quarter mile from home, and always insisted I stop in for cookies and a glass of milk. Later, I realized Sheriff Jason was lonely. His own two boys were grown and living several counties away.

Beth Little was Sheriff Jason's sister and kept house for him; she was small and bustling and sharp of tongue. Sheriff Jason's wife had died when his second son was born, and his sister had moved in to help raise the boys.

One afternoon when I'd stopped in Beth Little saw two buttons missing off my shirt. "Take that shirt off, Kyle, and I'll sew on those buttons while you have your cookies. Aggie has enough to do as it is."

I'd forgotten about the welts across my back until I heard her indrawn breath. "What happened to your back, boy? Has that Leroy Collins been beating you?"

I mumbled something and turned away, but Sheriff Jason took me by the arm and spun me around so my back was to him. "Darn that man!" he said fiercely. "Does he beat you often?"

I felt a flood of shame. "Sometimes. When I don't do my chores right."

"That man ought to be horsewhipped himself," Beth Little said, bristling. "Why don't you do something, Jason?"

"What would you have me do?"

"You're the sheriff, ain't you?"

"That doesn't cut any ice. It's not sheriff business. The boy's Aggie's kin. I haven't been in that house since she married Leroy and I'd not be welcome. Now if she'd make a complaint—"

"You know she'd never do that. Aggie's a proud woman, too proud for her own good. She made her mistake and she'll live with it until she dies. When I think that that man wouldn't have a dime if he hadn't married

Aggie and her already with that farm!"

My bedroom was a small, slant-roofed room on the second floor, directly over the kitchen. Only the lower floor was heated, all the heat for the upstairs rooms coming through grillwork vents in the floor, and when the fall nights turned chilly I often sprawled close to the vent while doing my homework. Usually my aunt and uncle went into the parlor after supper, where he read the paper and she sewed, but sometimes they stayed in the kitchen awhile or came out for a snack. I could hear every word spoken, but seldom heard anything interesting. They had little to say to one another besides the words needed for day-to-day living.

One evening about a week after I'd learned from Beth Little that my uncle had married Aunt Aggie for the farm, I heard their voices raised in anger.

"Adopt him! You must be out of your mind, woman! I was never for having him here in the first place. Now you want to go and adopt him!"

"He's my sister's child and should have folks of his very own."

"We're folks enough, worthless as he is around the place. We go and make him our legal kid and the place'd go to him anything should happen to us. I wouldn't put it past you to try and leave it to him anyway, you happen to go before me."

"That's all you ever think about, this farm!"

"Somebody'd better."

"Sometimes I think that's the only reason you married me."

"You *think!* For what other reason, I'd like to know?" His laughter was cruel, taunting. "Certainly not for your looks or your brains."

"Well, I'm going to adopt Kyle!"

"Not so long as I'm alive and have anything to say about it, and you'd have to have me agree to it. Now just shut up about it."

"You've got no right—"

"I've got every right!"

There was the sound of a slap, a cry from Aunt Aggie, followed by the heavy tread of his footsteps leaving the kitchen. Then the only sound I heard was Aunt Aggie's muffled sobs.

I suppose I'd hated him from the beginning, certainly from the first strapping he'd given me, but I'd never put voice to it before. Lying there beside the vent, school books forgotten, I clenched my fists and thumped my thighs as hard as I could. I whispered, "I hate him! I'll kill him!"

Aunt Aggie had never been very big, but now she seemed to get smaller and smaller. Her face gaunted until it was little more than a skull with the skin stretched tight over it. Her brown eyes sank into deep pits and her hands thinned down until the blue veins showed like wires under the transparent skin. She moved slowly and was often late with meals, her head bowing under my uncle's vocal displeasure. Often I would hear her pacing the floor late at night, sometimes moaning softly. She didn't eat enough to keep a bird alive.

If my uncle noticed it, he didn't say anything. Maybe he was happy about it. Maybe he was even poisoning her!

One day at Sheriff Jason's house, his sister said, "Kyle, is your aunt feeling poorly? I stopped in today, making sure first that that man was in the fields. Aggie looked like death."

I burst out, "Uncle Leroy's poisoning her!"

"Whoa now, boy," Sheriff Jason said quietly. "Let's not go off half-cocked."

"Maybe the boy's right, Jason."

He took my arm and turned me to face him. "You have any reason to back up what you say, Kyle?"

"She's sickly, always having to lie down, and she hardly ever sleeps at night."

"Well . . . Aggie's health has never been what you'd call good."

"If he hurts Aunt Aggie, I'll kill him!" I threatened.

"Well, now, I reckon you've reason not to like him but . . . How old are you now, Kyle?"

"Going on fourteen."

"And big for your age, too. But a little young to be talking of killing. Besides . . ." His craggy face grew still and cold. "If Leroy Collins does anything to Aggie, he'll rue the day!"

"Does anything?" his sister echoed. "It'll be too late then."

"What can I do, sis?" His voice was agonized. "Tell me, what can I do?"

A week later I overheard another conversation from the kitchen. They were talking as they came in.

". . . and he's sure?"

"He's sure," Aunt Aggie said. "That's why I want to adopt Kyle."

"I thought I told you to shut up about that."

"But things are different now! I want to see that he's taken care of."

"I'll see that he's taken care of." His laughter grated. "And I can't see that things are any different. With you maybe. Not with me."

"You're a mean man, Leroy Collins!"

"So folks keep telling me but you don't notice me losing any sleep over it, do you? What folks say about me never did bother me much."

"I'll never know why I married you."

"Why, you loved me and couldn't live without me. Don't you recollect?"

"I was wrong. I hate you!" she said in a low, intense voice.

"Hate away," he said carelessly, "but that kid's not getting any of this place so long as I'm alive. And there's not a blasted thing you can do about it."

"There *is* something I can do."

"What? Run to Jason Little? Run ahead. He's good at telling folks what to do."

"He's a better man than you are by far."

I heard the sound of a slap, a cry from Aunt Aggie, followed by a thump. Without even thinking about it, I was out of the room and down the narrow stairs. He was just coming through the kitchen door and I flew at him. Yelling hoarsely, "I'll kill you!" I hammered on his chest with my fists.

His long face was ludicrous with surprise, then flushed with anger. He gave me a stinging slap across the mouth, and the blow sent me crashing against the wall. I slid down to the floor, half-stunned.

He loomed over me, his face dark with rage. "You come at me again like that, kid, and I'll strap you within an inch of your life!"

From the doorway Aunt Aggie cried, "You leave him alone!"

He whirled, took two steps toward her, then turned on his heel and strode out into the night.

Aunt Aggie crossed the room to me as I struggled to my feet, and she folded me into her arms.

"I'm sorry, Aunt Aggie," I gulped.

"There, there, Kyle. It's all right. It's all right."

I came straight home from school the next afternoon, without stopping in at the filling station.

That evening I burst in on Sheriff Jason and his sister in their kitchen, with the news, "Uncle Leroy has left! He can't hurt Aunt Aggie anymore!"

Sheriff Jason stared. "Whoa now, boy. What's this all about?"

"He just packed up and left. And he won't ever be back!"

Sheriff Jason exchanged looks with his sister. "That don't sound like the Leroy Collins I know."

"Jason, you'd better—"

He got to his feet. "Yes, I reckon I'd better."

He went with me back to the farm. I was hurting to talk, but Sheriff Jason kept a brooding silence.

Aunt Aggie was reclining on the divan in the parlor, wan and tired looking. She gave Sheriff Jason a pale smile. "Jase . . . It's been a long time."

"Yes, Aggie. Too long." He went to her and took her hand for a moment, then dropped it and pulled up a chair, facing her. "Now, what's this about Leroy up and leaving?"

"Well, we'd been fighting about me adopting Kyle and . . ." Aunt Aggie turned to me and said, "There's cake in the kitchen, Kyle. You go have a piece and a glass of milk."

"Go on along, boy," Sheriff Jason said without a glance at me.

I went with dragging feet. Once out of sight in the hall, I sneaked back to the door and listened shamelessly.

". . . down by the pond clearing timber all morning. He's been working down there some weeks and I always carried his lunch down—"

"In your condition?"

"—and we started in again. You see, Jase, I wanted to make Kyle legally mine so he could get his share of the farm after I'm gone. Leroy wouldn't agree to it, so I finally told him to get out. He packed his things and left."

"That doesn't sound much like Leroy. You're sure that's the way it was, Aggie? I know how Kyle feels about him, and he's been making some wild threats. You sure he didn't—"

"Oh, no, Jase! Leroy was gone long before Kyle came home from school. He went walking down the road. That's the way I first saw him, remember? Walking toward the house carrying an old suitcase. He went carrying the same suitcase, in fact."

Sheriff Jason said slowly, "Yes, I remember, Aggie."

"I was a fool, Jase." Her voice had a choked sound. "If I had married you when you asked me . . . All those good years we've wasted, Jase. They're all gone!"

"We all make mistakes. We can whip ourselves to death with ifs." His voice softened, now it changed again. "But it doesn't make sense, his walking away from all this."

"I told him if he didn't I'd drive him out, take him to court if I had to."

"But why now? Why after all these years?"

"Everything's different now. Long as I knew I'd be here to see to Kyle's legacy, it didn't matter much. I'd long ago stopped loving him, if I ever had, but he was a man around to take care of the place, mean as he was. But all that changed."

"Changed how, Aggie?"

I heard her heavy sigh. "I didn't want to tell people but I have to tell you, Jase, so you'll see to Kyle. I went to a doctor last week. A few months at the most he gave me. . . ."

I fled from the sound of her voice. I stood in the kitchen, with my eyes clenched shut, weak tears squeezing past the lids.

Aunt Aggie took to her bed soon after that. Beth Little moved in to take care of us, and Sheriff Jason spent almost as much time there as at home. He did all the heavy chores around the place and helped me with mine. With him showing me, I became more handy doing farm chores, except I never did learn how to milk a cow properly. Every time I'd try, I would think of Uncle Leroy and his strap.

"Never mind, boy," Sheriff Jason said. "There're people grow up all the time who never learn to milk a cow."

Sheriff Jason didn't laugh as much as he once had, didn't yarn as much, but he was still at the filling station most afternoons to drive me home.

One Indian summer afternoon several men were grouped around him at the station. They didn't see me right away, and I heard one man say, "Don't see how you can be so all-fired sure the boy had nothing to do with it, Jason. Not that I could blame him, but right's right!"

Sheriff Jason said, "If you don't like the way I do my job, Pete—"

"Didn't say that," the man grumbled. "I just think it's almighty queer, the whole thing."

Sheriff Jason saw me then and motioned the man quiet. He stood up and said heartily, "Kyle! You ready to head out home?"

A doctor came to the farm every day now. I was seldom allowed in to see Aunt Aggie. Each time I did see her, she seemed smaller than the time before, her voice little more than a whisper. Late at night I could hear her crying out in pain, could hear Beth Little bustling in and out of her room.

One afternoon after I got home from school, a strange man came to the house; a lawyer, I later learned. He went into Aunt Aggie's room with Sheriff Jason and his sister, and they were in there for a long time with the door closed. While Beth Little was seeing the lawyer out, Sheriff Jason stayed behind in my aunt's room. I lurked in the doorway, listening, neither of them noticing me.

"I'd like to marry you, Aggie."

Aunt Aggie's weak voice took on a sudden lilt. "No, Jase. It's way too late for that. But thank you for offering. I can go happy now. Kyle's in my will, and the farm will go to him. I want you to promise me you'll take care of him until he's old enough."

Sheriff Jason said, "You have my solemn promise, Aggie."

Aunt Aggie died a week later.

Sheriff Jason took me home with him after the funeral and gave me a bedroom upstairs. "Aggie made me your legal guardian, Kyle, as well as the executor of her will. The farm will be yours when you're of voting age. Until then you're to live with me. I'll operate the farm and whatever profits there are will go toward sending you to college, the rest put into a trust. You'll never have a worry."

They didn't wake me the day after the funeral, and I slept past nine o'clock. When I did finally get up I went to the bedroom window and looked out. From there I could see the pond clearly. What I saw gave me a fearful start. Men were swarming around it like ants.

I hurried into my clothes and clattered downstairs. As I charged through the kitchen on my way to the back door, Beth Little stepped in my path.

"And just where do you think you're going?"

"A lot of men are over at the pond! I have to get over there!"

"You'll do no such thing. Jason told me to keep you in

today. Now, you just sit down and have your breakfast."

It was the longest day of my life. Late in the afternoon, again from my bedroom window, I saw Sheriff Jason coming across the fields toward the house. I hurried down the stairs and into the kitchen, where Beth Little was fixing supper. I said excitedly, "Sheriff Jason's coming!"

She went to the window and looked out. "I see he is."

Sheriff Jason spent several minutes on the back porch, scraping the mud off his boots. His glance found me at once when he came in.

"Well?" his sister questioned.

He nodded, without taking his gaze off me.

Beth Little turned to me. "Kyle, go to your room."

"No, sis," he said sharply. "He'll have to know. Now's as good a time as any. He should know the price of his legacy." He sighed and squared his shoulders. "Boy, we just dragged the pond. Found Leroy Collins, with his head bashed in. I swear, sick as she was, I don't know where she found the strength. Funny thing, he was caught in the roots of one of the trees where it had growed out into the water; one of those trees he was aiming to chop down."

"You knew all the time," his sister said accusingly.

"Not all the time. I suspicioned but I didn't know. Aggie told me just before she died."

"And you're the sheriff!"

"What would you have had me do, sis? She was dying. What more could the law have done to her?"

"But why now? You didn't do anything when she told you, why loose the dogs after she's dead and buried? Why didn't you just leave him down there?"

"Why, I figured he had a decent burial coming," Sheriff Jason said simply. "Even a man as mean as Leroy Collins had that much coming to him."

# 1938

# The Gettysburg Bugle

## by Ellery Queen

*Rural America in the late 1930s, with echoes of the Civil War fought generations earlier. . . . A story that ranks with Ellery Queen's Wrightsville novels as among the finest in the Queen canon.*

THIS IS A VERY OLD STORY as Queen stories go. It happened in Ellery's salad days, when he was tossing his talents about like a Sunday chef and a red-headed girl named Nikki Porter had just attached herself to his typewriter. But it has not staled, this story; it has an unwithering flavor which those who partook of it relish to this day.

There are gourmets in America whose taste buds leap at any concoction dated 1861-1865. To such, the mere recitation of ingredients like Bloody Angle, Minié balls, Little Mac, "Tenting Tonight," the brand of Ulysses Grant's whiskey, not to mention Father Abraham, is sufficient to start the passionate flow of juices. These are the misty-hearted to whom the Civil War is "the War" and the blue-gray armies rather more than men. Romantics, if you will; garnishers of history. But it is they who pace the lonely sentry post by the night Potomac, they who hear the creaking of the ammunition wagons, the snap of campfires, the scream of the thin gray line and the long groan of the battlefield. They personally flee the burning hell of the Wilderness as the dead rise and twist in the flames; under lanterns, in the flickering mud, they stoop compassionately with the surgeons over quivering heaps. It is they who keep the little flags flying and the ivy ever green on the graves of the old men.

Ellery is of this company, and that is why he regards the case of the old men of Jacksburg, Pennsylvania, with particular affection.

Ellery and Nikki came upon the village of Jacksburg as people often come upon the best things, unpropitiously. They had been driving back to New York from Washington, where Ellery had had some sleuthing to do among the stacks of the Library of Congress. Perhaps the Potomac, Arlington's eternal geometry, giant Lincoln frozen in sadness brought their weight to bear upon Ellery's decision to veer toward Gettysburg, where murder had been national. And Nikki had never been there, and May was coming to its end. There was a climate of sentiment.

They crossed the Maryland-Pennsylvania line and spent timeless hours wandering over Culp's Hill and Seminary Ridge and Little Round Top and Spangler's Spring among the watchful monuments. It is a place of everlasting life, where Pickett and Jeb Stuart keep charging to the sight of those with eyes to see, where the blood spills fresh if colorlessly, and the high-pitched tones of a tall and ugly man still ring out over the graves. When they left, Ellery and Nikki were in a mood of wonder, unconscious of time or place, oblivious to the darkening sky and the direction in which the nose of the Duesenberg pointed. So in time they were disagreeably awakened by the alarm clock of nature. The sky had opened on their heads, drenching them to the skin instantly. From the horizon behind them Gettysburg was a battlefield again, sending great flashes of fire through the darkness to the din of celestial cannon. Ellery stopped the car and put the top up, but the mood was drowned when he discovered that something ultimate had happened to the ignition system. They were marooned in a faraway land, Nikki moaned; making Ellery angry, for it was true.

"We can't go on in these wet clothes, Ellery!"

"Do you suggest that we stay here in them? I'll get this crackerbox started if . . ." But at that moment the watery lights of a house wavered on somewhere ahead, and Ellery became cheerful again.

"At least we'll find out where we are and how far it is to where we ought to be. Who knows? There may even be a garage."

It was a little white house on a little swampy road marked off by a little stone fence covered with rambler rose vines, and the man who opened the door to the dripping wayfarers was little, too, little and weather-skinned and gallused, with eyes that seemed to have roots in the stones and springs of the Pennsylvania countryside. He smiled hospitably, but the smile became concern when he saw how wet they were.

"Won't take no for an answer," he said in a remarkably deep voice, and he chuckled. "That's doctors orders, though I expect you didn't see my shingle—mostly overgrown with ivy. Got a change of clothing in your car?"

"Oh, yes!" said Nikki abjectly.

Ellery, being a man, hesitated. The house looked neat and clean, there was an enticing fire, and the rain at their backs was coming down with a roar. "Well, thank you . . . but if I might use your phone to call a garage—"

"You just give me the keys to your car trunk."

"But we can't turn your home into a tourist house—"

"It's that, too, when the good Lord sends a wanderer my way. Now see here, this storm's going to keep up most of the night and the roads hereabout get mighty soupy." The little man was bustling into waterproof and overshoes. "I'll get Lew Bagley over at the garage to pick up your car, but for now let's have those keys."

So an hour later, while the elements warred outside,

they were toasting safely in a pleasant little parlor, full of Dr. Martin Strong's homemade poppy-seed twists, scrapple, and coffee. The doctor, who lived alone, was his own cook. He was also, he said with a chuckle, mayor of the village of Jacksburg and its chief of police.

"Lot of us in the village run double harness. Bill Yoder of the hardware store's our undertaker. Lew Bagley's also the fire chief. Ed MacShane—"

"Jacksburger-of-all-trades you may be, Dr. Strong," said Ellery, "but to me you'll always be primarily the Good Samaritan."

"Hallelujah," said Nikki, piously wiggling her toes.

"And make it Doc," said their host. "Why, it's just selfishness on my part, Mr. Queen. We're off the beaten track here, and you do get a hankering for a new face. I guess I know every dimple and wen on the five hundred and thirty-four in Jacksburg."

"I don't suppose your police chiefship keeps you very busy."

Doc Strong laughed. "Not any. Though last year—" His eyes puckered and he got up to poke the fire. "Did you say, Miss Porter, that Mr. Queen is sort of a detective?"

"Sort of a!" began Nikki. "Why, Dr. Strong, he's solved some simply unbeliev—"

"My father is an inspector in the New York police department," interrupted Ellery, curbing his new secretary's enthusiasm with a glance. "I stick my nose into a case once in a while. What about last year, Doc?"

"What put me in mind of it," said Jacksburg's mayor thoughtfully, "was your saying you'd been to Gettysburg today. And also you being interested in crimes . . ." Dr. Strong said abruptly, "I'm a fool, but I'm worried."

"Worried about what?"

"Well . . . Memorial Day's tomorrow, and for the first time in my life I'm not looking forward to it. Jacksburg makes quite a fuss about Memorial Day. It's not every village can brag about three living veterans of the Civil War."

"Three?" exclaimed Nikki. "How thrilling."

"Gives you an idea what the Jacksburg doctoring business is like," grinned Doc Strong. "We run to pioneer-type women and longevity. . . . I ought to have said we *had* three Civil War veterans—Caleb Atwell, ninety-seven, of the Atwell family, there are dozens of 'em in the county; Zach Bigelow, ninety-five, who lives with his grandson Andy and Andy's wife and seven kids; and Abner Chase, ninety-four, Cissy Chase's great-grandpa. This year we're down to two. Caleb Atwell died last Memorial Day."

"A, B, C," murmured Ellery.

"What's that?"

"I have a bookkeeper's mind, Doc. Atwell, Bigelow, and Chase. Call it a spur-of-the-moment mnemonic system. A died last Memorial Day. Is that why you're not looking forward to this one? B following A sort of thing?"

"Didn't it always?" said Doc Strong with defiance. "Though I'm afraid it ain't—isn't as simple as that. Maybe I better tell you how Caleb Atwell died.

"Every year Caleb, Zach, and Abner have been the star performers of our Memorial Day exercises, which are held at the old burying ground on the Hookerstown road. The oldest of the three—"

"That would be A. Caleb Atwell."

"That's right. As the oldest, Caleb always blew taps on a cracked old bugle that's 'most as old as he was. Caleb, Zach, and Abner were in the Pennsylvania Seventy-second of Hancock's Second Corps, Brigadier General Alexander S. Webb commanding. They covered themselves with immortal glory—the Seventy-second, I mean—at Gettysburg when they fought back Pickett's charge, and that bugle played a big part in their fighting. Ever since it's been known as the Gettysburg bugle—in Jacksburg, anyway."

The little mayor of Jacksburg looked softly down the years. "It's been a tradition, the oldest living vet tootling that bugle, far back as I remember. I recollect as a boy standing around with my mouth open watching the

G.A.R.s—there were lots more then—take turns in front of Maroney Offcutt's general store . . . been dead thirty-eight years, old Offcutt . . . practicing on the bugle, so any one of 'em would be ready when his turn came." Doc Strong sighed. "And Zach Bigelow, as the next oldest to Caleb Atwell, he'd be the standard bearer, and Ab Chase, as the next-next oldest, he'd lay the wreath on the memorial monument in the burying ground.

"Well, last Memorial Day, while Zach was holding the regimental colors and Ab the wreath, Caleb blew taps the way he'd done nigh onto twenty times before. All of a sudden, in the middle of a high note, Caleb keeled over. Dropped in his tracks deader than church on Monday."

"Strained himself," said Nikki sympathetically. "But what a poetic way for a Civil War veteran to die."

Doc Strong regarded her oddly. "Maybe," he said. "If you like that kind of poetry." He kicked a log, sending sparks flying up his chimney.

"But surely, Doc," said Ellery with a smile, for he was young in those days, "surely you can't have been suspicious about the death of a man of ninety-seven?"

"Maybe I was," muttered their host. "Maybe I was because it so happened I'd given old Caleb a thorough physical checkup only the day before he died. I'd have staked my medical license he'd live to break a hundred and then some. Healthiest old copperhead I ever knew. Copperhead! I'm blaspheming the dead. Caleb lost an eye on Cemetery Ridge. . . . I know—I'm senile. That's what I've been telling myself for the past year."

"Just what was it you suspected, Doc?" Ellery forbore to smile now, but only because of Dr. Strong's evident distress.

"Didn't know what to suspect," said the country doctor shortly. "Fooled around with the notion of an autopsy, but the Atwells wouldn't hear of it. Said I was a blame jackass to think a man of ninety-seven would die of anything but old age. I found myself agreeing with 'em. The upshot was we buried Caleb whole."

"But Doc, at that age the human economy can go to

pieces without warning like the one-hoss shay. You must have had another reason for uneasiness. A motive you knew about?"

"Well . . . maybe."

"He was a rich man," said Nikki sagely.

"He didn't have a pot he could call his own," said Doc Strong. "But somebody stood to gain by his death just the same. That is, if the old yarn's true.

"You see, there's been kind of a legend in Jacksburg about those three old fellows, Mr. Queen. I first heard it when I was running around barefoot with my tail hanging out. Folks said then, and they're still saying it, that back in '65 Caleb and Zach and Ab, who were in the same company, found some sort of treasure."

"Treasure . . ." Nikki began to cough.

"Treasure," repeated Doc Strong doggedly. "Fetched it home to Jacksburg with them, the story goes, hid it, and swore they'd never tell a living soul where it was buried. Now there's lots of tales like that came out of the War"— he fixed Nikki with a stern and glittering eye—"and most folks either cough or go into hysterics, but there's something about this one I've always half-believed. So I'm senile on two counts. Just the same, I'll breathe a lot easier when tomorrow's ceremonies are over and Zach Bigelow lays Caleb Atwell's bugle away till next year. As the older survivor Zach does the tootling tomorrow."

"They hid the treasure and kept it hidden for considerably over half a century?" Ellery was smiling again. "Doesn't strike me as a very sensible thing to do with a treasure, Doc. It's only sensible if the treasure is imaginary. Then you don't have to produce it."

"The story goes," mumbled Jacksburg's mayor, "that they'd sworn an oath—"

"Not to touch any of it until they all died but one," said Ellery, laughing outright now. "Last-survivor-takes-all department. Doc, that's the way most of these fairy tales go." Ellery rose, yawning. "I think I hear the featherbed in that other guest room calling. Nikki, your eyeballs are hanging out. Take my advice, Doc, and follow suit. You haven't a thing to worry about but keeping the kids quiet tomorrow while you read the Gettysburg Address!"

As it turned out, the night shared prominently in Doc Martin Strong's Memorial Day responsibilities. Ellery and Nikki awakened to a splendid world, risen from its night's ablutions with a shining eye and a scrubbed look; and they went downstairs within seconds of each other to find the mayor of Jacksburg, galluses dangling on his pants bottom, pottering about the kitchen.

"Morning, morning," said Doc Strong, welcoming but abstracted. "Just fixing things for your breakfast before catching an hour's nap."

"You lamb," said Nikki. "But what a shame, Doctor. Didn't you sleep well last night?"

"Didn't sleep at all. Tossed around a bit and just as I was dropping off my phone rings and it's Cissy Chase. Emergency sick call. Hope it didn't disturb you."

"Cissy Chase." Ellery looked at their host. "Wasn't that the name you mentioned last night of—?"

"Of old Abner Chase's great-granddaughter. That's right, Mr. Queen. Cissy's an orphan and Ab's only kin. She's kept house for the old fellow and taken care of him since she was ten." Doc Strong's shoulders sloped.

Ellery said peculiarly: "It was old Abner . . . ?"

"I was up with Ab all night. This morning, at six-thirty, he passed away."

"On Memorial Day!" Nikki sounded like a little girl in her first experience with a fact of life.

There was a silence, fretted by the sizzling of Doc Strong's bacon.

Ellery said at last, "What did Abner Chase die of?"

Doc Strong looked at him. He seemed angry. But then he shook his head. "I'm no Mayo brother, Mr. Queen, and I suppose there's a lot about the practice of medicine I'll never get to learn, but I do know a cerebral hemorrhage when I see one, and that's what Ab Chase died of. In a man of ninety-four, that's as close to natural death as you can come. . . . No, there wasn't any funny business in this one."

"Except," mumbled Ellery, "that—again—it happened on Memorial Day."

"Man's a contrary animal. Tell him lies and he swallows 'em whole. Give him the truth and he gags on it. Maybe the Almighty gets tired of His thankless job every once in an eon and cuts loose with a little joke." But Doc Strong said it as if he were addressing, not them, but himself. "Any special way you like your eggs?"

"Leave the eggs to me, Doctor," Nikki said firmly. "You go on up those stairs and get some sleep."

"Reckon I better if I'm to do my usual dignified job today," said the mayor of Jacksburg with a sigh. "Though Abner Chase's death is going to make the proceedings solemner than ordinary. Bill Yoder says he's not going to be false to an ancient and honorable profession by doing a hurry-up job undertaking Ab, and maybe that's just as well. If we added the Chase funeral to today's program, even old Abe's immortal words would find it hard to compete! By the way, Mr. Queen, I talked to Lew Bagley this morning and he'll have your car ready in an hour. Special service, seeing you're guests of the mayor." Doc Strong chuckled. "When you planning to leave?"

"I *was* intending . . ." Ellery stopped with a frown. Nikki regarded him with a sniffy look. She had already learned to detect the significance of certain signs peculiar to the Queen physiognomy. "I wonder," murmured Ellery, "how Zach Bigelow's going to take the news."

"He's already taken it, Mr. Queen. Stopped in at Andy Bigelow's place on my way home. Kind of a detour, but I figured I'd better break the news to Zach as early as possible."

"Poor thing," said Nikki. "I wonder how it feels to learn you're the only one left." She broke an egg viciously.

"Can't say Zach carried on about it," said Doc Strong dryly. "About all he said, as I recall, was: 'Doggone it, now who's goin' to lay the wreath after I toot the Gettysburg bugle!' I guess when you reach the age of ninety-five, death don't mean what it does to young squirts of sixty-three like me. What time 'd you say you were leaving, Mr. Queen?"

"Nikki," muttered Ellery, "are we in any particular hurry?"

"I don't know. Are we?"

"Besides, it wouldn't be patriotic. Doc, do you suppose Jacksburg would mind if a couple of New York Yanks invited themselves to your Memorial Day exercises?"

The business district of Jacksburg consisted of a single paved street bounded at one end by the sightless eye of a broken traffic signal and at the other by the twin gas pumps before Lew Bagley's garage. In between, some stores in need of paint sunned themselves, enjoying the holiday. Red, white, and blue streamers crisscrossed the thoroughfare overhead. A few seedy frame houses, each decorated with an American flag, flanked the main street at both ends.

Ellery and Nikki found the Chase house exactly where Doc Strong had said it would be—just around the corner from Bagley's garage, between the ivy-hidden church and the firehouse of the Jacksburg Volunteer Pump and Hose Company No. 1. But the mayor's directions were a superfluity; it was the only house with a crowded porch.

A heavy-shouldered young girl in a black Sunday dress sat in a rocker, the center of the crowd. Her nose was as red as her big hands, but she was trying to smile at the cheerful words of sympathy winged at her from all sides.

"Thanks, Mis' Plum . . . That's right, Mr. Schmidt, I know . . . But he was such a spry old soul, Emerson, I can't believe . . ."

"Miss Cissy Chase?"

Had the voice been that of a Confederate spy, a deeper silence could not have drowned the noise. Jacksburg eyes examined Ellery and Nikki with cold curiosity, and feet shuffled.

"My name is Queen and this is Miss Porter. We're attending the Jacksburg Memorial Day exercises as guests of Mayor Strong"—a warming murmur, like a zephyr, passed over the porch—"and he asked us to wait here for him. I'm sorry about your great-grandfather, Miss Chase."

"You must have been very proud of him," said Nikki.

"Thank you, I was. It was so sudden— Won't you set? I mean—Do come into the house. Great-grandpa's not here . . . he's over at Bill Yoder's, on some ice . . ."

The girl was flustered and began to cry, and Nikki took her arm and led her into the house. Ellery lingered a moment to exchange appropriate remarks with the neighbors who, while no longer cold, were still curious; and then he followed. It was a dreary little house with a dark and damp parlor.

"Now, now, this is no time for fussing—may I call you Cissy?" Nikki was saying soothingly. "Besides, you're better off away from all those folks. Why, Ellery, she's only a child!"

And a very plain child, Ellery thought, with a pinched face and empty eyes; and he almost wished he had gone on past the broken traffic light and turned north.

"I understand the parade to the burying ground is going to form outside your house, Cissy," he said. "By the way, have Andrew Bigelow and his grandfather Zach arrived yet?"

"Oh, I don't know," said Cissy Chase dully. "It's all such a dream, seems like."

"Of course. And you're left alone. Haven't you any family at all, Cissy?"

"No."

"Isn't there some young man—?"

Cissy shook her head bitterly. "Who'd marry me? This is the only decent dress I got, and it's four years old. We lived on Great-grandpa's pension and what I could earn hiring out by the day. Which ain't much, nor often. Now . . ."

"I'm sure you'll find something to do," said Nikki, very heartily.

"In Jacksburg?"

Nikki was silent.

"Cissy." Ellery spoke casually, and she did not even look up. "Doc Strong mentioned something about a treasure. Do you know anything about it?"

"Oh, that." Cissy shrugged. "Just what Great-grandpa told me, and he hardly ever told the same story twice. But near as I was ever able to make out, one time during the War him and Caleb Atwell and Zach Bigelow got separated from the army—scouting, or foraging, or something. It was down South somewhere, and they spent the night in an old empty mansion that was half burned down. Next morning they went through the ruins to see what they could pick up, and buried in the cellar they found the treasure. A big fortune in money, Great-grandpa said. They were afraid to take it with them, so they buried it in the same place in the cellar and made a map of the location and after the War they went back, the three of 'em, and dug it up again. Then they made the pact."

"Oh, yes," said Ellery. "The pact."

"Swore they'd hold onto the treasure till only one of them remained alive, I don't know why, then the last one was to get it all. Leastways, that's how Great-grandpa told it. That part he always told the same."

"Did he ever say how much of a fortune it was?"

Cissy laughed. "Couple of hundred thousand dollars. I ain't saying Great-grandpa was cracked, but you know how an old man gets."

"Did he ever give you a hint as to where he and Caleb and Zach hid the money after they got it back North?"

"No, he'd just slap his knee and wink at me."

"Maybe," said Ellery suddenly, "maybe there's something to that yarn after all."

Nikki stared. "But Ellery, you said—! Cissy, did you hear that?"

But Cissy only drooped. "If there is, it's all Zach Bigelow's now."

Then Doc Strong came in, fresh as a daisy in a pressed blue suit and a stiff collar and a bow tie, and a great many other people came in, too. Ellery and Nikki surrendered Cissy Chase to Jacksburg.

"If there's anything to the story," Nikki whispered to Ellery, "and if Mayor Strong is right, then that old scoundrel Bigelow's been murdering his friends to get the money!"

"After all these years, Nikki? At the age of ninety-five?" Ellery shook his head.

"But then what—?"

"I don't know." But when the little mayor happened to look their way, Ellery caught his eye and took him aside and whispered in his ear.

The procession—near every car in Jacksburg, Doc Strong announced proudly, over a hundred of them—got under way at exactly two o'clock.

Nikki had been embarrassed but not surprised to find herself being handed into the leading car, an old but brightly polished touring job contributed for the occasion by Lew Bagley; for the moment Nikki spied the ancient, doddering head under the Union Army hat in the front seat she detected the fine Italian whisper of her employer. Zach Bigelow held his papery frame fiercely if shakily erect between the driver and a powerful red-necked man with a brutal face who, Nikki surmised, was the old man's grandson, Andy Bigelow. Nikki looked back, peering around the flapping folds of the flag stuck in the corner of the car. Cissy Chase was in the second car in a black veil, weeping on a stout woman's shoulder. So the female Yankee from New York sat back between Ellery and Mayor Strong, against the bank of flowers in which the flag was set, and glared at the necks of the two Bigelows, having long since taken sides in this matter. And when Doc Strong made the introductions, Nikki barely nodded to Jacksburg's sole survivor of the Grand Army of the Republic, and then only in acknowledgment of his historic importance.

Ellery, however, was all deference and cordiality, even to the brute grandson. He leaned forward, talking into the hairy ear.

"How do I address your grandfather, Mr. Bigelow? I

don't want to make a mistake about his rank."

"Gramp's a general," said Andy Bigelow loudly. "Ain't you, Gramp?" He beamed at the ancient, but Zach Bigelow was staring proudly ahead, holding fast to something in a rotted musette bag on his lap. "Went through the War a private," the grandson confided, "but he don't like to talk about that."

"General Bigelow—" began Ellery.

"That's his deef ear," said the grandson. "Try the other one."

"General Bigelow!"

"Hey?" The old man turned his trembling head, glaring. "Speak up, bub. Ye're mumblin'."

"General Bigelow," shouted Ellery, "now that all the money is yours, what are you going to do with it?"

"Hey? Money?"

"The treasure, Gramp," roared Andy Bigelow. "They've even heard about it in New York. What are you goin' to do with it, he wants to know?"

"Does, does he?" Old Zach sounded grimly amused. "Can't talk, Andy. Hurts m'neck."

"How much does it amount to, General?" cried Ellery.

Old Zach eyed him. "Mighty nosy, ain't ye?" Then he cackled. "Last time we counted it—Caleb, Ab, and me— came to nigh on a million dollars. Yes, sir, one million dollars." The old man's left eye, startlingly, drooped. "Goin' to be a big surprise to the smart alecks and the doubtin' Thomases. You wait an' see."

Andy Bigelow grinned, and Nikki could have strangled him.

"According to Cissy," Nikki murmured to Doc Strong. "Abner Chase said it was only two hundred thousand."

"Zach makes it more every time he talks about it," said the mayor unhappily.

"I heard ye, Martin Strong!" yelled Zach Bigelow, swiveling his twig of a neck so suddenly that Nikki winced, expecting it to snap. "You wait! I'll show ye, ye durn whippersnapper, who's a lot o' wind!"

"Now, Zach," said Doc Strong pacifyingly. "Save your

wind for that bugle."

Zach Bigelow cackled and clutched the musette bag in his lap, glaring ahead in triumph, as if he had scored a great victory.

Ellery said no more. Oddly, he kept staring not at old Zach but at Andy Bigelow, who sat beside his grandfather grinning at invisible audiences along the empty countryside as if he, too, had won—or was on his way to winning—a triumph.

The sun was hot. Men shucked their coats and women fanned themselves with handkerchiefs and pocketbooks.

*"It is for us the living, rather, to be dedicated . . ."*

Children dodged among the graves, pursued by shushing mothers. On most of the graves there were fresh flowers.

*"—that from these honored dead . . ."*

Little American flags protruded from the graves, too.

*". . . gave the last full measure of devotion . . ."*

Doc Martin Strong's voice was deep and sure, not at all like the voice of that tall ugly man, who had spoken the same words apologetically.

*". . . that these dead shall not have died in vain . . ."*

Doc was standing on the pedestal of the Civil War Monument, which was decorated with flags and bunting and faced the weathered stone ranks like a commander in full-dress uniform.

*"—that this nation, under God . . ."*

A color guard of the American Legion, Jacksburg Post, stood at attention between the mayor and the people. A file of Legionnaires carrying old Sharps rifles faced the graves.

*"—and that government of the people . . ."*

Beside the mayor, disdaining the simian shoulder of his grandson, stood General Zach Bigelow. Straight as the barrel of a Sharps, musette bag held tightly to his blue tunic.

*". . . shall not perish from the earth."*

The old man nodded impatiently. He began to fumble

with the bag.

*"Comp-'ny! Present—arms!"*

"Go ahead, Gramp!" Andy Bigelow bellowed.

The old man muttered. He was having difficulty extricating the bugle from the bag.

"Here, lemme give ye a hand!"

"Let the old man alone, Andy," said the mayor of Jacksburg quietly. "We're in no hurry."

Finally the bugle was free. It was an old army bugle, as old as Zach Bigelow, dented and scarred in a hundred places.

The old man raised it to his earth-colored lips.

Now his hands were not shaking.

Now even the children were quiet.

Now the Legionnaires stood more rigidly.

And the old man began to play taps.

It could hardly have been called playing. He blew, and out of the bugle's bell came cracked sounds. And sometimes he blew and no sounds came out at all. Then the veins of his neck swelled and his face turned to burning bark. Or he sucked at the mouthpiece, in and out, to clear it of his spittle. But still he blew, and the trees in the burying ground nodded in the warm breeze, and the people stood at attention listening as if the butchery of sound were sweet music.

And then, suddenly, the butchery faltered. Old Zach Bigelow stood with bulging eyes. The Gettysburg bugle fell to the pedestal with a tiny clatter.

For an instant everything seemed to stop—the slight movements of the children, the breathing of the people, even the rustling of the leaves.

Then into the vacuum rushed a murmur of horror, and Nikki unbelievingly opened the eyes which she had shut to glimpse the last of Jacksburg's G.A.R. veterans crumpling to the feet of Doc Strong and Andy Bigelow.

"You were right the first time, Doc," Ellery said.

They were in Andy Bigelow's house, where old Zach's body had been taken from the cemetery. The house was full of chittering women and scampering children, but in this room there were only a few, and they talked in low tones. The old man was laid out on a settee with a patchwork quilt over him. Doc Strong sat in a rocker beside the body, looking very old.

"It's my fault," he mumbled. "I didn't examine Caleb's mouth last year. I didn't examine the mouthpiece of that bugle. It's my fault, Mr. Queen."

Ellery soothed him. "It's not an easy poison to spot, Doc, as you know. And after all, the whole thing was so ludicrous. You'd have caught it in autopsy, but the Atwells laughed you out of it."

"They're all gone. All three." Doc Strong looked up fiercely. "Who poisoned their bugle?"

"God Almighty, don't look at me," said Andy Bigelow. "Anybody could of, Doc."

"Anybody, Andy?" the mayor cried. "When Caleb Atwell died, Zach took the bugle and it's been in this house for a year!"

"Anybody could of," said Bigelow stubbornly. "The bugle was hangin' over the fireplace and anybody could of snuck in durin' the night. . . . Anyway, it wasn't here before old Caleb died; *he* had it up to last Memorial Day. Who poisoned it in *his* house?"

"We won't get anywhere on this tack, Doc," Ellery murmured. "Bigelow. Did your grandfather ever let on where that Civil War treasure is hidden?"

"Suppose he did." The man licked his lips, blinking, as if he had been surprised into the half-admission. "What's it to you?"

"That money is behind the murders, Bigelow."

"Don't know nothin' about that. Anyway, nobody's got no right to that money but me." Andy Bigelow spread his thick chest. "When Ab Chase died, Gramp was the last survivor. That money was Zach Bigelow's. I'm his next o' kin, so now it's mine!"

"You know where it's hid, Andy." Doc was on his feet, eyes glittering. "Where?"

"I ain't talkin'. Git outen my house!"

"I'm the law in Jacksburg, too, Andy," Doc said softly. "This is a murder case. Where's that money?"

Bigelow laughed.

"You didn't know, Bigelow, did you?" said Ellery.

"Course not." He laughed again. "See, Doc? He's on your side, and he says I don't know, too."

"That is," said Ellery, "until a few minutes ago."

Bigelow's grin faded. "What are ye talkin' about?"

"Zach Bigelow wrote a message this morning, immediately after Doc Strong told him about Abner Chase's death."

Bigelow's face went ashen.

"And your grandfather sealed the message in an envelope—"

"Who told ye that?" yelled Bigelow.

"One of your children. And the first thing you did when we got home from the burying ground with your grandfather's corpse was to sneak up to the old man's bedroom. Hand it over."

Bigelow made two fists. Then he laughed again. "All right, I'll let ye see it. Hell, I'll let ye dig the money up for me! Why not? It's mine by law. Here, read it. See? He wrote my name on the envelope!"

And so he had. And the message in the envelope was also written in ink, in the same wavering hand:

Dere Andy now that Ab Chase is ded to—if sumthin happins to me you wil find the money we been keepin all these long yeres in a iron box in the coffin *wich we beried Caleb Atwell in.* I leave it all to you my beluved grandson cuz you been sech a good grandson to me. Yours truly Zach Bigelow.

"In Caleb's coffin," choked Doc Strong.

Ellery's face was impassive. "How soon can you get an exhumation order, Doc?"

"Right now," exclaimed Doc. "I'm also deputy coroner of this district!"

And they took some men and they went back to the old

burying ground, and in the darkening day they dug up the remains of Caleb Atwell and they opened the casket and found, on the corpse's knees, a flattish box of iron with a hasp but no lock. And, while two strong men held Andy Bigelow to keep him from hurling himself at the crumbling coffin, Doctor-Mayor-Chief of Police-Deputy Coroner Martin Strong held his breath and raised the lid of the iron box.

And it was crammed to the brim with moldy bills of large denominations.

In Confederate money.

No one said anything for some time, not even Andy Bigelow.

Then Ellery said, "It stood to reason. They found it buried in the cellar of an old Southern mansion—would it be Northern greenbacks? When they dug it up again after the War and brought it up to Jacksburg they probably had some faint hope that it might have some value. When they realized it was worthless, they decided to have some fun with it. This had been a private joke of those three old rascals since, roughly, 1865. When Caleb died last Memorial Day, Abner and Zach probably decided that, as the first of the trio to go, Caleb ought to have the honor of being custodian of their Confederate treasure in perpetuity. So one of them managed to slip the iron box into the coffin before the lid was screwed on. Zach's note bequeathing his 'fortune' to his 'beloved grandson'—in view of what I've seen of his beloved grandson today— was the old fellow's final joke."

Everybody chuckled; but the corpse stared mirthlessly and the silence fell again, to be broken by a weak curse from Andy Bigelow and Doc Strong's puzzled: "But Mr. Queen, that doesn't explain the murders."

"Well, now, Doc, it does," said Ellery; and then he said in a very different tone: "Suppose we put old Caleb back the way we found him, for your re-exhumation later for autopsy, Doc—and then we'll close the book on your Memorial Day murders."

Ellery closed the book in town, in the dusk, on the porch of Cissy Chase's house, which was central and convenient for everybody. Ellery and Nikki and Doc Strong and Cissy and Andy Bigelow—still clutching the iron box dazedly—were on the porch, and Lew Bagley and Bill Yoder and everyone else in Jacksburg, it seemed, stood about on the lawn and sidewalk, listening. And there was a touch of sadness to the soft twilight air, for something vital and exciting in the life of the village had come to an end.

"There's no trick to this," began Ellery, "and no joke, either, even though the men who were murdered were so old that death had grown tired waiting for them. The answer is as simple as the initials of their last names. Who knew that the supposed fortune was in Confederate money and therefore worthless? Only the three old men. One or another of the three would hardly have planned the deaths of the other two for possession of some scraps of valueless paper. So the murderer has to be someone who believed the fortune was legitimate and who—since until today there was no clue to the money's hiding place—knew he could claim it legally.

"Now of course that last-survivor-take-all business was pure moonshine, invented by Caleb, Zach, and Abner for their own amusement and the mystification of the community. But the would-be murderer didn't know that. The would-be murderer went on the assumption that the *whole* story was true, or he wouldn't have planned murder in the first place.

"Who would be able to claim the fortune legally if the last of the three old men—the survivor who presumably came into possession of the fortune on the deaths of the other two—died in his turn?"

"Last survivor's heir," said Doc Strong, and he rose.

"And who is the last survivor's heir?"

*"Zach Bigelow's grandson, Andy."* And the little mayor of Jacksburg stared hard at Bigelow, and a grumbling sound came from the people below, and Bigelow shrank against the wall behind Cissy, as if to seek her pro-

tection. But Cissy only looked at him and moved away.

"You thought the fortune was real," Cissy said scornfully, "so you killed Caleb Atwell and my great-grandpa so your grandfather'd be the last survivor so you could kill him the way you did today and get the fortune."

"That's it, Ellery," cried Nikki.

"Unfortunately, Nikki, that's not it at all. You all refer to Zach Bigelow as the last survivor—"

"Well, he was," said Nikki in amazement.

"How could he not be?" said Doc Strong. "Caleb and Abner died first—"

"Literally, that's true," said Ellery, "but what you've all forgotten is that Zach Bigelow was the last survivor *only by accident.* When Abner Chase died early this morning, was it through poisoning, or some other violent means? No, Doc, you were absolutely positive he'd died of a simple cerebral hemorrhage—not by violence, but a natural death. Don't you see that if Abner Chase hadn't died a natural death early this morning, *he'd still be alive this evening?* Zach Bigelow would have put the bugle to his lips this afternoon, just as he did, just as Caleb Atwell did a year ago . . . *and at this moment Abner Chase would have been the last survivor.*

"And who was Abner Chase's only living heir, the girl who would have fallen heir to Abner's 'fortune' when, in time, or through her assistance, he joined his cronies in the great bivouac on the other side?

"You lied to me, Cissy," said Ellery to the shrinking girl in his grip, as a horror very like the horror of the burying ground in the afternoon came over the crowd of mesmerized Jacksburgers. "You pretended you didn't believe the story of the fortune. But that was only after your great-grandfather had inconsiderately died of a stroke just a few hours before old Zach would have died of poisoning, and you couldn't inherit that great, great fortune anyway!"

Nikki did not speak until they were twenty-five miles from Jacksburg. Then all she said was, "And now there's nobody left to blow the Gettysburg bugle," and she continued to stare into the darkness toward the south.

# 1942

# The Adventure of the Double-Bogey Man

## by *Robert L. Fish*

*We conclude with a story whose nominal setting is wartime England—one of a series which Anthony Boucher once called, "the funniest and most adroitly plotted of all the innumerable parody-pastiches of Sherlock Holmes." Bob Fish's parody harks back to that Holmesian era, when hansoms prowled the streets of London and the game was forever afoot. Thus we end our book not with a view toward the future, but with a turning back once again to those Dear Dead Days. . . .*

A PERUSAL OF MY NOTES for the year '42, made in September of that year and recounting the many cases in which I had engaged with my friend Mr. Schlock Homes, gave me as rude a shock as ever I have suffered. It was in February of '42 that I had begun the study of a new method of speedwriting, feeling that a facility in this science might well aid me in both quickly and accurately annotating our adventures. Unfortunately, a sharp increase in my medical practice, possibly caused by a section of slippery pavement near our rooms at 221B Bagel

Street, left me little time for my studies, and I came back to my casebook to find I was unable to translate my own hieroglyphics. In desperation I took my Pitman notebook to an expert, but when he announced that it was all Gregg to him, I found myself without recourse.

Even Homes, with his vast background of cipherology and cryptology, was able to be of but small help. He did manage to decipher one title as The Sound of the Basketballs; but since we could recall no case involving sports that year, we were unable to go further. These adventures are therefore lost to posterity, and I bitterly hold myself to blame for their loss.

October, however, brought a case of such national importance that it dwarfed all work Homes had previously done that year; for beyond furnishing him with an opportunity once again to demonstrate his remarkable ability to analyze distortions in their proper perspective, it also gave him a chance to serve his country as few men have been able to serve her. In my notes, now meticulously kept in neat English, I find the case listed as The Adventure of the Double-Bogey Man.

I had returned from carefully sprinkling powdered wax on the offending section of pavement, in the hope that this might resolve its slippery condition, to find that in my absence Homes's brother Criscroft had arrived and was ensconced with my friend on the sofa before the bare fireplace. As I entered, they were engaged in a favorite game of theirs, and as always I stood back in reverent silence as they matched their remarkable wits in analytical reasoning.

Their subject appeared to be an old-fashioned tintype of a mustached gentleman dressed in the clothing of yesteryear, stiffly seated in a bower of artificial flowers, his bowler held woodenly before him, and his frozen face reflecting the ordeal of the portraiture.

"An ex-student of the Icelandic languages, dedicated to the growing of rubber plants," hazarded Criscroft, eyeing the discolored photograph closely.

"Color-blind and left-handed," returned Homes languidly, as I held my breath in admiration.

"A one-time trampoline acrobat, adept at playing the twelve-toned gas-organ," observed Criscroft.

"A victim of the hashish habit," Homes said, smiling. "Went before the mast at an early age, and has traveled widely in Bournemouth."

"The son of a Northumbrian bell-ringer," offered Criscroft. Then, turning and noting my presence, he held up his hand. "But enough of this, Schlock. Watney has arrived and we can get down to the real reason for my visit. Put Father's picture away now, and let me tell you why I left the Home Office in such troubled times and hurried here as quickly as possible. We are in serious need of your help!"

Once I had placed drinks in their hands and Homes had lit a cubeb, Criscroft proceeded to lay his problem before us.

"As you are probably aware," he said, "we have recently allowed some of our former colonies to join us in confronting the present unpleasantness emanating from Berlin. The representative of the recent American colonies is a certain General Isaac Kennebunk, Esquire; and in confidence I tell you that it appears this gentleman will be selected to assume the duties of Chief of Staff of our combined Allied forces." He cleared his throat and leaned forward impressively. "With this fact in mind, you can readily understand our perturbation when I inform you that, as of yesterday, General Kennebunk is missing!"

"Missing?" I cried in alarm, springing to my feet. "Missing what?"

"General Kennebunk *himself* is missing," said Criscroft heavily. "Since yesterday morning, when he left a War Council meeting to return to his rooms, he has been neither seen nor heard of. Suffice to say that the General is knowledgeable of all our secret strategy. Should he have fallen into the hands of our enemies or their sympathizers, it could prove to be quite embarrassing for us."

"And you wish me to locate him," stated Homes positively, rubbing his hands together in that gesture that I well knew indicated both extreme interest and poor circulation.

"Precisely. Needless to say, as quickly as possible."

"Then permit me a few questions. First, where was the General in digs?"

"The War Department arranged a suite for him at an old inn, The Bedposts, in Bolling Alley."

"He stayed there alone?"

"Except for his military aide, a certain Major Anguish McAnguish, who temporarily was sharing his quarters."

"And the Major?"

"He has also not been seen since the disappearance, but as you can well imagine, our principal interest is in General Kennebunk."

"Naturally. And what steps have been taken so far?"

Criscroft rose and leaned against the chill fireplace, his face ashen with the strain of his great problem and overwhelming responsibility. "The War Department brought in the Military Police at once—in the person of a former police agent named Flaherty, whom I believe you know. As soon as the Home Office was notified, we insisted on taking the assignment out of his hands and contacting you. The War Department agreed enthusiastically. However, they still wish to retain Flaherty, although they admit you are the possessor of the sharpest analytical brain in England today."

"Flaherty will get them nowhere," replied Homes seriously, although it was plain to see that the compliment had pleased him. "I assume, then, that I have a free hand. The rooms are under guard?"

"I have seen to it that they were immediately sealed, and guards posted. Orders have been issued to allow only you and Watney permission to enter."

"Fine!" said Homes, rising and removing his dressing-gown. "In that case let us proceed there at once. One moment while I don suitable raiment, and we shall be on our way."

Criscroft's hansom deposited us at the mouth of Bolling Alley, and the Home Office specialist leaned down from his seat to grasp his brother's hand gratefully. Then, with a wave, he drove off and we turned down the narrow lane in the direction of the famous old inn.

Our credentials gave us immediate access to the floor that had housed the missing officer, and after ascertaining from the rigid soldier on duty that there had been no visitors, we unlocked the door and passed within. At first view there was certainly nothing to indicate the forcible removal of the General. The beds were neatly made up, the furniture properly placed and but recently dusted, and the late autumn sun passing through the white starched curtains gave the apartment a cheerful air.

Homes paused in the doorway a moment, his piercing eyes sweeping the scene closely; then, closing the door firmly behind us, he began his search.

The dresser drawers gave no clue of anything untoward. The articles of clothing therein were neatly arranged and concealed nothing. Homes dropped to his knees to search beneath the bed, but other than some regulation army boots and a pair of what appeared to be spiked mountain-climbing shoes, the space was bare.

Stepping to the closet, Homes stared at the rows of uniforms neatly arranged upon the rack; then, with sudden resolve, he pushed them aside and probed beyond. I heard a low cry of triumph from my friend, and knew he had discovered his first clue.

With gleaming eyes, he withdrew some oddly shaped sticks, several oversized white pellets, and some tiny wooden pins. Handling these objects with great delicacy, he laid his find upon the bedspread and stepped back to contemplate them, showing inordinate interest.

"Homes!" I cried in amazement, reaching for these odd objects. "What can these be?"

"Take care!" he advised, grasping my arm and drawing me back. "It is more than possible that these are strange weapons, and it would not do to destroy ourselves before our investigation has fairly begun. Let us leave them for the moment and continue our search."

The very cleanliness of the room seemed to mitigate against finding more—the wastebasket was empty, the desktop cleared of all but essentials. Opening the desk drawer, Homes withdrew a blank white writing pad, and was about to replace it when his keen eyes noted faint markings on its surface. Carrying it swiftly to the window, he held it horizontally at eye level against the light.

"Quickly, Watney," he exclaimed in great excitement. "We have something! My bag!"

Dusting charcoal over the empty sheet, he blew it gently until it settled in the crevices left by the pressure of the quill upon the previous page, and a message appeared as if by magic. Homes placed it carefully upon the desk and I bent over his shoulder to read the missive with him.

*"Mammy,"* it said (or Manny—the inscription was not quite clear), *"Only time for nine today; back up to fifty-six! Started off four, but I won't talk about the rest. The trouble is still my right hand, and the result is the old hook! Talk about the bogey man; the double-bogey man has me!"*

This perplexing message was simply signed with the initials of the missing colonial officer, I.K.,E. I raised my eyes from the strange paper to find Homes with such a fierce look of concentration upon his lean face that I refrained from speaking. At last he looked at me frowningly, his mind returning from the far places of his thoughts.

"We must return to Bagel Street at once, Watney!" he said, his voice taut with urgency. "I believe I begin to see a pattern in this, and if I am correct we must waste no time if we are to save this General Kennebunk!"

"But, Homes," I cried, "do you mean that the answer lies in decoding this cryptic message?"

"This is no code, Watney, although there is no doubt that it contains a hidden message. Come, we have much to do!" Folding the paper with great care, he thrust it into his waistcoat pocket and turned to the door.

"But these objects," I said. "Shall I take them with us?"

"No," he replied, staring at them with great loathing. "They will always be here should we require them, but I believe I already know their foul purpose. Come!"

We locked the door behind us, handed the key to the guard, and hurried to the street. A passing cab picked us up at once, and throughout our journey, Homes leaned forward anxiously, as if in this manner he could hasten our passage. While the cab was slowing down before our quarters, Homes thrust the fare into the cabbie's hand and sprang to the pavement even before the horses had fairly stopped. I hurried up the stairs behind him, anxious to be of immediate assistance.

"First, Watney," he said, turning up the lamp and hurriedly pulling his chair close to the table, "if you would be so kind as to hand me the Debrett's, we can get started!"

I placed the tome in his hand and he slid his strong finger down the alphabetical list rapidly. "McAnguish, McAnguish," he muttered as he noted each tine. "Ah, here we are! Anguish McAngush, 224 Edgware Road, Hyde Park 6-24 . . . No, no, Watney! This is the telephone list! The Debrett's, please!"

I replaced the volume, blushing slightly, and he fell to studying it while I watched his face for some clue to his thoughts. He scribbled some data on a pad and handed the book back. "And now the World's Atlas, if you please!" He looked up as he spoke, and noting the look of befuddlement on my face, smiled and spoke in a kindly tone.

"No, Watney, this time I am not attempting to mystify. In time you shall know all. It is simply that every minute may count, and there is no time at present for explanations. So if you will excuse me, I shall get on with my work!"

I waited as he flung the Atlas open, then seeing that he had already forgotten my presence, I quietly left and went to my room.

I awoke to find the first faint strands of dawn feathering the windowpane, and even as I wondered what had aroused me so early, I felt again the urgent pressure of Homes's hand upon my arm.

"Come, Watney," he said in a low voice, "our train leaves in thirty minutes. I have a cab waiting and you must hurry if we are not to miss our connection. Get dressed quickly, and I shall meet you below."

His footsteps diminished as he left the room, and I groped for my oxford bags, my mind awhirl, sleep fighting to resume control. I entered our sitting room to find that Homes had already descended, and even as I picked up my overcoat, I noted that the table was still covered with many volumes from Homes's vast reference library, and that the lamp was still lighted. It was evident that my friend had spent the night at work. I was turning down the lamp when a faint cry from below caused me to slip quickly into my coat and hurry down the steps.

Homes was already seated in the cab, and even as I came running up he gave the driver instructions to start, his strong hand pulling me into the moving vehicle. "Forgive me, Watney," he chuckled, as we rattled off towards Euston Station. "The complete answer came to me but a short while ago, and I still had to telegraph Flaherty to meet us with some of his agents at the train. I also had to arrange our passage on the Ayr Express and see that a cab was waiting to take us to the station. I'm afraid that I left the problem of awakening you until the last."

"And the answer lies in Scotland?" I asked.

"It does indeed," replied my friend, smiling. Then, leaning forward, he cried, "Tuppence extra, driver, if we do not miss our train!"

We came clattering into Euston Station at a terrific clip, and Homes had me by the hand, dragging me from the moving vehicle while it was still moving smartly. We ran down the deserted platform, peering into the compartments of the steaming train, and then, as the cars began to move, Homes flung open a door and sprang aboard, pulling me behind him. I had scarcely time to catch my breath when we passed beneath the tunnel, and Homes then seated himself comfortably in the first smoking compartment we came upon.

"Flaherty and his men are aboard," he said, reaching into his pocket for his briar. "I noticed him in the car behind as we came along the platform. With any luck we should have this case finished by nightfall."

"But I do not understand any of this, Homes!" I cried perplexedly. "I have seen all that you have seen, and none of it makes any sense at all! Do you mean you have deduced the General's whereabouts, and the plot behind his disappearance, simply from the little data of which I am cognizant?"

"Little data?" he replied in honest surprise. "Actually, Watney, I have never had a case so replete with data. Allow me to demonstrate!"

He drew the folded paper containing the cryptic message from his pocket and placed it upon the small table beneath the window. I moved to face him, and he began his explanation.

"First, Watney," he said, smoothing the sheet so that I could once again read the scrawled words, "listen carefully to what the General says. He begins by saying 'only time for nine'—meaning quite clearly that he only has time for a few words. He follows this with 'up to fifty-six' and the words 'off four.' What can these words possible indicate? Only one thing: directions! The most positive directions that exist, Watney—*latitude and longitude!* Up fifty-six. Off four. Obviously fifty-six degrees north latitude and four degrees west longitude!

"Do we have anything to support these deductions? What else does he say? He says, 'The trouble is my right hand.' And who is his right hand? Major Anguish McAnguish! And Debrett's gives the home seat of the McAnguish family as Carnoustie in Scotland—*at exactly this latitude and longitude!*"

Homes leaned back, puffing furiously upon his briar. "Let us go a bit further," he said, as I sat wide-eyed at this brilliant exposition. "The General next states, 'The result is the old hook.' I do not know if you are familiar with the slang speech of America, Watney, but the 'old hook' means that he is being pressured into something which is, to say the least, distasteful to him. And he finishes by saying, 'The double-bogey man has me!' We all know what the bogey man is—one of the superstitions of our childhood. And the double-bogey man can only be twice as terrible in the imagination of this poor chap!

"On this basis, then, let us restate the message as the General might have written it had he not attempted to conceal his meaning from his enemies. He would have said: 'Just time for a short note. I must go back to Carnoustie, because McAnguish is blackmailing me. There I shall be forced to participate in some pagan rites which are too terrible even to discuss!' "

I sat up in alarm. "Pagan rites, Homes?"

"There can be no doubt—remember the bogey man, Watney! I do not know if you are familiar with Voodoo, or Macumba, or any of the other pagan religions based upon sorcery, but human sacrifice often plays a part, and often using the most primitive of weapons! You recall, I am sure, the war-clubs and the wooden darts which we discovered in the rooms of General Kennebunk, which are also, I might point out, the rooms of Major McAnguish!"

Homes leaned back once again and eyed me grimly. "Remember, Watney, our Aryan enemy has made paganism its official religion. And Scotland has many Nationalists who are not out of sympathy with these enemies. There can be no doubt that some where on the heaths of Carnoustie this rite is either in progress or being prepared! I can only hope that we are in time to rescue General Kennebunk from these fiends before it is too late— for it is quite evident who the victim of this sacrifice is to be!"

"How horrible, Homes! And for this reason you brought Flaherty and his men?"

"Precisely. There may well be fisticuffs, and besides, we have no official position in this, particularly in Scotland. However, grim as the situation may be, it is certain we shall be of small use if we do not rest a bit before our arrival. I would suggest twenty winks while we can, for we may be quite busy before the day is over."

I awoke to find Homes in conference with a heavy-set gentleman whose pocket sagged under the weight of a truncheon, and who could be none other than the police agent Flaherty.

"I understand, Mr. Homes," this person was saying respectfully. "It shall be as you say."

"You have a photograph of this colonial officer?"

"I do, Mr. Homes. He is a balding gentleman much given to wearing colorful knickerbockers and rather dashing shirts when off duty, and I am sure I shall have no trouble recognising him."

"Good. Then we are ready. I have studied a one-inch map of the area and am convinced that there is but one heath sufficiently isolated as to be suitable for their nefarious purpose. The engineer of the train has agreed to stop close by to allow us all to descend and deploy. Come, Watney, I feel the brakes being applied at this very moment!"

Seconds later we found ourselves beside the track while the express slowly gathered speed again. In addition to Homes and myself, Flaherty was accompanied by three large men, all similarly attired, and all weighted down by their truncheons. At a signal from Homes, we crossed the tracks and spread out in a widening curve, fanning across the heath.

The section of heath we fronted was well landscaped, with flags, probably marking watering holes, spaced about. We were advancing slowly when of a sudden there was a sharp whistle in our ears and a white stone flew past us to disappear in the distance.

"It's a trap, Homes!" I cried, flinging him into a nearby sand-filled depression and covering him with my body.

"I believe in Scotland they call these ditches 'bunkers,' " he replied, rising and dusting himself off carefully. "Come, men, we must be close!"

He leaned over the edge of the depression, studying the landscape, Flaherty beside him. Suddenly the police agent stiffened, and peering into the distance, pointed his finger excitedly.

"It's him, Mr. Homes," he cried. "I don't know how you ever deduced it, but as always you were right! And he is surrounded by three others, all of whom are armed with heavy sticks! But wait!" The police agent turned to Homes with a bewildered air. "He, too, is armed!"

"It is as I feared," said Homes, watching the four men approach. "Either hypnotism or drugs, both quite common in this type of affair. I fear in his present condition he may struggle, but at least we have discovered him before they can put their odious plan into practice. Come, men, let us surround them!"

"I'm sorry, Mr. Homes," said Flaherty, placing his hand on Homes's arm. "My instructivns are very clear. You have found him, and a fine piece of work, but it is my duty to effect the rescue. You must go back to London at once."

"Nonsense!" Homes cried, incensed. "Come, men!"

"No, Mr. Homes," Flaherty replied quite firmly. "The instructions come from the Home Office itself. You are far too valuable to risk in an operation such as this. But fear not; I promise you I shall get him safely away from these culprits!"

"Do not fail then," Homes replied sternly. "Come, Watney, we have but forty minutes if we are to catch the next train south!"

I had opened the morning journal and was engrossed in attempting to open my eggs and turn the pages simultaneously when Homes entered the breakfast room and seated himself opposite me.

"I believe you are wasting your time, Watney," he remarked genially. "I have already been informed by Criscroft that the General is back in London, and I seriously doubt that the censors would allow an account of yesterday's proceedings to reach the public columns."

"I am not so sure, Homes," I replied, noting a small article buried in one corner. "It is true that no great details of the affair appear, but it does say that because of a nerve-racking event that took place yesterday, General Kennebunk is under doctor's orders to take a few days' rest."

"I can well imagine how nerve-racking it must have been," said Homes, his eyes warm with quick sympathy. "However, I would judge that several days engaged in one of our pleasant English sports could well erase this terrible memory. I believe I shall suggest this to the Home Office. A letter to my brother Criscroft, if you please, Watney!"